ONE STEP PAST SUNDOWN

ONE STEP PAST SUNDOWN
THE HELSING SOCIETY™ BOOK ONE

BRADFORD BATES
MICHAEL ANDERLE

DISRUPTIVE IMAGINATION

This book is a work of fiction. All of the characters, organizations, and events portrayed in this novel are either products of the author's imagination or are used fictitiously. Sometimes both.

Copyright © 2022 by LMBPN Publishing
Cover by Fantasy Book Design
Cover copyright © LMBPN Publishing
A Michael Anderle Production

LMBPN Publishing supports the right to free expression and the value of copyright. The purpose of copyright is to encourage writers and artists to produce the creative works that enrich our culture.

The distribution of this book without permission is a theft of the author's intellectual property. If you would like permission to use material from the book (other than for review purposes), please contact support@lmbpn.com. Thank you for your support of the author's rights.

LMBPN Publishing
PMB 196, 2540 South Maryland Pkwy
Las Vegas, NV 89109

Version 1.01, September 2022
eBook ISBN: 979-8-88541-873-7
Print ISBN: 979-8-88541-874-4

THE ONE STEP PAST SUNDOWN TEAM

Thanks to our beta readers
Mary Morris, Kelly O'Donnell, John Ashmore, Rachel Beckford

Thanks to the JIT Readers

If we've missed anyone, please let us know!

Dorothy Lloyd
Zacc Pelter
Diane L. Smith
Wendy L Bonell
Jackey Hankard-Brodie
Dave Hicks
Deb Mader
Christopher Gilliard
Peter Manis
Paul Westman
Angel LaVey

Editor
The SkyFyre Editing Team

CHAPTER ONE

2026

The situation must have been urgent because Saul called instead of leaving one of his notes.

"Dylan, I need your help." Saul's voice was a whisper but carried a breathless sense of panic.

This was bad. Saul only called when there was real trouble on the horizon. Like, "humans in danger, come with guns blazing" problems. The fact he wasn't shouting orders already made this feel personal. Was someone dumb enough to go after one of the Helsing brothers?

I owed Saul a lot. I'd never ignore his calls.

"Tell me what's happening."

There was silence on the other end of the line as Saul collected himself. "It's Megan. She's in trouble."

All the air rushed out of my lungs, leaving me lost for words. Megan was Greg Helsing's daughter and the first Champion of the Helsing Society in decades. The world of man had been defenseless against the supernatural for three generations, but that all changed when Megan's powers manifested. It was a monumental moment for the Helsing Society and meant a lot less work for me.

I'd been Saul's problem-solver for the last twenty years. When Greg and his Templars couldn't handle something, it was my job to fix it. Being a half-blood—half human and half vampire—gave me some advantages over a normal human.

Well, maybe The Rock was up to the job, but I wasn't entirely sure someone that big and charismatic could be fully human. I heard he might even run for president. As awesome as a Dwayne Johnson presidency would be, it would have the stink of supernatural manipulation all over it.

So did Megan's capture. It surprised me that the Helsing Society hadn't kept a better handle on their most prized asset, but since Saul was calling there was still time to rescue her.

"Tell me where."

With a click, I transferred the audio from my phone to my earbuds and started getting ready.

Fluffy, my imp, watched me from the coffee table. She knew something was up, but she didn't know what. She surprised me by turning off all our home electronics. I guess the little demon decided she was coming with. It never hurt to have a little demon power on your side. Even if mine spent most of her time smoking weed and running away from the fights I ran toward. She was probably the first demon pacifist in recorded history.

Despite our different takes on life, she was my friend. I had a demon for a friend. What a crazy world.

Papers rustled in the background. Despite his Watchers'

use of technology, the older man never felt comfortable around it. He liked to print documents and hold them in his hands. It didn't stop him from using the people at his disposal to hack every damn camera in the city when he wanted to find something. Think your network was secure? Not when the Helsing Society hunted for fledglings.

"Remember the silos?" Saul asked as though he thought I'd forgotten them.

"Didn't they tear those down?" The longer I lived, the more I saw old things replaced with shiny new ones.

Saul sounded worried again. I knew he didn't want a repeat of the past. "They did. It's a series of storage warehouses now."

Neither of us wanted to say it, but I had to know before going in. "Is there a master?"

"I don't know." Saul said it like he knew he was asking me to storm the beach at Normandy.

What he didn't know, or maybe didn't want to, was that I had a massive crush on Megan. It was crazy to think I'd met a girl who looked my age but was damn near half of it. I couldn't stop thinking about her.

I'd lusted after women before, even pined like a lovesick puppy, but I'd never met a woman who robbed my brain of oxygen like she did. When I saw her, everyone else ceased to exist. It was like I'd met the other half of my soul. While Saul might not know how I felt, I'd walk into the fires of hell to get her back.

I'd even go there pro-bono, and I never did anything for free.

"Don't worry, Saul. I'll get her back." I meant every damn word.

I hung up the phone, pulled on my steel-toed boots, and

laced them up. A few seconds later, the nine-millimeter was out of the safe and holstered to the waistband of my jeans. I grabbed my hoodie—a gift from a witch Saul and I helped out of a jam a long time ago. The stake on the back was a little on the nose, but I loved the deep red color. It might simply look like a cool sweatshirt to others, but it was bulletproof and would ward off low-level magic attacks. It was priceless.

Fluffy flew off the table and landed on my shoulder. "Are we going to save the princess?" Imps were notoriously good eavesdroppers.

"Just like Link and Mario." Saving the princess was a story as old as time, and I'd never stop fighting for this one.

Fluffy grinned. "Old-school. I like it."

Sometimes old-school was the best.

I armed the security system and ran down the stairs. We were in my two-door Wrangler a few seconds later and headed toward our destination. If the vamps found out who Megan was, things would escalate quickly.

What was she doing out on a mission alone? Her powers had just manifested. She didn't know the extent of her capabilities. Neither did I. The only thing I knew for sure about every Champion of the Helsing Society was that they died violently.

Not Megan. Not on my watch.

I parked a mile from the entrance to the industrial complex.

Saul sent some satellite pictures. I pulled them up on my phone and sent copies to my laptop for larger viewing as I inventoried the gear in the cargo area. Science supplied us with an endless wealth of super cool stuff to fight vampires. Silver-tipped stakes, knives with silver in the blades, and an assortment of colloidal silver paintballs for the custom rifle I had made. The weapon might be overkill for this mission, but this was Megan, so I took it anyway. Besides, it was the perfect weapon against younger vampires vulnerable to silver.

I grabbed another tube of silver ammunition and one of witch juice. There weren't many magic users in the Phoenix metro area, but it never paid to take chances.

Walking down the street with a weapon that resembled an M16 strapped to my back was bound to attract attention even in an open carry state like Arizona. That's why I wouldn't walk. Running at vampire speed, I could cover the distance to the warehouse in about two minutes.

I looked over the satellite images one last time. Everything but the gate and one warehouse at the back of the property was unguarded. It seemed too easy until I remembered the security equipment. In addition to a standard alarm system, there could also be motion sensors, pressure plates, cameras, and infrared or temperature sensors in use.

I closed the rear gate, locked the Jeep, and turned to Fluffy. "I'm not going to offer you a deal. I just need you with me on this one."

The imp looked touched. "Let's say you owe me one."

I glared at the little bugger. "Within reason."

Fluffy landed on my shoulder. "Don't worry, Dylan. We'll get her back."

My demon was hard to figure out. She wanted to help but had an internal block that stopped her unless we made a deal. I still got angry about it on occasion but realized that in her strange way, Fluffy was trying to assist me.

The asphalt thundered beneath my feet as I sped down the road, headed for the warehouse complex.

Of course, waltzing straight in the front would be a mistake. Instead, I did what any good burglar would do. I broke into the lot next door. It was full of junked cars and heaps of rusty scraps. I didn't see the value, but maybe someone else did. When I was a kid, junkyards like this had aggressive dogs for security, but nowadays even the canines were being put out of work by technology.

With any luck, I'd be long gone before the establishment's employees checked their surveillance tapes.

Being spotted on film wasn't a concern unless they called the police or worse, alerted the on-duty staff at the warehouse. I wasn't worried about being recognized. Mirrors muddled our features. Photographs and videos made us look out of focus and washed out like an overexposed photograph. The effects made us harder to identify. It was a damned handy personal security feature when answering questions inside a police station at three in the morning.

That could be anyone on that video, Officer, I swear.

I ignored the cameras and kept my eye on the fifteen-foot tall razor wire-topped wall that separated the lots. It seemed like overkill to protect a few simple warehouses, but they probably did it to save on insurance. The bean counters loved it when they didn't have to worry about easy theft.

I walked along the wall until I found a pile of cars that looked tall enough for me to use as a springboard to get over the barrier. I nodded at Fluffy. "It's your time to shine."

She flew over the wall and came back a minute later. "All clear on the other side."

I jumped once, landing on top of three stacked cars. I leapt a second time and landed on the other side of the wall. It would've been cool to say I landed silently, but no. My two-hundred-pound frame slammed into the ground, hard. My knees didn't like it, but by the time I stood, any damage caused by the drop had already healed.

Fluffy landed on my shoulder. "Circle back for the guards at the gate, or go straight for the princess?"

It was a good question. I didn't like the idea of leaving armed men behind me. They could be trouble when we tried to exit.

At the same time, all that mattered was getting to Megan as quickly as possible. I couldn't let anything happen to her. She might never feel anything for me, but I was smitten with stupidity when it came to her. If she died tonight, I'd never get to see where things might go. Not to mention, her loss would devastate Saul and Greg.

"I have to save her, Fluffy." I didn't like the desperation in my voice.

The imp flew off my shoulder. "One security system going down. They'll never see you coming."

I winked at the imp. "Thank you." I swore I saw a little color in her cheeks as she flew off.

My guess was demons didn't get many thanks. It was kind of like working at a fast-food place without any acknowledgment. How hard was it to say thank you after ordering food? A little common courtesy went a long way to brighten people's days. In this case, it wasn't an empty platitude. I meant it.

Imagining a perplexed security person trying to figure out why their entire system was down for no reason made me snicker mentally. *Get Imped, sucker!*

I gave Fluffy a few minutes to work, then crept forward. Vampiric hearing had advantages when it came to sneaking around. If anyone were close, I'd be able to hear them. The guards at the gate were too distant to pick up, but nothing moved in my immediate vicinity.

I kept the rifle raised as I peeked around the building's corner. The guards at the gate faced the street. It made sense. If there was a threat, it shouldn't be coming from inside the secured area.

Turning away from the gate revealed the other two guards I'd seen on the satellite images. This was the only building with additional security. It had to be where they were holding Megan. Guards wouldn't be stationed outside a warehouse unless there was something inside to protect.

The men didn't move with the grace of vampires, so I realized they were Renfields. I hated humans willing to sell out their species by working for vampires.

I glanced at the gate to confirm no one was looking and sprinted across the space between the large buildings. The narrow alleys between several structures provided cover until I was close enough to hear the guards breathing. Neither man spoke. They were attentive to their task, which wasn't easy to do late at night. Even when a person worked the graveyard shift for years, something about the three am hour brought most people down.

Not these guys.

The two men guarding the front of Warehouse Fourteen were alert and twitchy, suggesting they were wired with enough coffee to power an army. It wouldn't be easy to sneak up on them. Thankfully, they were humans. They didn't stand a chance against me.

I pulled my knife from its sheath, slipped around the

edge of the warehouse, and took off like a rocket. I drove the blade into the first man's chest as I slammed into him. Momentum carried us into the second guard.

Before he could reach for his gun, I'd pulled my knife free and plunged it into his heart. The gentle sucking sound as I pulled the blade out wasn't loud enough for the guards at the gate to hear. The growing pool of blood by the door *was* a cause for concern.

I pushed the bodies up against the side of the building. They weren't out of sight but weren't out in the open anymore. I couldn't do anything about the blood. I had too much dignity to lick it off the asphalt. As a wise woman once said, ain't nobody got time for that.

With the two Renfields down, I pulled the rifle off my back and ensured it was ready to fire. Fluffy appeared a moment later. She glanced at the bodies, then drifted to the door. As far as I knew, there wasn't a building on the planet Fluffy couldn't get into. Fort Knox was lucky she hadn't taken my vacation idea seriously.

Between my face blurring on surveillance cameras and her ability to open locks, we could have stolen enough money to buy our own country. *Dyltopia? Nope. Maybe Fluff Island? Shit, that was even worse. Maybe I'd settle for enough money to pay my property taxes.*

The door slid open, and I slipped through it with my rifle raised. Stacks of boxes on pallets occupied most of the space. I rushed toward the first set, using it for cover as I searched for more guards.

I'd never had formal training on how to breach a building. I only knew what I learned from playing video games and watching John Wick movies. I wasn't an expert, but I knew enough not to get shot.

Then something hit me in the back. *Always clear the door, dumbass.*

I hadn't checked either side of the doorway in my haste to get inside, and now I was paying for it. A bullet hit the magical hoodie and bounced off. That didn't stop the round from cracking one of my ribs. Before the shooter could fire again, I dodged, picked him up by the throat with one hand, and let my rifle hang to grip his wrist. I squeezed, crushing the bones until he dropped his weapon.

I wanted to feed on him to speed up the healing, but I didn't know what Megan would think if she saw my mouth covered in blood. She knew I was different, but I didn't believe she knew the whole story. Greg was probably dying to fill her in. The last thing he wanted was his daughter getting involved with a monster. To him, I was more vamp than human.

I snapped the guard's neck and dropped him.

There was a lot of human security for an allegedly simple mission. Megan could deal with one fledgling on her own, maybe more. The newer, less experienced vampires weren't as powerful as their elders. For her to get captured meant the intel was off or she'd made a big mistake in her calculations.

I silently moved through the warehouse with my rifle in my hands, slipping from one laden pallet to the next. In some places, they'd been stacked almost to the twenty-five-foot ceiling. It made the warehouse feel like a rattrap or a maze instead of an organized distribution center. My gut said to slow down because I was moving too fast to hear or see anything important, but my feet had other ideas.

Saving Megan was all that mattered.

"You're going to tell us where the Templars' headquarters is." The man who spoke wasn't asking a question.

It sounded like Megan spat on him. Then he slapped her.

I didn't think as I rounded the last obstacle between us with my rifle raised to fire. I wanted to look at Megan and ensure she was okay, but I stayed focused on the vampire standing before her. My finger reflexively squeezed the trigger and held it for auto-fire. Paintballs flew and exploded on impact, burning his skin where the colloidal silver touched him. Each hit stripped away some of his strength.

Two fledglings charged me, trying to defend their sire. It was easy to stop the first one by firing a steady stream of flying silver paintballs at him. The younger vampire reacted violently to the shots. He fell to the floor, screaming in pain. I turned to shoot the last fledgling and managed to block her sword as she swung it at me.

Who the fuck brings a sword to a gunfight?

The blade stuck in my rifle's barrel, and when she tried to yank the sword free, I let go of the gun. The woman flew backward, and I charged her holding my silver-tipped stake. She burst into ashes a moment later when it tore through her heart.

The other fledgling was too busy clawing the silver from its skin to notice me coming. I ashed that sucker with a smile. There was only one person left in the room to deal with.

The vampire.

"It wasn't nice to kill my children." He had one hand around Megan's throat.

His three-inch-long nails pressed into her skin. It would only take a small squeeze to rip her throat out. The craziest thing was Megan didn't look worried. Her long black hair was tied back in a ponytail, making her vibrant blue eyes stand out. I could have looked into those eyes forever. Right now, they shone with laughter.

"It's not him you should be worried about." Megan tugged on the vampire's forearm.

The limb didn't move a fucking inch.

She kept tugging on it, and the vampire laughed. "When the master sees who I've brought him, he will shower me with riches."

Megan kept her hands on the vampire's arm, but she wasn't tugging anymore. Her blue eyes almost glowed. The idiot was still too focused on me to realize something was happening.

A golden aura appeared around Megan's hands. I had no idea what she was doing, but I'd back her play. All I had to do was keep this vampire busy for a little longer.

"Do you think your master is going to be happy with you? This location is compromised, and he's lost several assets." I nodded at one pile of ashes. "I wouldn't count on a warm welcome home."

The vamp's smug expression didn't falter. He tried to lift Megan, but all that rose was a stump. He waved it as he tried to comprehend where the rest of his limb had gone.

The vampire lunged to grab Megan and screamed, "The master will restore me."

"That would be a neat trick." Megan dodged the vampire's grasp and kicked his back as he passed to create space between them.

I was still getting used to her magic, but if I wasn't mistaken, she'd Harry "My scar will protect me" Pottered that guy's arm.

It was like when Voldemort tried to touch Harry at the end of the first movie and started to dissolve. Except she'd actively used her magic to hurt him. *Remind me never to piss her off.* There were a few parts of my anatomy I wanted to keep intact.

The vampire realized how much trouble he was in when my stake tore through his heart. I stepped back, pulling the stake free as flames burst from the wound. The vampire exploded, and fire spread to some of the boxes behind him. It was time to go. As soon as the boys out front saw the flames, they'd call in the cavalry.

Megan pulled me into a hug. "Thanks for coming."

"Always." I grinned like a lovesick moron. "What happened to the leg?"

Seeing her wound made me want to kill that vampire again.

"I was scouting the place, and one of the guards got off a lucky shot." She looked more embarrassed that she'd made a mistake than the fact a vamp had almost killed her.

I looked at the wound, trying not to think about what her blood would taste like. "You can't run on that leg." I knelt and offered her a piggyback ride. "Hop on."

Megan didn't know the extent of my abilities, but she was about to get a preview.

I slipped my hands under her thighs and lifted. She winced so I set her down. Holding her like that was going to be a problem. My hand was on the bullet wound.

My heart ached to know she was in pain. I'd been shot so many times I had forgotten how much it could hurt. The last face I wanted to see grimace was hers.

I stepped in front of her and lifted her into my arms. Realizing what I wanted, Megan wrapped her legs around my waist. I put my hands under her butt, keeping them well away from her wound.

Megan bit her bottom lip in a way that made my heart race, then buried her head into my neck. "What are you waiting for? Get me out of here."

"As you wish." We took off at full speed.

I wasn't going to stop until she was safe.

Fluffy and I sat on the couch. I took a hit off my dry herb vape and passed it to the imp. Megan was back in her family's arms and resting. Seeing how much they loved her made me think about my family. I hadn't thought of them in years. Time had a way of eating away at the pain of their loss, but the emotional wound stung as freshly as the day it happened whenever I picked at it.

Fluffy passed the vaporizer back, and I took another hit. Life had been simple before all of this started. I was a kid fresh out of high school. Now my remaining human friends were in their fifties.

There were still so many unanswered questions, things that needed resolution. To know what I wanted for the future, I had to examine my past. Tonight was the right night to do it. Leaning back, I exhaled and let my body sink into the couch.

Reliving the past was never easy, but I couldn't avoid it forever.

CHAPTER TWO

1999

"Dylan, you sound like a cheap wind chime." Enrique laughed as he tossed an empty beer bottle into the woods.

The glass bottles in my backpack *clinked* as I walked, but I didn't hear him complaining about getting free beer. It was a great night when you were under twenty-one and your buddy scored a few bottles. Neither of us had fake IDs, and there weren't many merchants willing to risk the fine for selling to minors. This beer stash was courtesy of the fridge in my family's garage. Thanks to the holiday season's upcoming parties, it was packed. Or had been, until I got frisky and grabbed a whole damn twelver off the top.

It was too bad there wasn't a beer tree we could harvest when we wanted a few drinks.

I was nineteen and living at home. I spent my days helping my dad keep the sandwich shop running and my nights trying to sneak girls into my bedroom. If I could get them past Mom. The woman possessed a sixth sense when it came to interrupting my chances of getting lucky.

"Did you toss that in the forest?" I pulled another beer from my backpack and waggled it. "If you want this one, you gotta promise to put the empty back in the bag."

Enrique stopped and held out his hand. "Give me the beer, eco-warrior."

If being an eco-warrior nabbed me a date with Joey Laureen from *Bio-Dome*, I was all in.

Pulling the beer away from his outstretched hand, I *tsked* like his grandma did when she was upset with him. "Not until you give me your word."

"You sound like a girl on the third date." Enrique grinned like he'd promise me the world if I gave him what he wanted. "I won't chuck this one in the trees if it unwinds your panties."

It was my turn to smile as I pulled the beer away from his outstretched hand again. "I don't know. They're still kind of bunched up from all the excitement."

When a man accused you of wearing panties, you had two choices. Let him humiliate you or push it further until they were too uncomfortable to bring it up again. I wasn't there yet, but if Enrique dropped another panties joke, I would mention how hot his older sister was.

It was a real shame Marissa didn't come home for Christmas anymore. She was a real hottie. I could go on and on about when she washed her car in the driveway. Sometimes I still dreamed about it.

Enrique snatched the beer from my hand before I could pull it away again. My buddy did whatever he wanted, regardless of how I felt about it. That was his MO. If he hadn't been my best friend since I moved to Illinois, I would have kicked him to the curb in a heartbeat.

We were on different paths. I wanted to get back into school, and he was content being a small-time hustler. He wasn't perfect best friend material, but I tried to work around the flaws.

No one was perfect. I had plenty of flaws of my own.

That was why I created the Path to Greatness—a little roadmap in my head of where I wanted to be in the future. Whenever I had to make a serious choice, I pulled up the Path to see if the decision got me closer to success or farther away. Then I picked the option that moved me closer. At least I did most of the time.

Sometimes you had to throw the plan aside and live a little.

"Hate calling it a night so early, but I have to work tomorrow." I looked down at my feet, shuffling them a bit. I hated disappointing my best friend, but I wasn't going to underestimate my father's wrath. "You know how my dad gets if I show up late and hungover."

Taking a long pull of his beer, Enrique lifted his brows. "Fine, but before I let you off the hook, you gotta do me a solid."

Here we go.

Favors for Enrique typically ended with us running from the cops or an angry boyfriend and his crew. I couldn't afford to get into any more trouble if I wanted to get into college. Taking a year off school to help at the store had put me behind on applying to universities as it was, and schools wouldn't think criminal histories were badges of honor.

I knew my friend wouldn't take no for an answer, but

my days of blindly following his lead were over. "Tell me what it is first."

There were certain lines I wouldn't cross on one of Enrique's little adventures. It was all fun and games when we hit the beer bong and ran down the street to get Taco Bell, but I wasn't the kind of guy who broke into buildings or sold drugs for a living. I had different ideas about what I wanted out of life. Enrique wanted to get ahead, but he was willing to cut corners. I'd learned not to underestimate his lack of scruples when it came to making money a while ago.

"I gotta go make a deal with Dabbler." He handed me the empty bottle and motioned for another.

I frowned as I pulled a fresh beer out of my bag and slapped it into his hand. "Didn't he try to stab you once?"

This trip didn't sound like it was on the Path to Greatness.

"We might have entered into aggressive negotiations on occasion, but that's all in the past." Enrique waved his free hand as if warding off further discussion on the matter. "Now, we do business."

Alarm bells went off in my head. "Do you only need a ride, or are you looking for backup?" Going to meet with Dabbler was on the edge of my "fuck off I'm going home" radar.

I would need some convincing before I said yes.

As far as drug dealers went, Dabbler wasn't so bad. I'd never seen him with a gun. That didn't mean if I wanted a little ganja, there weren't a hundred other people I'd call first. Dabbler tended to traffic with a harder crowd than I was comfortable with.

I liked to smoke and relax. I wasn't about the lifestyle. Hard drugs had a higher chance of ending in violence, and I had other plans for my future. Dreams that didn't include serious injury or jail time for trafficking.

All I wanted was a chance to shine.

Enrique waved away my concerns and hit me with the "aw shucks" smile. "Grams won't let me take the car tonight, so I need a ride. You don't have to come up. You can wait downstairs. It won't take more than a few minutes. I swear." Enrique sipped his beer.

"What are you picking up?" I wasn't driving him home with something I didn't know about in my car. Police officers didn't tend to believe pleas of ignorance.

"You gotta relax, bro. Dabsie Doo Little just got a shipment of the dankest dank. You remember that stuff from last summer that smelled like blueberries? I'm going to buy a quarter pound. Shit is going to sell itself."

That Blueberry Skunk was some damn fine weed.

Going to Dabbler's house with a thousand bucks in his pocket and no backup seemed stupid. Once a deal crossed that financial threshold, people started to get a little twitchy. Dabs wasn't hardcore, but that didn't mean he wouldn't lash out if Enrique tried to screw him over. This was starting to feel way out of my comfort zone, but I couldn't let my friend go alone. If something happened to Enrique because I didn't go, I wouldn't be able to live with myself.

Picking up a quarter pound was a little beyond my scope. That wasn't a weight you carried around for recreational use with your friend while watching movies. I needed to think of the trip as a ride, or I needed to back out. Then there was the blueberry factor. It was good, and it'd been out of circulation for almost a year.

"Are you sure he has the blueberry?" I had my doubts, but it might be worth it if he had this strain.

Enrique grinned. "I'm sure." He put a hand on my shoulder. "I wouldn't buy a quarter pound of just anything. I've got standards to uphold."

For the blueberry, I was in, but that didn't stop my mind from running into worst-case scenario territory. I doubted the cops would believe I was only giving Enrique a ride if we got pulled over with a quarter pound of marijuana in the trunk.

The police in St. Charles tended to act like marijuana was as dangerous as heroin, but that was the line the Federal government still fed them. I simply found their logic difficult to follow. The number of friends I had who smoked a little herb and still got straight A's bordered on absurd. I was pretty sure if they all started chasing the dragon, there wouldn't be a single one left on the academic honor roll.

At least California figured out the truth. One day the rest of the states would follow.

The St. Charles police department didn't play games, and Illinois wasn't California. Getting caught with a QP would mean serious jail time. It was too much pot for them to believe it was for personal consumption, which meant we'd face a distribution charge on top of possession. If Enrique had any baggies or a scale on him, we were up shit creek without a paddle. I designed the Path to keep me from getting into this kind of trouble, but I was a sucker for dank. Nothing made making sandwiches for a living feel cooler than smoking a little before work.

The family sandwich shop was struggling and not because the food was bad. Someone wanted to buy the strip mall out from under my dad, and he wasn't playing ball. They started to play dirty. It meant I had to work more when I should have been out meeting ten thousand new and incredible women at school. Eight more months and I could move somewhere warm.

Short-shorts and flip-flops for days.

"Are you sure you want to do this?" It was the only way I could think of to get him to change his mind without making me feel like I was leaving him hanging.

Instead of answering, he walked toward my Jeep. Halfway there, he turned. "Come on, bro. Let's get this done."

I dumped our empties into the park's trash can and put my bag and the six-pack we had left in the trunk. The hardest thing in the world was to say no to your friends when they wanted your help. I decided to drive Enrique despite the risks. Mostly because I wanted another chance to enjoy some of the blueberry, and I wasn't too worried about the cops. As long as we stuck to the side streets, we might not see a squad car.

The still, small voice inside me said this trip was a major detour on the Path to Greatness, but I was going for it. "I'm in."

"Yes!" Enrique fist-pumped like Tiger Woods winning the Masters. "Let's do this shit. I gotta swing by my place and get the cash."

It was hard not to get caught up in his enthusiasm. "Where'd you get the money?"

"You know me. I've been hustling." Enrique jumped into the passenger seat and rubbed his hands together to warm them. "If you turn on the heat, I'll ask Rosa to make us something to eat."

The thought of food from Rosa's kitchen was enough to get me moving. She made the best Mexican food on the planet, and I would have eaten it every day if I could. I slammed the rear gate closed, and a minute later I had the heater cranked to max. By the time we reached Enrique's house, we'd be sweat-covered. I'd gladly pay the price if that's what it took to get a seat at Rosa's table.

It was amazing what I'd do for some shredded beef tacos.

Dabbler looked like someone who still lived in his mom's basement, but he'd managed to rent a shitty studio apartment. I'd been in some real dumps before, but his place above The Melrose Bar was one of the worst.

The siding on the back of the building was peeling off, and the staircase didn't look sturdy enough for a person to climb. This was not the kind of place I wanted to end up living. It shattered my perception of drug dealers. They always lived in fancy places in the movies, but they usually wound up dead or in jail.

I wasn't going to end up like those guys. At least, I wouldn't if I stuck to the Path.

You could say it was a work in progress.

As we moved single file up the rickety staircase, the walls shook from the bass vibrations of the band playing in the bar. All I could think of was the money in Enrique's pocket might cover Dabbler's rent for a year. How could a guy sell so many drugs and still live in such a shithole? It didn't make sense unless he spent recklessly.

Or maybe consumed recklessly.

There was a single naked bulb lighting the hallway. It gave off a weak, yellow light that made the crusty linoleum floor look like dried urine patches. Enrique glanced at me and smiled in a way that said, "never say I don't take you to the finest places." I hoped my expression reminded him that I was doing him a solid, and he could fuck right the fuck off. Rosa's tacos weren't worth another trip to this dump.

We came to a pentagon-shaped foyer with five doorways. One of the entrances was the way we came in. Three had apartment numbers, and a fourth looked like a communal bathroom. Enrique headed toward a door on our right. The linoleum cracked under our feet as we walked, and I mentally listed all the reasons why I shouldn't be there.

It's the tacos. I fall for that shit every time.

Enrique paused at the door and looked at me. "Dude, you're going to love this."

He pulled his beeper from his pocket and looked at it. After tucking the device back into his jeans, he knocked using a pre-arranged signal pattern. Two knocks, followed by four, a single knock, and three more.

The door opened a bit, and Dabbler peered through the crack. "One second." The door slammed closed and reopened quickly. "You're late, Enrique."

"Blame Wonder Kid here. He scored us some beers." He walked into the apartment with ease, looking like he'd spent a lot of time there. "New TV?"

Dabbler smiled. "I got the PlayStation hooked into the stereo. The sound is unreal."

The inside of Dabbler's studio didn't match the outside. The place had hardwood floors and a pimping woodstove tucked into the corner by his bed. Comfortable-looking couches and the biggest TV I'd ever seen dominated the rest of the space.

"It's HD." Dabbler hit me in the chest as he passed. "Come check it out."

There were moments in life when things got turned around. Working at my dad's shop for seven bucks an hour suddenly didn't seem like the best way to save for college. This place was awesome. If Dabbler could afford all this, maybe I could make enough money to help my dad get out of trouble. Then I could go to school guilt-free.

Dollar signs flashed before my eyes, and I reminded myself to calm down. Every movie I'd seen about a successful drug dealer ended with them in a box.

The Path to Greatness wasn't achievable if I was dead. Which meant my dream of running the streets like a mafioso was over before it started. Making deals like a bad Bond villain wasn't my style anyway.

Sure, it was probably my imagination running away with me. Small-time drug dealers didn't get bumped off unless they stepped on bigger toes. Who would waste their time killing someone as insignificant as Dabbler?

The guy's studio might be nice, but it was only four hundred square feet.

I marveled at the size of the TV, though. He'd paused *The Fifth Element*, and Mila Jovovich looked better than ever. High definition suited her.

I loved this movie. It was probably the best I'd seen since my dad took me to *Braveheart* in the theater. We didn't have HD at our house yet. With the time Dad spent at the store, all of our HD TVs were there so he could watch baseball, and I was stuck watching my old VHS videos at home.

I'd been worried we were walking into a trap, but Dabs had the funds to pull off this kind of transaction. There had to be more than a pound of cannabis in the giant bag sitting on the table by the TV. It could have been as much as three. It was the most marijuana I'd ever seen in one place.

The sense of calm I'd felt began to deteriorate. There was enough weight on that table to rack up some serious jail time. The fantastic apartment above the sketchy bar suddenly seemed super conspicuous. The kind of thing cops would catch onto pretty quickly. We hadn't even smoked yet, and I was paranoid as hell.

The voice in my head said it was time to go, and when that voice spoke, I listened to it. My Spidey-sense kept me from getting busted at parties on more than one occasion.

Enrique met my eye. "You're doing that thing."

"It's fine." *It wasn't.* "I need to call it an early night." I looked at Dabbler and shrugged. "Gotta work in the morning."

Looking at the bag on the table, Dabbler grinned. "Some of us are working right now."

"See, he wants us out of his hair too, bro." Enrique pulled out the cash. "Let's do this thing."

Dabbler counted the money, tossed it in a drawer, pulled out a prepackaged bag, and handed it to Enrique. "Always a pleasure, but I've got some other business tonight. You've gotta bounce."

The deal was done. It was time to go. I walked toward the door, and there were three hard knocks. I froze and looked at Dabbler and Enrique. Both of them had frozen in place, too.

Dabs hadn't expected this interruption. It was like a giant game of red-light, green-light. We stood paralyzed for a moment, but the second the shock wore off, Dabbler burst into motion. He grabbed the weed so he could hide it.

The front door exploded in a shower of splintered wood.

I didn't move. I thought it was the cops and didn't want to get shot for acting squirrely. My philosophy about the police was don't give them a reason to feel twitchy. That involved a lot of yes sirs, no sirs, and not resisting. I put my hands up, and two men with guns ran past me into the studio.

They weren't cops.

A third man in a nice black trench coat stepped inside. He wedged the broken door's remains back into the frame and strolled into the room like he owned the place. He glanced around and looked unimpressed with what he saw.

"I don't appreciate waiting for what's mine." His eyes locked on Dabbler like he was a bug that needed squashing.

This reinforced the "don't become a drug dealer" vibe I'd felt earlier. If I was going to get shot, I wanted it to be while doing something heroic. I didn't want to die trying to make a few extra bucks. It wasn't fucking worth it. I'd only gotten laid a couple of times, and I wanted to experience a lot more of that before I bit the big one.

This was why I should have stuck to the Path. All I could do now was pray I didn't die in a drug dealer's apartment above a bar I wasn't old enough to drink in.

"S-s-sorry," Dabbler stammered. It wasn't much of an apology.

The man took off his coat and laid it on a couch before sitting down. He looked at the giant bag of marijuana and frowned. "I hope you didn't pay for that with the money you owe me." His voice lowered to a growl.

Dabbler didn't say a word, so the man turned his gaze on us. "How do you know Mr. Dabbler?"

"We were buying some weed." Enrique held up his package as I nodded enthusiastically.

One of the men put his gun away and snatched the package out of Enrique's hands. He opened it and dumped it on the floor. "No money here, boss."

"Dabbler, why don't you fill another bag for these two young men?" He crossed his legs and leaned back. "I'd like to send them on their way so we can have our talk in private."

I didn't know who this man was, but he was the baddest motherfucker I'd ever seen. He made Jules Winnfield—Samuel L. Jackson's character in *Pulp Fiction*—look timid.

The law didn't matter to him. He controlled this situation, and there was nothing we could do about it. If I wasn't scared shitless, I would have been impressed. I'd met my first real gangster, and I didn't know his name.

Everyone in the room knew the man on the couch had issued a command we couldn't ignore. Dabbler filled a new bag while Enrique and I made ourselves as invisible as possible. When he finished, Dabs thrust the bag at the man with the gun.

You knew shit was about to get real when a drug dealer didn't weigh his product.

The gunman snatched the bag from Dabbler and pressed it against Enrique's chest. "You were never here, and you're never coming back. Do you understand?"

"Yes, sir," we both managed to croak.

The boss nodded. "The sirs were a nice touch, boys."

The guard nodded and pushed Enrique toward the door. "Get the fuck out of here."

Neither of us questioned our good fortune. We ran for the door as if our lives depended on it. The damn thing fell off its hinges when I touched it, but I didn't stop. I jumped through the gap and kept running. Laughter followed us as I pulled my keys from my pocket and thundered down the stairs.

I ran so fast I wasn't sure my feet touched down. I wanted to get out. An Olympic sprinter wouldn't have caught me. I was in the Jeep and had it in gear when Enrique pulled his door open and dove inside.

"Holy shit, bro!" He held out the bag of weed. "Can you believe it? This is like double what I paid for."

I peeled out of the parking lot and sped off into the night. "We could have died, and you're focused on the deal you got?"

"We're in one piece, and I'm going to make a lot of money. Win-win, dude." Enrique was riding high.

My adrenaline was pumping, too. I never wanted to do that again, but this was the most alive I'd felt since bungee jumping. Escaping a near-death experience had a way of putting things into perspective. It was time to take the Path to Greatness more seriously and not as a set of loose guidelines to follow when it was convenient. That and I needed a girlfriend.

I really wanted to get laid again before I died.

I slammed the Jeep into fourth gear, then poked Enrique's shoulder. "I want a quarter of it for free, no bullshit."

"Done." Enrique was probably thinking of ways to rope me into his next scheme, but this would be my last one.

All I needed to do was get him home, grab some tacos, and never do anything this stupid again. Smoking a little weed was fine, but I couldn't be out there making deals. I didn't want to be a criminal or a sandwich maker. I wanted to go to college, meet some girls, and figure out what I was passionate about. Why was that so fucking hard?

"For the record." I couldn't let it go. My heart was still beating like a jackhammer. "Almost getting shot at Dabbler's is never a win-win."

Enrique laughed. "This is one of those moments we'll look back on in twenty years when our kids are all grown up, and we'll laugh."

Best friend shit.

I could see that, but I knew he and I were on very different paths. I wanted to live a dream that didn't include a felony rap sheet. Tonight was supposed to be about having a few beers and shooting the shit. How did things get all twisted up?

"We ride together; we die together." I hit the 25 and headed back to his house.

Enrique slapped his hand against the dash. "Bad boys for life!"

CHAPTER THREE

"Bro, *Varsity Blues* just came in the mail today. Can you say the words whipped cream bikini? You gotta bail on work and watch this with me," Enrique pleaded over the phone.

Could I say the words? Since I'd heard about the scene, I hadn't thought about anything else. After last night's action, smoking a little and watching a movie sounded like just my speed, but there was no way I could ditch work early. Dad was my boss and landlord, so bailing on work wasn't a great idea. Besides, I wasn't quite ready for another episode of the Enrique Show.

When your family needed help, you did what you had to do. That meant staying late, covering extra shifts, and working on weekends. It didn't hurt that I got paid, too. I'd heard stories of kids working in the family business and not being paid for their work. While I didn't get overtime, I got paid for every hour. All of it went into savings for tuition.

When I got to school, all I'd have to focus on was hitting the books. I was going to engross myself in the entire college experience.

The Path to Greatness didn't allow taking the night off or more of Enrique's shenanigans. I felt bad for letting him down, but tonight I was choosing me.

"Sorry, Enrique. I can't make it tonight. Maybe tomorrow before work?" I wanted to see that whipped cream bikini before he sent the DVD back in the mail.

Enrique sighed. "Come on, Dylan, you know how Rosa gets. She wants those things back in the mail so we maximize our subscription. You gotta come over tonight, or the bikini goes back in the box."

He almost had me.

"I'll be there tomorrow, bro, promise." Either he'd understand or he wouldn't, but I could always soften the blow. "I'll bring you a sandwich from the shop if you can wrangle me up some more tacos."

"Seriously, dude? You think because we're Mexican that we eat tacos every day?" Enrique sounded offended, but I knew it was a negotiation tactic.

The bastard knew I wasn't asking about the tacos because they were Hispanic. I asked because I was tired of eating sub sandwiches, and his grandma made the best fucking tacos on the planet. I'd eaten four of the damn things last night. If I could sit at Rosa's dinner table every day and twice on Sundays, I'd always be satisfied.

But not Menudo Day. That was the one time you'd find me as far away from their house as possible. Any other day, Rosa would have me waiting outside the kitchen, begging like a puppy for a taste of something delicious. She was good enough to start a restaurant. Wouldn't that be something? Rosa's Cafe. Sounded like a dream.

I laughed. "Bro, if you take the phone in the kitchen right now and ask Rosa what's for dinner, and if the answer isn't tacos, I'll bring you two sandwiches in the morning."

"Fuck off." The line went silent as Enrique thought about it. "I'll ask, but if I win, one of the sandwiches has to be meatball double cheese."

His grandma made the tacos. My mom made the meatballs.

"It's a deal, but you hold the phone up so I can hear." No way I was taking his word for it.

Mama didn't raise a sucker.

I heard Enrique moving, then he said, "*Abuelita*, what are we having for dinner?"

"We're having chicken tacos smothered in salsa verde. I've been simmering the green chili sauce all day." Rosa's voice drifted over the line.

It wasn't shredded beef, but chicken tacos still counted for the W!

"I still want a meatball, double cheese," Enrique whispered, sounding defeated.

I knew how to make his day. "Meatball extra cheese, and a side of potato salad, coming your way."

"You're the best, man." Knowing Enrique, he imagined the sweet marinara sauce dripping off the crunchy white bread.

Maybe I'd bring him two.

There was a bang on the storeroom door. It was my dad. "You better not be chatting on the phone before seven!"

"Gotta go. I'll see you tomorrow." I hung up the cell phone my parents bought me and opened the storeroom door. "Sorry, Dad. It was only a few minutes, I swear."

Tony pointed at the sandwich table. "Wash your hands

and make a number forty-two with fries for the man in the lobby."

It didn't pay to argue when you got caught abusing your phone privileges three days after a phone responsibility talk. "I'm on it."

"I'll be in my office. If you get busy, holler at me." Dad sauntered down the hallway with a lazy wave.

It was good to be king.

Maybe not so great if he was heading to the office. Dad was a goddamn sandwich maestro. The man lived and breathed cold cuts. The one thing he never did was leave the kitchen to go to his office. It usually took Mom hours of nagging to pull him away from behind the deli counter, and even then, all he thought about was getting back to it.

I could count the number of times he set foot in that office on one hand. Mom did the books. That was their deal. She'd be part of the restaurant if she didn't have to work in the kitchen. Unless it was the meatballs. Nobody made those but Mom.

Things hadn't been easy for Tony since Sweeny showed up with his first offer. From there, the situation got progressively worse. The bastard had the balls to show up at our house this morning with his checkbook out. Dad must have had the mental fortitude of Michael Jordan taking the last shot of a championship game to not wipe the smug smile off the smarmy bastard's face.

Sweeny made me angry in a way I'd never felt before. He chased away our other tenants and scared off our best employees. He was the reason I was here instead of at college. It was like the man woke up one day and decided to ruin my life.

Sweeny should have known better. Dad was never going to sell.

Dad built this place from the ground up. He started by owning the shop on the corner. Now he owned all ten storefronts.

He could have retired years ago and lived off the rent, but making the perfect sandwich was his higher calling. No one was going to take that away from him. Whatever Sweeny offered, it would never be enough to force Tony out. No one made him do anything he didn't want to do. He was tough as nails.

Or as stubborn as a disgruntled mule.

The forty-two was pastrami on white, Swiss cheese, mayo, onions, lettuce, and tomato with a kiss of spicy mustard. It was a damned fine sandwich. If I hadn't spent the last fifteen years wolfing them down, I probably would have been hungry the second I heard the order number. Fries were on the ticket, so I dropped those first and got to work slinging bread.

A lot of places like to toast the bread with everything on it. That was fine when the customer wanted something hot like a meatball or cheesesteak, but it ruined a good cold cut sandwich. You always toast the bread first, was what Dad liked to say.

Toast the bread, mayo, mustard, cheese, and onions on the bottom. Then the meat, with lettuce and tomatoes sprinkled on top. That was how Tony made them, and twenty years of continued success couldn't disagree with his process.

Tony's Famous Subs had the best damn sandwiches in the city, and everyone knew it.

I placed the masterpiece in the basket, salted the fries,

and dumped them on top. When I saw Sweeny in the lobby, smiling as if he didn't have a care in the world, I almost spat in the food. It was a good thing my parents had raised me to value myself as a person, or I would have done it in an instant. At least now I knew why my dad needed a break.

It never pays to punch the customers. If I said it enough, I might avoid going to jail today. Sweeny would have loved for me to slug him. It would make it easier for him to steal the store from under us.

"Pleasure to see you again, Mr. Sweeny." I set the basket on his table with a bottle of ketchup. "Can I get you anything else?"

He picked up a fry and took a bite. "I swear, these are the best damn fries in the state. It's going to be a real shame when you go out of business."

The greasy little shit.

"My dad might be too polite to tell you to fuck off, but you're not welcome here." Everything inside me wanted to lunge forward and find out how many times I had to smash his head on the table before it cracked open like one of Gallagher's watermelons.

Sweeny picked up the sandwich and weighed it in his hand. "If he'd sell to my employer, Tony would have enough money to open a new shop anywhere."

"You've met my dad. He'd rather go bankrupt than give in." Tony didn't like being squeezed even if the offer was double the property value.

This was his baby. He wasn't going to sell.

Sweeny swallowed a bite of food. "I'm looking out for you, kid. My employer gets what she wants, and she's not worried about how it gets done."

"Is that a threat?" The salesman had always struck me as sleazy but not dangerous.

Sweeny set the sandwich down and stood. "Think of it as a friendly warning." He walked to the counter and grabbed a paper bag. "I think I'll take this to go."

I watched as Sweeny bagged his food and left. I wanted to lock the door behind him, but a jingle from the back door distracted me. We weren't expecting deliveries, and I knew Mom wasn't in the office. So why had the door jingled?

What in the hell was going on?

Sweeny the Sleaze had me on edge, so despite the reaming I might get from Tony, I locked the doors to the lobby and flipped the sign to closed. If we missed a couple of dinner customers, so be it, but no one was coming through the front while I went to see what was happening in the back. With the front doors locked behind me, I felt a bit safer. As soon as I picked up my knife from the kitchen, I'd feel downright peachy.

Millions of peaches, peaches for me, I silently sang.

My brain was already at work trying to calm me down. Who would have thought one of the most popular songs in recent years would be about peaches? I shook off the random factoid and looked for the right knife.

The big one we used to shave meat was intimidating enough. Probably wouldn't work for shit in a fight, but it was damn near the size of a machete. With this thing in my hand, anyone without a gun would think hard about fucking with me.

A woman screamed. There shouldn't have been a woman in the building unless Mom had come in and didn't tell me she was here. I ran to the back.

The sub shop wasn't big. There was only one turn

between the hallway and the single office in the back of the shop. The doors to the alley looked closed, but the lock had been pushed open, and they wouldn't close completely. *What in the world was going on?*

The office door swung open, and my mom ran out. Blood dripped down the side of her face and covered her shirt. She froze when she saw me, and panic filled her eyes.

She glanced at the office, then back at me. "Run!"

The lights went out.

She screamed, and there was a *whoosh* like the air was being sucked out of the room before the office door slammed shut.

Fuck! I froze and listened. I wanted to run, but my feet had other ideas. My family was in there. I couldn't run while they were being attacked. I had to do something. My parents would never leave me. I wouldn't leave them.

The backup generator on the roof kicked in, and the lights flickered on. I sighed in relief. Whoever cut the power didn't know about Dad's backup plan. After losing an entire refrigerator full of imported meat, Tony bought one. He was a big believer in never making the same mistake twice.

The momentary comfort I felt when the lights came on faded when I saw the trail of blood on the floor. Mom's office door stood ajar and looked like someone had slammed it so hard the lock broke. There was no noise from inside, but the lights were on.

I felt like I'd become trapped in a movie without the sound reel playing. It was deadly silent, but that wouldn't last for long. I raised the knife, ready to strike. *Please be okay*, I repeated to myself. When I reached the door, I drew a deep breath and screamed as I kicked it the rest of the way open.

Mom sat in the guest chair with her body facing the desk, but her head unnaturally twisted toward the door. She stared at me with lifeless eyes. I didn't know how to process what I saw. The scream died on my lips, and I went numb. I knew other people were in the room, but I had trouble tearing my eyes away from her corpse.

"Your mother was a fighter." A slender woman licked a bit of blood from her lips.

In any other circumstance, I would have spent the next day telling Enrique about the hot babe that came into the store. She was five-seven but looked taller with boots on. Her hair was platinum blonde, but her eyebrows were raven black. She wore dark eye makeup, and her wing-tipped eyeliner gave her eyes a slight upward tilt.

She looked like a goddess, but she had her hand wrapped around my father's throat. I'd cut her with the knife the same as if she were a three-hundred-pound man named Big Jim.

"Your dad, on the other hand, is meat for the grinder." She pulled his head to the side and bit down hard on his neck.

I screamed again and swung the knife at her head. Then my arm stopped moving. Reacting on instinct, I turned and punched whoever was holding me. I might as well have hit a brick wall for all the good it did.

The man holding my arm let out a small grunt when my fist bounced off his chest. He squeezed my arm until I dropped the knife, then kept me in place and made me watch as the woman drank from my dad's neck.

Sometimes, the news reported Satanic cult shit, but it always sounded like a bunch of teenage crazies. I'd never put much stock in Satan. It seemed he showed up about as much as God did, which, as it turned out, wasn't all that often.

Killer cults sounded as ludicrous as saying video games turned kids into killers and listening to rap music destined you for life as a thug. Clearly, the media was hip to something I'd been missing because these weren't your average high school weirdos.

Tony finally stopped jerking as the life drained from his eyes. The woman looked at me and smiled. Tiny bits of flesh stuck in her teeth and blood dripped from her lips. I wasn't sure one person could rip out another's throat with their teeth, but I was learning a lot of new things tonight.

The man behind me grunted in satisfaction and bent my head to the side.

"Ivan, wait. This one is so innocent. Do you think the prince would like him?"

What were they talking about? This was America. We didn't have princes.

The big man let go of my head. "He likes them younger. Stop wasting time, Krista. The cleaners are waiting outside."

What in the actual fuck?

Krista smiled as she walked toward me. Her bloody fangs gleamed in the white fluorescent lights. "Shame, he would have made a nice plaything."

Ivan let me go so Krista could grab me. I saw one slight chance to get away, and I took it.

I dropped to the floor and got my hands on the knife. Krista spun me around, and I brought the blade up in a wild slash. Blood spattered across my face. The copper tang filled my mouth and nose. Ivan snapped my wrist like a twig, and I howled as he shoved me to the floor.

Krista loomed over me. I'd sliced open her cheek, and

the wound ran through her eye. Raw fury blazed in her good eye as she pushed the flap of skin back in place with one finger. The torn flesh knit back together and the color returned to her injured eye.

Sweeny must have poisoned me somehow. Whatever was happening now *couldn't* be real.

"I hope you taste as delicious as the sandwich maker." Krista opened her mouth as her fangs extended. "Time to find out how far the apple has fallen from the tree."

Seeing death standing right in front of you and knowing there was nothing you could do about it felt odd. When her fangs pierced my neck, it made Ivan breaking my wrist feel like a tickle. Why was she biting me on the neck? There had to be easier ways to kill someone.

I never thought I'd die in such a ridiculous situation. Everything started to feel heavy, and my legs gave out. A wave of euphoria washed over me. I knew I was dying, but all the pain was gone. I floated on a cloud of ecstasy, and it was fucking delightful.

If I could bottle this feeling, I'd be a trillionaire.

Krista tossed me aside when she finished. "Call in the cleaners. I'm going back to the city."

The light slowly faded, and as much as I tried, I couldn't open my eyes.

CHAPTER FOUR

I woke up in the dumpster behind our building. Reality wasn't nearly as enjoyable as the dream I had about flying. I didn't know how Enrique got me in the dumpster, but if he thought he was getting a meatball sub after this shit, he had another think coming.

Then it hit me. This wasn't some stupid prank. It wasn't Enrique who threw me in the dumpster. It was Ivan. Bastard took me out the back door and tossed me in the bin like I was the evening's trash.

It was all coming back to me.

Being stuck in the garbage wasn't the worst thing that could have happened. I could have been dead. Holy shit, maybe my parents were still alive. I fumbled around in the dark, but all I felt was a slick and sticky mess.

"Mom?" I croaked. "Dad?"

There was no answer.

Gingerly, I felt my neck. There was dried blood but no other wounds. I'd seen how Krista destroyed my dad's, so it was a hell of a shock to find mine intact.

I slowly shifted my weight, trying to figure out which way was up. Dumping bodies in a dumpster wasn't exactly criminal mastermind shit unless you owned the garbage company or had the cops on your payroll. The most basic rule of getting away with murder had to be not leaving the bodies where anyone could find them.

Sanitation workers tended to notice when an arm was sticking out of the bin.

Someone who thought they were a vampire had bitten me. It was fucking nuts, but it happened. Did Sweeny work for the vampire wannabes? I felt like I was losing my mind.

I needed to get out of this dumpster. Then I had to find a cop and tell them what had happened. There was always a chance my parents were still alive but too weak to answer. All that mattered was my family. They had to be okay. They were all I had.

The memory of my desperate escape attempt came back to me. I'd slashed Krista with the knife, and Ivan had broken my wrist. I twisted my right hand in a circle. Damn thing felt fine.

Maybe I had been drugged and imagined the entire thing? That would explain Krista's face healing before my eyes. They couldn't even pull off that kind of special effect in the movies yet.

Then there were the teeth. I'd see them in my nightmares.

I would freak out if I didn't get out of the dumpster soon. Who could I tell about what happened? The story was outlandish at best, a coverup for a horrific crime at worst. *I didn't believe it, and I was fucking living it.*

This wasn't a video game or a comic. The things that

went down shouldn't be possible. What kind of freak bites a person to death?

Shoving the dumpster's lid open took some doing, but once I got my leg wedged against the wall for leverage, it flopped back when I pushed it. The lights behind our shop were bright like the sun after being trapped in the dark. I couldn't see more than a few feet in front of me until I shaded my eyes.

I blinked a few times and waited for my vision to clear so I could check whether my parents were in the dumpster too. All I wanted to do was run and pretend like this wasn't happening, but I did what I needed to do.

Mom looked right at me from her awkward sprawl, but her eyes were glazed over, and her head was still unnaturally twisted in the wrong direction. Not much hope for her, but there was a chance Dad was still alive. It took me a minute to wriggle close enough to his body to check for a pulse, but there was nowhere on his neck to put my fingers without them slipping into the wound.

It didn't matter anyway. He was gone.

I sobbed. This must have been how Enrique felt when his dad died of cancer. The man had run marathons in his spare time for shits and giggles.

Healthy people like that shouldn't drop dead. His death served as a reminder that life could be fleeting so you had to enjoy it. Enrique had taken the message more liberally than I had, but now I was learning the same hard lesson.

Life was a relentless, raging river, and I was a pebble in the stream.

I looked down at Dad's neck again, then slowly raised a hand toward mine. I'd checked it once, but the whole situation still felt dream-like. I felt the dried blood, and the area was sore, but there weren't any big ragged holes. My brain was so full of horror movies and books about creatures of the night that I was starting to buy into the delusion.

"Holy shit, am I a vampire?" The thought made me laugh out loud.

The statement's absurdity would have made my dad ask if I'd smoked something before work. Why were they dead but I was walking around? It didn't make sense.

I touched my lips. My body answered before my mind had a chance to catch up. I remembered the taste of Krista's blood when it spattered on me. Could that be it? Was her blood in my system?

This was madness. Vampires weren't real. I said it to myself again to ensure the voice of reason dominated and held on to the mantra like it was a lifeline. *Vampires aren't real.*

The bodies of my parents were very real. It was conceivable that grief might make me delusional enough to think I'd become a creature of the night. Sweeny had to be smarter than to hire assassins to get the property. I heard about stuff like that on the news but never thought it would happen to me.

An attack on our family couldn't be random. It had to be tied to Sweeny's employer somehow. Hulking Russian Bond villains didn't just show up to take out small business owners. They certainly didn't bring gorgeous, mentally unstable serial killers for backup. My mind was still trying to process what was happening when I should have been running.

It was the worst night of my life, and it'd be nice to explain it all away with the supernatural. Instead, I would spend the night in a police station, and that was if they believed my story. If the police didn't believe me, I'd probably get the Menendez treatment and spend the rest of my life in a cell. The only difference was I didn't kill my parents. This felt like a Lifetime movie waiting to happen.

What Really Happened to Tony and Mary McCormick, tonight at nine.

I climbed out of the dumpster, letting my mind wander into the absurd to keep it distracted from the nightmare of reality. Becoming a vampire or a werewolf had always been a "dream come true" idea.

I was always under the impression they didn't have to be mindless killers, that most supernatural creatures were victims of circumstance. They weren't good or bad because someone turned them. Being bitten only amplified who a person was before. But what did I know? My brain tried to piece together every fragment of supernatural lore I'd ever heard. I should have been running instead.

Things had gone sideways, and the fact I was trying to talk myself into a vampire-killed-my-parents story meant my judgment wasn't exactly sound. I needed to speak to someone who wouldn't bullshit me and would tell me if I was having a psychotic breakdown. I looked in the dumpster again and confirmed that everyone I loved was still there.

I only had one place to go.

A wave of thirst hit me. I was parched, like a man wandering the desert with no oasis in sight. Why was I so thirsty?

I'd heard blood loss could dehydrate a person. There wasn't as much blood in the human body as people thought. A gallon and a half was it. Lose more than half a gallon, and you were in real trouble. I don't know where I picked up that little factoid, but my brain was full of useless tidbits of information scrounged from late-night Internet reading.

See, Mom? I use the Internet for more than looking at boobs.

Standing next to the dumpster in the bright lights seemed like a terrible idea, so I walked to the parking lot. If my Jeep was still there, I could get to Enrique's before this got any worse. He'd know what to do. Right now, I was running on pure instinct and a thousand hours of *Goldeneye* video game experience to make my bid for freedom. Stay stealthy, stay out of sight, stay the fuck alive.

At least vampires didn't use proximity mines.

My Jeep was still in the back lot. I ran toward it. All of this would hit me like a ton of bricks later, but right now, I was too caught up in the moment to think things through. Getting the hell out of Dodge was my only priority. The fact that nothing would ever be the same without my family wasn't something I could consider right now. I just wanted everything to go back to normal.

It was too bad this wasn't like that Michael Douglas movie where everything was a game his brother set up. I wouldn't even be mad if my parents crawled out of the dumpster right now. I'd hug them and cry until I couldn't cry anymore. Then I'd let them have it. All I wanted was for them to be alive.

I reached into my pockets for my keys, but they were empty. My fucking pockets were empty.

Not only did Krista and her thug try to murder me, but they also took my brand-new phone, my wallet, and my keys. For some reason, I was more pissed about the wallet and keys than anything else. Maybe it was because they were tangible and real when I wanted so desperately for my parents' deaths not to be. Theft was normal, and I needed to cling to normality like a cliff diver needed water below them when they jumped.

Since I didn't have my keys, I needed Plan B. I could run to Enrique's house, but by the time I got there, shit might have hit the fan even worse. Someone had to have seen something. You couldn't simply erase three people. I looked at the restaurant's back door and thought about my dad bringing in deliveries. Then a different memory came to mind. I'd thought it was stupid at the time, but Tony insisted on putting a Hide-a-Key thing in my rear tire well.

I love you, Dad.

I reached above the back left tire and found the box with the spare key. My dad was always a sucker for having a backup plan, and my mom was responsible for putting them into action. I thanked God for both of them and the key in my hand. When the Jeep roared to life a moment later, I almost lost it. Tears formed at the corners of my eyes, but I wasn't safe yet. I drew a few deep breaths to steel my nerves and put the Jeep in reverse.

Something slammed into the driver's side door hard enough to dent it. The window shattered, and Ivan bounced backward. Holy shit, he just threw himself at my car like a fucking cannonball. My first instinct in an accident was to stop and make sure everyone else was okay, but in this case, I popped the Jeep into first gear and gunned it. Ivan reached through the broken window and tried to pull me out of the car as the back tires caught and the Jeep lurched forward.

The bastard was strong and didn't show signs of letting go as he clutched the broken window. He ran next to the Jeep while snarling something, but his voice was drowned out by Billy Corgan screaming about being locked in a cage. *Mom would be so pissed about the music volume.* I popped it into second gear and floored it. We hit the curb and bounced over the dip before hitting the sidewalk.

We fishtailed in the fresh slush. The skid caused Ivan to lose his footing, and I left him lying in the street. I glanced in the rearview mirror and saw him standing in the center of the road, staring at the back of my ride like he was searing the image into his memory for later.

I hoped there wouldn't be a later.

Holy blazing shitballs. That was closer than a shave with a straight razor. I looked out the broken window and realized Ivan had crushed the frame with his grip. Who in the hell was strong enough to dent a door like that? If I hadn't shaken him, would he still be holding onto the door?

That was close, too close.

I kept checking the side and rearview mirrors. I didn't see anyone following me, but I wasn't about to drive straight to Enrique's house. The last thing I wanted to do was lead trouble straight to my best friend's door, but like Princess Leia once said, he was my only hope.

I drove to my best friend's home using the side streets. One street from his place, I took a hard left, pulled into an alley between two rows of houses, and cut the engine. I needed to get myself under control. Speeding down side roads while looking behind me would only get me pulled over.

The cops would probably tell me to lay off the chronic until they saw the blood on my clothes. I looked more like I belonged in the Manson cult than making sandwiches.

Why did this happen to me? I just wanted to go to school and live a boring middle-class life, maybe have a kid or two. Now I was in some kind of crime drama, and I wanted it to stop. *Vampires are not real.*

Just because I loved to dream that the supernatural was real didn't mean it was. I also dreamed Salma Hayek would do that dance in the movie *From Dusk Till Dawn* right into my bed, but it never fucking happened. Vamps were something someone created in their head because they were afraid to die, and being immortal was the one true way to cheat death.

What happened wasn't possible. This was reality. There were certain rules—the corporations got rich, and the poor people got screwed. In no fucking scenario did the possibility of vampires exist.

If they did, I had some velociraptor DNA in a shaving cream can for sale on eBay.

My mind was spinning, and all I could think of was getting to Enrique. No one got out of more trouble than that slippery bastard. If anyone knew what to do, it would be him. There had to be a way to fix this and get back to normal. Your life shouldn't be allowed to go from gently chugging along to totally fucked in a matter of moments.

Part of me still hoped none of this was real. It was so farfetched I'd have trouble believing it as a movie plot, let alone reality. Sleazy sales guys working for vampires as they tried to squeeze the owners of a strip mall for their property. It was like someone wrote a *Sopranos* and vampire mash-up, and it wasn't working for me.

Why did I keep saying vampires? They weren't fucking real. Krista was just some bitch with a blood fetish and expensive fake teeth.

I drew a few deep breaths and tried to calm down. Jumping to all kinds of wild conclusions wasn't helping anything. I pulled out my bowl and the bag of blueberry Enrique had given me from the center console.

Usually, I saved the sticky for my after-work video game session, but if there was ever a time to get stoned it was now. Smoking all the time wasn't a Path to Greatness-approved pastime, but it was a great mental health pick-me-up in the right situation.

Two puffs later the rough edges began to smooth out.

A light came on in one of the houses, and I put the Jeep back in gear. Before pulling out of the alley, I stashed my bowl back in the center console. My hands stopped shaking, and my mind stopped spinning out-of-control fantasies about my life.

I wasn't in a good place mentally, but at least I was back in control for the most part. Maybe it was the weed or all of the stress, but the thirst I'd been feeling intensified. Enrique could get me a glass of water while I told him my story.

He's going to think I'm fucking nuts. I feel batshit.

The driver's side door was all the reminder I needed that this was happening. I tried to ignore the subarctic wind blowing through the shattered window by thinking about the heated seats. They were the best invention since functional plumbing. Warming my lower back felt great after a long day of slinging sandwiches. On a good day, the gentle heat almost made me fall asleep, but tonight it kept me Zen enough to keep going.

Five minutes more and I'd be at Enrique's house. I pulled Mellon Collie and the Infinite Sadness out of the tape deck and loaded something happier. For this drive, I needed something with a little more bounce. Sublime's *40oz. To Freedom* thumped from the overhead soundbar. "On the East side…that's where I live."

Feel the flow.

Within minutes, I parked in front of Enrique's place and

climbed out of the Jeep. My clothes were stiff and crunchy from the dried blood and the cold. The stuff caked my hands and hair. I needed a shower and some fresh clothes. Then maybe I'd be ready to spill my guts.

Enrique's room was at the front of the house, and he still had his light on. I decided to tap on his window instead of coming in like he always told me to. Interrupting a man's whipped cream bikini watching, Jergens for jerking time seemed rude without at least knocking first. The guy deserved time to wash his hands before answering the door.

The thought of his shocked face when I tapped on the window was priceless. Sadly, the speed at which his head popped into view discredited the Jergens theory. I headed for the door after a sheepish wave.

When the front door opened, Enrique stepped out grinning. "Dude, I knew you couldn't pass up chillin' with your homie."

"My schedule seems to have freed up." When I was stressed, the sarcasm always came out before I could stop it.

His smile faded. "What did you get into? Is that blood?" He backed away, and I couldn't blame him.

It wasn't every day someone showed up at the front door drenched in blood like an extra from an *Evil Dead* movie. I honestly couldn't say if my reaction would have been different if he showed up at my house looking like this. Except I probably would have run.

Holding my hands up, palms out to show I wasn't dangerous, I dropped to one knee. "I need help."

"Yeah, I can fucking see that man." Enrique stood still. "What in the hell happened to you?"

"Language, Enrique!" his grandma shouted from inside. "Invite your friend in or close the door."

This wasn't where I planned to tell him my story, but he closed the door so I wouldn't get inside without telling him something. "Sweeny showed up at the store."

Enrique shivered. "Guy makes my skin crawl."

You're not the only one.

"He tells me I better be careful. Next thing you know, there's this huge dude and some crazy lady in Mom's office."

"Holy shit, man. Did they hurt your parents?" Enrique pulled me to my feet and into an embrace.

I returned his hug, not knowing how badly I needed it until right then. "They're gone, man."

"You gotta call the cops. Sweeny can't get away with this shit." Enrique pulled me into the house. "Let's get you cleaned up. I'll take care of everything."

There was so much more he needed to know. "She bit their necks." My hand went up to my throat. "She bit my neck."

"Well, you're not bleeding now, but if you're hurt, we'll clean it up once we can see it. My bathroom, now. I'll grab a bag for those clothes and get you something to wear."

Being locked in the bathroom felt safe, and the sound of water hitting the shower floor put me at ease. My clothes crackled when I pulled them off and shoved them in a plastic bag from the Blue Goose Market. Little rust-colored flakes fell around me like I was shedding lice. Before I left, I would have to vacuum the floor.

The warm water felt so good when I stepped into the shower. I never wanted to leave. If Enrique was calling the cops, I needed to hurry up. The last thing I wanted was to get dragged out of the shower and taken downtown naked as the day I was born. It'd probably be better if I was waiting outside when the officers showed up. Rosa couldn't afford a new front door.

At least when they arrived, I wouldn't be covered in blood.

Pink water swirled down the drain, and I prepared myself for the flood of questions. Tonight was already the worst night of my life, and it wasn't about to magically get better. At least Enrique cared enough to let me get cleaned up. I could get through anything with my best friend there to support me. There was a path out of this mess.

I just had to find it.

CHAPTER FIVE

A detective was waiting in the living room.

At least, he didn't look like a beat cop. He wasn't wearing a uniform and didn't have a military haircut. He wasn't wearing funny clothes that made him look like a plain-clothes officer. Detectives always wore a suit, even when it was hot out. Bet they didn't realize when they got the paygrade bump they'd be spending the whole damn thing on a new work wardrobe.

The suit was inexpensive enough to be on the money for a detective, who risked it getting damaged on the job. This guy's coat was next-level elegant for a simple tan trench, though. My family might not have been rich, but I had enough friends with money that spotting the difference in superior quality wasn't that difficult. This guy wasn't shopping off the rack during the Burlington coat sale.

The man on the couch was a higher-ranking detective.

The detective looked up from where he sat talking to Enrique and saw me watching him. The look in his eyes was sad, but it wasn't the "sorry your parents just got murdered" kind. It was the resignation someone felt when they had to deliver bad news. I could already see it in the papers. *Dylan was smoking that marijuana again, and this time things went a little too far.* It was right out of the reefer madness playbook.

The worst thing I ever did while stoned was finish the ice cream and put the empty container back in the freezer instead of throwing it away.

My defenses were up. Not the right attitude to have when talking to the cops. They could spot a defensive personality from a mile away, which only made them suspicious.

Sniffing out changes in people's moods and their stories is what cops did for a living. They had to be good at it, or more killers would run free. I drew a deep breath and reminded myself I didn't do anything wrong.

Everything was going to be fine.

The detective offered Enrique a reassuring smile and stood. "Hi, I'm Detective Fraiser. Your friend here was filling me in on what you told him."

"Have you found my parents yet?" I couldn't stop myself from asking, no matter how guilty it might make me look.

The detective motioned toward the couch. "Maybe you'd like to sit."

"I'm fine where I am." Not the best answer, but I was too nervous to sit.

Rosa walked by and smacked me on the arm with a newspaper. "Manners."

I sat in the nearest chair. "Can you please tell me what happened?"

Detective Fraiser looked perplexed. "I hoped you could fill me in on some details. So far, we've got a cut power line and animal blood sprayed around the office. No bodies, business left wide open, and the generator ran out of gas. What happened there?"

Animal blood?

"Wait, you think this is some kind of prank?" All I could think of was crawling out of that dumpster and the cold dead look in my parents' eyes.

This was no prank.

The only explanation must be that Krista had someone inside the force or forensics covering things up. I didn't know much about the science of testing blood, but I knew all about government bureaucracy. There was no way they had a sample tested for anything this late at night in the time it took me to take a shower.

I drew a deep breath and tried to think about it more logically. Did it make more sense that the detective treated me as a suspect or that a woman who thought she was a vampire had cops on her payroll? I almost laughed but managed to keep a straight face. Of course, Fraiser was trying to trip me up. The people closest to the victims were always the best suspects.

That's what I told myself, but I wasn't a cop. I was a kid who watched a lot of late-night crime fiction. Sometimes those writers got the details right, and sometimes they were way off. I knew one thing for sure: it hadn't been animal blood covering the office.

Detective Fraiser nodded like this was all a waste of his time, and he would be better off spending it on something else. "All the evidence leads to this being some kind of hoax. I hear your family has been dealing with some problems from an aggressive real estate agent?"

"Sweeny?" He was slimy, but did he have the balls to hire an assassin? "Detective, until you locate my parents, I think we have to assume something bad happened to them."

Snapping his notepad closed, Detective Fraiser met my gaze. "I hope that isn't the case. Right now, I think we should take you to the hospital. Your friend here said you showed up covered in blood."

He didn't say the blood from the prank, but I knew he was thinking about it.

"I'm not injured." I looked at Enrique. He was supposed to have my back, but he wasn't saying a word.

"We should get you checked out. The last thing the department needs is some idiot from social services breathing down our necks because we didn't do our due diligence. It'd help me out if you'd agree to come with me. Then I can check you off the list and look at other suspects. I'll start with this guy Sweeny you mentioned."

Detective Fraiser smiled reassuringly. "It's not out of the realm of possibility for someone to damage property to hurry a sale along."

I should have nodded and kept my damn mouth shut, but I knew what I saw. "They're dead. I saw it with my own eyes."

With pity in his eyes, Detective Fraiser stood and motioned for me to do the same. "Let's get you to the hospital for an evaluation, and I'll look into it further. I can tell you for certain we haven't found any bodies. Not at the restaurant or your house."

They already searched our house? I'd greatly underestimated the efficiency of the St. Charles police department. Clearly, they were on it. I didn't know why, but I felt like the detective was lying to me.

Enrique and Rosa didn't look put off by his statements,

though. Maybe I was being paranoid. After what happened tonight, anything was possible.

"We've seen some local activism against butcher shops recently." Fraiser walked toward the door. "It's been mostly harmless until now, but let's get you to the doc so we can start looking into alternative theories."

Rosa called from the kitchen doorway, "As long as you bring him back when you finish. I mean it. I'll be checking up on him."

Right now, I couldn't think of a person I loved in this world more than Rosa.

The detective looked annoyed as he glanced at Enrique, and smiled and waved at the kitchen door. "I will, and if the hospital needs to keep him for any reason, I'll call and let you know."

"I expect a call from you personally, Detective Fraiser." She gave him the stare that only grandmas can muster when they feel exceptionally feisty.

The detective held the front door open. "I might even stop by personally to discuss it with you." He turned his gaze to Enrique. "Hopefully that won't be necessary."

Enrique moved past the detective and hugged me. "I don't know what's up, bro, but you're always welcome here."

My head spun in a million different directions. I had Rosa looking out for me, my best friend promising me a home, and a detective who was wildly off base with his animal rights theory. Granted, a few animal rights activists sloshing blood around a deli was more believable than a vampire stalking the sandwich makers of the city. I wanted to believe Fraiser's version of events, but I knew it wasn't true.

My parents would never put me through this.

It wasn't like I had a lot of options. When it came to the police, you either did what they said or ran. Risking the consequences for non-compliance wasn't an option. Running would only make me look guilty.

If I wanted to get out of this, I had to face it head-on. I'd go to the hospital and comply with their checkup. The only problem was Sweeny was still out there, and Enrique could be in danger. I had to give him a heads up.

"Don't trust anyone," I whispered to Enrique. His eyes bulged. I spoke louder. "I'm sure this is all a misunderstanding, and they'll have it cleared up by morning."

I was laying it on thick, but what else could I do?

I yelled toward the open kitchen door, "Thank you for everything, Rosa!"

Rosa popped her head out and waved away my thanks like she'd do it for anyone. "Like Enrique said, you are welcome here any time for as long as you need."

The sheer honesty in her voice brought tears to my eyes. I couldn't say anything to her without breaking down, so I stepped outside. "Let's go."

Fraiser closed the front door behind him. "Hope you don't mind riding in the back. It's regulation."

"As long as I don't have to wear your bracelets, it's all good." The only way I would put the cuffs on was if he arrested me.

"I don't think that will be necessary." The detective opened the car's rear door. "At worst, you've made some bad decisions that will cost your folks some cash to clean up. My money is leaning on these crazy vegan warriors. They don't think anyone should eat meat, and Tony runs the best deli in St. Charles. It makes him a logical target."

The fact he still thought this was a prank made me

reassess the police department. He wasn't filling me with any hope they'd find the real killers because they didn't think there had been a murder. I chose to go with him, and there was no getting out of it now.

Looking into his eyes, I spoke with conviction. "Whatever we need to do, detective. I'm all in."

I climbed into the car, and the door slammed shut behind me. I jumped, but the detective didn't notice. After starting the car, he switched the police radio off and played some music. Seeing the police radio made me feel better about the situation. Fake cops didn't call into dispatch. Fraiser glanced at me through the cage to ensure I was all set and pulled out into the street.

"This shouldn't take too long. Any kind of music you prefer?" Detective Fraiser was making small talk.

I had other things on my mind besides music. "Put on whatever you want."

He peered into the rearview mirror. "Suit yourself. Hope you like Power Hour."

Metallica started playing through the speakers. If there was anyone cooler than them, I hadn't found them yet. Metallica took the world by storm. Every album they dropped was better than the last. I tried not to relax too much. The last thing I wanted to do was answer a bunch of questions. Maybe the detective asked about the music I liked because he thought metalheads worshipped Satan and kids who played video games had destinies as killers.

As if those things had any correlation.

It was crazy that people thought kids who played a certain kind of violent video game were more predisposed to violence. I knew hundreds of gamers. Most of them couldn't kill a mosquito with a can of bug spray let alone get in a physical fight with a real person. If the detective asked, I'd talk about *Madden* and *Cool Boarders*. Talking about sports games instead of first-person shooters would probably put his mind at ease.

Seriously, I could listen to John Madden yell "BOOM" for hours on end.

Thinking about my favorite games reminded me of the delicious snacks my mom used to bring me. My belly rumbled. The unbearable thirst was one thing, but now I was so fucking hungry. I felt like I hadn't eaten in a week, and people were starting to look real appetizing. With the night I had, you'd think food would be the furthest thing from my mind. It kind of was, but my body had other ideas. What I felt was more like a compulsion than a desire.

I had to eat, and it needed to be soon.

Asking for food wasn't going to make me popular with the detective. I looked up, wondering where we were. I could probably talk one of the nurses at the hospital into a snack if they admitted me.

It couldn't be much longer until we were there, but I didn't see any buildings that looked like the hospital. We weren't even on the freeway yet. A detective would have known where the nearest hospital was.

Where in the fuck were we going?

"Which hospital are you taking me to?" It was an innocent enough question.

He glanced at me in the mirror before returning his gaze to the road. "It's a small private clinic."

Not very reassuring. "I think I'd rather go to Delnor Hospital."

"Trust me. This is the right place for the job." Fraser

turned the music up loud enough that further conversation was impossible.

A hunger pain lanced through my belly. It was bad enough that it doubled me over. Something wasn't right. I'd never been this hungry in my life. Not even after fasting and running laps in sweats to make weight for wrestling. The hunger was all-consuming. It was all I could think about.

"I need something to eat!" I banged on the cage separating us.

What was left of my rational thinking was quickly deteriorating. I knew I shouldn't be acting this way. Hell, I'd be the first to admit it made me look like a psycho, but I couldn't stop myself. Detective Fraiser hadn't said a single word since I started banging on the cage, but he'd had enough of my shit.

He turned left and circled into the mall parking lot from behind. If his dashboard clock was correct, it was three in the morning. The mall was devoid of signs of life. No one was out on the roads with the light snowfall and the cold. We were completely isolated, and I had serious doubts about the detective's good intentions.

The car stopped, and Fraiser cut the music. "Time to shut the fuck up, kid."

He turned to face me, pulled his service weapon free, and dragged the barrel across the metal barrier between us as though taunting a caged animal. "I was going to make this quick and easy for you, but I'm tired of your shit. This is the end of the road for you."

I knew he wanted to hurt me, but all I could think of was eating.

"Just get me something to eat." I snarled and lunged at the bars hard enough to shake the car. It could have been my imagination, but it looked like the steel bent where my hands smashed into the cage.

"I've got an extra burger up here." Detective Fraiser opened his door and snow flew in. "If you get out of the car, you can have it."

That slimy motherfucker didn't have a burger. I would have smelled it. Never lie to a hungry person about food. You're liable to get your arm ripped off. I tracked the detective as he closed his door and moved around the car to open mine. The bright white snowflakes looked beautiful against the black sky, but I was losing control.

He should have used the cuffs.

My muscles were tense, like a jaguar ready to spring on its prey. The second the door opened, I would attack whether I wanted to or not. It wasn't instinct that took over. It was more like I was the fucking Terminator, and the detective was my primary target.

My mouth was on fire. It felt like the time at the golf course when the guys tricked me into eating a habanero. I thought I'd die from the heat, but there was a pain in my mouth now that no glass of milk could cure.

When the door handle jiggled, my mouth flooded with saliva.

The detective smiled. The next events felt like I was watching the cut-scene in a video game instead of controlling my actions. I'd never been able to move like this before. I was a B-grade athlete at best, but today it felt like I could have taken on the best in the world and won with ease.

Violence was my purpose, and I was earning straight A's.

I kicked the door open. It hit Fraiser, and he stumbled backward. He was off-balance, and he fell on his back when he slid in the slush. I stalked forward, ready to savor my kill.

The detective wasn't smiling anymore. His hand shook as he lifted the gun and fired. The bullet hit my chest. Then I was on him like a spider on a fly. He was a big man, but I moved his neck to the side like there wasn't an ounce of resistance.

My teeth ripped into him like he was a juicy watermelon. The gun went off a few more times before Fraiser stopped fighting. I didn't know if the last bullets fired hit me. All I could focus on was the liquid bliss running down my throat. It was the best burger I ever had.

I was riding on Cloud Nine, floating gently above the world. Nothing hurt. There was nothing to be worried about. I was at the top of the food chain, a super predator, and it felt good.

Too damn good.

Shoving Detective Fraiser's lifeless body to the ground, I screamed into the night. The sound was primal, the kind of noise that would have sent villagers running for the safety of the fort hundreds of years ago. Tonight, the noise traveled through the empty mall parking lot, carried away by the snow.

My belly was full, and control returned to my limbs as I looked down at the detective's body.

"You fucking shot me." I kicked him, and his bones made a satisfying crunch on impact.

Then it dawned on me exactly what I'd done, and the wonderful taste in my mouth wasn't something that should have tasted so wonderful. "Oh shit. Oh shit, oh shit, oh shit."

Oh man, I'd totally screwed the pooch now.

There was getting caught with beer, and then there was killing someone. There was no way out of this situation. Not unless the detective wasn't a cop. The badge and the radio made that theory far-fetched, but I was willing to grasp at any straws right now. I was pretty sure the other officers wouldn't take kindly to one of their own having his throat ripped out.

The entire St. Charles Police Department was about to start hunting for me like it was the Middle Ages. Only they had SWAT teams and helicopters instead of pitchforks and torches.

What in the hell even happened?

The gunshots weren't quiet, and there was a neighborhood behind the mall. Someone would have heard the noise. I had to get the fuck out of there, but I couldn't leave Fraiser's body out in the open. What was I going to do?

There were two frozen ponds at the back of the mall. One was close enough that I could drag the body over, but how would I break the ice? Maybe I should give up and wait for the cops to sort it out. I was tired and wanted all of this to be over.

Screw that.

Detective Dickwad tried to kill me at the mall. He got what he deserved. It was a cold hard truth. Fraiser was a dirty fucking bastard. Just like Sweeny. As much as I wanted to deny the vampire situation, I'd just drained a man dry. When confronted with all the evidence, there wasn't a more reasonable explanation. It was almost too much for me to wrap my head around. I needed a place where I could lie low and figure things out.

It would have been a nice time to have Internet access, but that would mean going home and hoping no one was on the phone. The house wouldn't be safe, and it wasn't like Googling vampirism would produce any actionable results.

I had to get as far away from St. Charles as I could. There was only one place I could think of going.

Arizona.

We'd only lived in Illinois for five years. I knew enough about Arizona to feel comfortable there, and I'd grown up in Tucson. If I stayed in Phoenix, the chances of anyone recognizing me were slim to none. God help me. I might even have to buy an ASU shirt as a disguise.

Sorry, Wilbur.

It wasn't really a plan, but having an idea got my feet moving. Picking up the body should have been hard, but I lifted Fraiser with ease. Despite being in decent shape, I knew lifting a two-hundred-pound man shouldn't have been as easy as lifting my backpack at school. But it was.

There wasn't much time, so I ran toward the pond. When I reached the edge, I skidded to a stop and threw the body as far as possible. The detective landed on the ice with a *crunch* but didn't fall through. The ice was too thick, and my plan was all shot to shit. Maybe it was time to run.

"I can't believe I'm doing this." I stepped onto the ice, hoping it would hold the detective and me.

There was no cracking sound, so I took another tentative step, then another. I should have brought something to crack the ice, but I had never disposed of a body before. Next time I'd have a plan. Holy crap, was there going to be a next time? I lifted the body easily enough. Maybe I could break through the ice.

"Here goes nothing." I slammed my fist into the ice with all my power. The bones in my hand snapped like twigs. I fell backward, clutching the ruined limb against my chest, and screamed in pain.

Then the pain turned off like my body had flipped a

switch. It distracted me from my hand, which looked like a steamroller had run over it. Without warning, the bones snapped back into place.

By the time I stood, my hand had healed. The detective's body slid through the crack in the ice. When his feet disappeared, I felt a lot better. Hopefully, the snow would cover up any footprints before the police got here, and all they would find was an empty squad car behind the mall.

A siren sounded in the distance, and I ran. No need to press my luck any further. I felt too alive to spend eternity in jail. My broken hand felt perfectly new when I flexed it. The cold didn't bite nearly as hard as it had before.

Who would have known drinking a little blood could be so damn rewarding? It was like I'd found the Fountain of Youth. All I had to do was be the kind of asshole willing to kill so I could live. There would be time to contemplate my existence later.

The sun would come up soon. There had to be a farm or cemetery where I could find someplace to hide. No one was farming in this weather or visiting the dearly departed. Tomorrow night, I'd sneak over to Enrique's, get my Jeep, and disappear into the night.

It'd be nice to see my best friend one last time. He deserved to know what happened and why I was leaving. Then I'd go to sunny Arizona, the land of my youth. Not exactly the kind of place you'd expect to find vampires.

Which made it perfect for me.

CHAPTER SIX

It was snowing again.

It wasn't the Norman Rockwell picture-perfect Christmas kind of snow. This was the kind that bordered on sleet. It was cold enough that it almost formed full flakes but not cold enough for them to do anything but melt what was already on the ground. I liked to refer to it as black snow because it was the type that led to black ice as soon as the temperature dropped.

There was no trickier mistress on the planet than black ice.

Ice on the roads was bad enough. Normally you could see it and slow down or avoid the patch, or you had chains or studs on your tires to deal with the issue. You couldn't see black ice. It looked like regular asphalt until your car began to spin. The lucky drivers were the ones who didn't flip their vehicles, or their tires caught pavement again before they slid off the road.

The unlucky ones often didn't make it back home.

It was worse at night when the darkness stripped away

the heat produced by the muffled winter sun. Staring into the falling icy pinpoints left a subdued feeling in my belly. Was the lonely twinkle in the dark the last natural light I'd see for the rest of eternity? If I knew I'd be full-on nocturnal by nineteen, I would have spent more time out in the light and less time locked in the basement playing *Final Fantasy VII*.

Life had a way of tossing hand grenades at you, and when one of those babies landed in your lap, everything changed instantly. It was like when we moved from Arizona to Illinois. It happened in the blink of an eye. All I could do was roll with the punches and look for the next lifeline to grab. No sun, I could deal with that. Extra speed and strength with a dose of immortality had me looking at the upside of my current situation as much as the down.

Yes, I was willing to admit it. I might happen to possibly be a vampire.

Okay, maybe I wasn't ready to admit it. Denial is a thing.

Was this situation fucking unreal? Yes. Was I losing my mind? If only it were that simple. There was a new world for me to discover, an entirely new set of rules to learn and live by. When it came to vampires, what was myth and what was real? I had no clue how to start figuring it out. I was a baby deer taking its first steps on instinct alone. All I kept thinking was that if I had to give up eating human food forever, the perks of transition better be worth it.

A life without pizza was no life at all.

Sleeping in the broken-down shed at the back edge of Garfield Cemetery wasn't exactly what I would call a perk, but life would get better. It would take a little while to get my feet wet. It was too bad there wasn't a Boys and Girls Club for the newly supernatural.

At least I'd been smart enough not to take the detective's car. When the cops found Fraiser's empty ride and not the man, they would be on high alert. Unless he was impersonating a cop. Then his car would be towed away as abandoned.

Having a radio and a badge didn't mean anything. I could buy an old police uniform and a fake badge at a million thrift shops in downtown Chicago. Besides, real cops didn't make a habit of executing teenagers in empty mall parking lots. Then again, if Fraiser wasn't a cop, how did he know to show up at Enrique's house?

Did Sweeny have him under surveillance?

I wouldn't have put anything past that rat-faced Judas. It wasn't like Rosa and Enrique would know how to contact a vampire. Plus, my best friend would never sell me out. We'd been joined at the hip for the last five years and were like brothers.

The Garcias were rock-solid, not the kind of folks who turned their backs on friends for money. You couldn't buy their loyalty even for an amount of cash that would change their lives forever. It was a damned fine quality to have in a best friend.

Yes, it made sense that Enrique could have called Fraiser, but I was doing my best to talk myself out of it. It wasn't out of the realm of possibility that the dispatcher at the precinct diverted my best friend's call. Shit, if Sweeny had enough cash and an officer was desperate enough, he might even have one on the payroll. It felt better casting Fraiser as the bad guy.

I still felt guilty for killing him, even if he was trying to murder me at the time.

Based on the holes in my clothes, the detective put at

least five rounds into my chest. When it came to being shy with a firearm Frasier wasn't your guy. He didn't hesitate when he realized what was happening. But here I was, up and moving around. Not only that, but I felt great. I felt fucking fantastic!

I couldn't say the same for the guy beneath the ice.

Were my actions justified? I liked to think so, but the thought of his warm blood filling my mouth had me on edge. Part of me wanted to throw up, and the other screamed for more. The blood made me feel like I was walking on sunshine or was Popeye with his can of spinach. Only my spinach was a guy who introduced himself as a detective.

My stomach growled. It was one thing to know I had to drink blood to survive, and another realizing the meal had to be a person. *Did it have to be?*

In some vampire stories they lived off animals, but human blood always called to them above all else. In other lore, anything but human blood made vampires sick. There was no way to figure it out without a little experimentation, but I wasn't quite hungry enough to start chasing down stray cats.

Sleeping in the ruined shack all day probably would have killed me if I was still human. At the very least I would have lost a few fingers or toes to frostbite. Now that I had changed, I didn't feel the cold.

My eyes had adjusted to the darkening sky, and it was time to start moving. I would look strange walking down the side of the road in the frigid temperatures, but there was nothing else I could do. Dad never taught me how to hotwire a car, so I was stuck hoofing it.

I had to make it back to Randall Road. From there I could track down a phone and call a cab. A wave of anger washed over me when I remembered Krista and her thug had taken all of my possessions. I would have attacked without hesitation if either was standing in front of me. It wasn't like me to be this angry, but I'd never dealt with a situation quite like this.

All I wanted to do was see my best friend one last time before leaving town and affirm my belief that he had nothing to do with this. I walked until I reached the road and started jogging. Acting like I was out for a run might attract less attention than trudging along with my head down. The last thing I wanted was for a concerned citizen to stop. It might be the last time they could be a Good Samaritan.

Running was one of my least favorite activities. I avoided it at all costs, but it didn't strain me as I jogged back to town. Randall Road came into view, and I followed it north to St. Charles. Enrique's house was close to the middle school in the center of a working-class neighborhood. None of the lots were huge, but good families who cared about their community filled them.

The neighborhood looked like a great place to grow up. It was easy to see the area was full of other kids by the clutter in the front yards. Our neighborhood was full of retirees, and if something was left out front, you heard about it in four seconds flat. It was like someone forgot to tell my neighbors that people over sixty were still allowed to have fun.

There were probably some hot girls around here, too. All

I had at home was Mrs. Morrison and her flower-covered nightie.

Not exactly spank bank material.

My stomach growled, and I laughed. That was the first time thinking of Mrs. Morrison made me hungry for anything. It felt good to laugh. For a while, it felt like I'd never smile again.

If my folks could see me running like this now, it would have blown their minds. Who needed a cab? I'd crushed seven miles without getting winded. Whatever changes my body was going through, the new stamina was something else.

My enhanced vision was cool, too. I could see in the dark like a bright, sunshiny day, and it wasn't distorted or weird colors like night vision goggles. It was more like the moon provided as much light as the sun.

Rounding the corner onto Enrique's street, I slowed into a casual walk and ducked into Mr. Pearlstein's pristine yard. There were a ton of bright lights up ahead, and that wasn't usual. Neither was the bigass moving truck parked out front. Did something happen to Enrique because of me? My sense of calm started to deteriorate. If anyone hurt Rosa because of me, I was going to lose it.

Nothing in my life made sense anymore. There were only two reasons there would be a truck here this late at night. The first scenario was that Enrique and Rosa were dead, and evidence they'd ever lived there would be gone by morning.

The other was a road I didn't want to go down. No one wanted to think their best friend would turn on them, but that was the only other way I could see this going. What should I root for? That my best friend was dead, or that he sold me out?

There were problems, and there were economy-sized cans of whoop-ass problems.

I knew where a betting man would put his money. Who moves out of their house at sundown the day after a detective escorts their best friend off the property? Not only that, but where did they get the money? Selling the extra blueberry wasn't going to do more than cover the cost of the moving truck, let alone a down payment on a new place. Something wasn't adding up, and I was going to figure it out real fucking quick.

If Rosa weren't involved, I would have prayed for the less likely scenario of the vamps snuffing out Enrique because he knew too much. I had no idea why the vamps would waste the energy when no one would believe Enrique's story, even if he shouted it from downtown rooftops. But what did I know about vamps?

Maybe they'd just kill anyone. I had no reason to think otherwise. God knows there were plenty of unsolved murders.

I didn't want to be one of them, so going through the front was out of the question.

I jumped over Pearlstein's white picket fence back to the sidewalk and followed it to the alley in the back. As I ducked into the shadows, my stressed-out brain tossed out random factoids. Most houses in Arizona didn't have these access routes since almost every garage was in front. Illinois had alleys almost everywhere, often serving as the main entrance to most homeowners' garages. The mental babbling's muddled link was that the passages offered alternate ways to get around.

The alley was clear of any activity. It was too cold for anyone to want to do anything except huddle by the fireplace and watch TV. Even Mr. Stevenson's dog Sparks would be inside tonight. It was too cold to leave the yappy little fucker outside.

Reminding myself to stay calm, I walked down the center of the alley like I owned the place. I was still wearing Enrique's clothes, so any neighbors glancing out their window would think I was him. One thing I'd learned a long time ago was that looking like you belonged somewhere was the best way to be forgettable.

When I reached Enrique's driveway, I crouched in the shadows and peered around. My Jeep was sitting in his garage, but Rosa's car was gone. The light above my ride burned brightly, not leaving me anywhere to hide once I moved forward.

I turned my attention to the house. Rosa and Enrique usually left the back door unlocked. I could get in that way. It looked like whoever was inside was getting ready to leave soon. I still didn't have any clue what was going on. I *was* sure I wouldn't find any of the answers hiding in the backyard.

One way or another, it was time to find out the truth.

I entered the garage and crept around the driver's side of the Jeep, watching the door leading into the house the whole time. The dent in the Wrangler's driver's side door was gone, and someone had fixed the glass. What in the fuck was going on? My life was rapidly deteriorating into a *Twilight Zone* nightmare, and all I wanted to do was wake up.

My hands shook, but fear of the truth wouldn't stop me from moving forward. It was always better to know, right?

If I wanted to give up, I should have stayed in the dumpster.

Still using the Jeep for cover, I moved to the door and turned the knob. The hinges screeched like a dying cat when the door opened. How many times had I told Enrique put some WD-40 on it? After being so careful with my approach, how had I forgotten such a crucial detail?

I froze, ready to run at the first unexpected noise.

The door didn't explode in a hail of gunfire, so I finished pushing it open. My imagination was working on overdrive. There could have been an entire circus troupe performing in the living room, and it wouldn't have surprised me. I needed to calm down, but my heart was beating like a jackhammer.

It was nice to know it could still do that.

No one was in the tiny mudroom at the back of the house, so I was safe for the moment. I drew a few deep breaths to steady my heart rate. Coming here was stupid. It wasn't like Enrique could help me. If he didn't sell me out, my being here was only putting him in further danger.

One thing life never ran short of was choices.

I'd made mine when I opened the back door, so I pushed forward. The back stairs were on my left, and the kitchen opened before me. Using the stairs was out of the question. Damn things were twice as noisy as the back door. I could check out the upstairs once I made sure the lower level was clear.

The home was an older two-story house. The rooms were essentially squares linked with doorways. At least it wasn't an open floor plan. That would be pure shit when it came to finding places to hide. A lot of extra walls made staying out of sight easier.

Especially when there was no furniture.

What in the fuck? Where was all the furniture? Yes, part of me understood there was a moving truck outside for a reason, but seeing the entire house empty hit me like a kick in the balls. The pit in my stomach grew, and I finally knew how Julius Caesar must have felt. *Et tu, Brute?*

Nothing hurt as much as a knife in the back.

Staying hunched as I moved toward the window felt silly. I straightened to my full height and looked where the couch used to sit. Movement outside the front windows caught my attention. People were loading the last boxes into the truck while Enrique and Rosa watched outside the covered front porch.

Rosa looked back at the house and out into the street. "I don't know about all of this, Enrique. This is our home."

Always full of confidence, my best friend responded, "Trust me, Abuelita, Mr. Sweeny said everything is taken care of. Our new house is completely paid for. You own it."

"But how?" Her tone suggested she knew her grandson was a fuck up, and a new house was beyond his reach. "Something doesn't feel right."

Enrique laid on the guilt. "This was my one shot at doing something special for you, and look, Grandma, it all worked out. Go with Carlos, and he'll get you set up at the new place. I need to turn off the lights and lock up."

"Keep your secrets, Enrique. But know that God is looking down on you. Even you can't keep secrets from Him." She didn't hug her grandson like usual, only moved toward the truck with slow, deliberate steps.

The front door opened a moment later. My mind was still trying to wrap itself around Enrique knowing Sweeny. My best friend said the greasy little shit took care of everything. He confirmed selling me out at least once. What kind of person would offer up their best friend to die for something as trivial as a bigger house?

There was a sharp pain in my mouth as my fangs dropped. I couldn't help it. I was fucking furious. What a sucker I'd been coming here to say goodbye. Enrique had already moved on. The bastard was even driving my Jeep.

When it came right down to it, if Enrique was helping Sweeny, he helped kill my parents. Then he served me up to Fraiser on a silver platter. Imagine the balls it would take to pull something like that off.

Enrique must have thought his were the size of basketballs.

There were a million ways Enrique could justify to himself what he'd done, but he'd never be able to make it right with me.

I slipped into the downstairs bathroom as Enrique walked into the house. The front door closed and locked, and the lights out front turned off as well as the lights to the living room. Enrique went up the stairs, flipping switches as he went. I took a moment to step into the living room and look out the front window. The vehicles were on the move, and he was all alone with me.

And I was hungry.

My Jeep was in the garage, and it was Enrique's ride into his bright new future. Since I knew where he would end up, I moved through the house like a rocket. The door to the garage *squeaked* behind me, but the footsteps thundering down the creaky back stairs masked it. Missing each other at the back door was a minor miracle and the first bit of good luck I'd had since making it out of Dabbler's apartment alive.

I was so fucking mad my fangs hurt.

If I was going to eat people, it would only be those of questionable character. So far, I had a decent-sized list of candidates to pick from. The world was full of shitty people. I could be the Vampire Punisher, making the streets safer for everyone.

So what if I wanted to pretend to be the coolest comic book character ever invented? I needed to think of something to lighten the mood or I might explode. The villains of St. Charles would have to wait because tonight's snack was walking toward me.

Hope those thirty pieces of silver were worth it, Judas.

In the space of a day, I'd gone from never killing anything more than a fish to contemplating wiping out multiple people. I needed to get this rage under control. Maybe there was a support group for angry supernaturals.

The door opened, and rational thought became a thing of the past.

Enrique walked into the garage with a huge smile. It was the worst thing he could have done. I was on him in a second. I hit him so hard we flew through the closed door and ended up sprawled on the mudroom floor. He tried to scramble away, but I was stronger. It was easy to pin him in place while he wriggled like a worm at the end of a hook.

I grabbed him by the coat, lifted him, and slammed him back onto the floor hard enough that one of the tiles cracked. "Why?"

The words came out as half-sob, half-scream. It was all I could say as I looked down at my former best friend. My heart was broken. My family was gone. I could back-trace all my misery and grief to the man I had pinned to the floor like a bug.

"Come on, bro. You know I'm never going to amount to anything. I'm a hustler. This was my chance to get out from under it." Enrique tried to hit me with a guilt trip.

I'd let Enrique talk me into doing a lot of stupid shit over the years, but he wasn't going to weasel out of this. Looking back at our friendship with fresh eyes, I realized we were never best friends. I was someone he used to feel good about himself.

So many things became clearer. Today I learned that Enrique cared about one thing and one thing only. Himself.

"So if I killed your grandma for a new pair of shoes, you'd be cool with it?" I snarled and slammed him against the floor again. "I can't believe I thought you were my friend."

Enrique's warm brown eyes were dark and hard. It was like looking at an entirely different person.

"That's the thing, bro. You have big dreams, but all you ever do is make sandwiches. I seized an opportunity when someone presented it to me. Sometimes you gotta make the hard calls if you want to be on top." Enrique pulled a gun from his jacket pocket.

The first shot tore through my chest. I fell backward, clutching the wound in shock. When I hit the floor, Enrique stood and moved toward me as I gasped for air. I was tired of being shot, but my body had already flipped off the pain and started healing.

"Looks like I win again." Enrique pointed the weapon at my head.

Headshots were cool in video games, but people didn't take them very often in real life if they wanted to hit their target. The head was a smaller target than the body, and I was faster than before Krista bit me. The gun went off, but the bullet smashed into the mudroom floor instead of my face. Before Enrique could aim again, I grabbed him above the wrist and snapped his forearm like a Thanksgiving wishbone.

He screamed and dropped the gun. I kicked it away. His hand flopped around at the end of his broken arm like he was an extra on the beach in *Saving Private Ryan*.

Everything had spiraled out of control. Someone in the neighborhood would have heard the gunshot. Knowing Mr. Jones, he was already on the phone with the police. Hopefully he couldn't hear Enrique squealing like a stuck pig.

I needed to shut him up and get the fuck out of there.

I thought about leaving him on the floor to live with the shame of what he'd done, but Enrique didn't feel any guilt about serving my family up as sacrificial goats. My body was healing the gunshot, but it was happening slower than the night before. There was one thing that would make it all better, and he was lying in front of me.

"You would have done it too," Enrique pleaded as I grabbed his hair.

I wrenched his head to the side and screamed as my fangs tore into his throat. Then I was lost in the pleasure of feeding. His blood filled me with energy, and the last of my wounds closed.

People had shot me two days in a row. That had to be some kind of record. It was the worst pain I'd ever experienced, but the pain always became a fleeting memory as soon as I started to feed.

I pushed his lifeless body to the side and stood. My hoodie was a mess, and there was nothing left in this house for me to change into. I stripped off Enrique's coat and tossed the bullet hole-riddled hoodie on his body.

My mental debate about leaving his corpse didn't take long. I didn't want Rosa to see him like this. It was better for all of us if Enrique disappeared.

I fished my keys out of his pocket and strapped him into the Jeep's passenger seat. It was like I'd stepped onto a set filming a vampire, *Weekend at Bernie's* mash-up. The thought almost made me laugh. Enrique's blood had made me giddy. I wondered if anyone would notice I was driving around with a corpse as my copilot.

It was dark out, so I'd be safe unless I got pulled over. The cemetery's shed should be fine to crash in for one more night, but then I'd have to move on. In the morning I'd stash Enrique's corpse in the graveyard and try to pull enough money together to get out of town.

Back in the driver's seat of my baby, I asked myself the one question I'd been afraid to until now. Could I live my life as a vampire? It was hard to separate myself from the grief to see things clearly. My parents were dead. My life had shattered into a million pieces. The one person I thought cared about me turned out to be the bastard who sold us out.

I patted Enrique's leg. "Not doing much winning now, are you, buddy?"

Drawing a few deep breaths, I tried to let go of everything. Being sad wouldn't keep me alive, and neither would being angry. I reached past Enrique, popped open the glove box, and found my spare lighter. The locked center console still had the blueberry and my bowl in it. Not long after filling the pipe, I had the Jeep full of delicious smoke. I felt better as I put the Jeep in reverse and turned on the tunes.

Ben Harper's *I Want to Burn One Down* came on my playlist.

Ben's mellow voice drifted out of the speakers as I drove out of the neighborhood. What I wanted to do was ditch Enrique's body and go to the sandwich shop. If Krista or Sweeny were there, I'd take them out. She'd probably love the chance to kill me again.

Unlike the plucky action hero who gets struck down and rises again to take his revenge, I had the feeling if she saw me again, it would be the end of my adventure. Not killing me the first time was a mistake. I wanted to live long enough to make her regret it. My world was upside down, and the only thing keeping me going was a will to survive.

That and a belly full of hate.

I'd get the chance to go after Krista at some point, but first I had to level up. This was my origin story. If I went for the kill too quickly, there wouldn't be a sequel.

Instead of a spider, a vampire had bitten me. This was my chance to do some good in the world. I could see the comic's cover now, almost like Spawn, but without the wicked cool cape.

A glance at the corpse riding shotgun made me realize I better not get ahead of myself. Superheroes weren't exactly known for murder sprees, and I was pretty sure none of them fed on humans. I'd never really been a superhero kind of guy. More like the reluctant hero, the anti-hero. Seriously, don't call for help before I've had my coffee.

"Holy shit, bro, I'm a vampire superhero." I hit Enrique's chest with a smile.

He didn't think it was funny.

Then it hit me like a ton of bricks. Was he really dead? I'd come back to life a few hours later, and it wasn't like I knew how turning a person worked. What if I'd accidentally turned him?

The last thing this world needed was an Enrique supervillain running around. He'd murder anyone who got in his way without a second thought. I had to make sure he didn't come back, but how in the hell was I supposed to do it?

The fact is, when it came to vampires, all I had in my head were stories. From *Fright Night* to *Sunglasses After Dark*, there was a whole world of fiction in between. Some of it felt more realistic, but who knew when everyone claimed it was all made up? I'd always assumed the authors had fantastic imaginations. I'd never thought for a second that the stories were real.

Maybe being undead wouldn't be the worst thing in the world. I needed to get a handle on it.

It was kind of cool, like being an explorer. A little chuckle slipped out. I always thought the next great adventure would be colonizing Mars, but it turned out there was an entire world on Earth I never knew existed. It was an exciting prospect that had me thinking of the future.

The deserted cemetery looked the same. Lots of old plots and not many new visitors. I parked the Jeep behind the same half-rotted storage shed I'd slept in the day before. Inside the shed was a little hole in the ground with a tarp over it. Not exactly the Four Seasons, but it worked out well enough yesterday. A quick look around didn't show anything out of place from the night before. This location probably wouldn't be safe for longer than another day or two, but it was fine for now.

With my hidey-hole against the sun secure, I went back to the Jeep. It was odd how quickly I was getting used to dead bodies. In one day I'd gone from never seeing one to hiding them around town. Killing people for food was a slippery slope not only on moral grounds but because someone could discover me. How did the other vampires do it? Could they feed without killing?

It was an interesting prospect—the idea of being able to survive without killing. There was also a chance I could drink the donated stuff. Less likely on the list of options was animal blood. Almost everything I'd ever read said animal blood was a no-go, but I had to give it at least a shot. An image of me getting bucked off a cow while trying to bite its neck rolled through my mind, and I laughed again. Cow one, Dylan big fat zero.

Having a full belly still had me feeling loopy.

If the tales about vampires' immortality were true, I had all the time in the world to get a handle on the situation.

Lifting Enrique out of the car was easy. The enhanced strength I had after feeding was pretty freaking awesome. I wouldn't be jumping across buildings like Neo in *The Matrix*, but I'd be able to handle my own in a fight with any human. Even without training. I could heal from any punch a human could throw, and one of mine would end things.

With supernatural gifts comes a certain level of responsibility, one I was trying to use as the sun rose. I laid Enrique's body out in the open where the rays would hit it and backed up toward the shed to watch from a distance. If he were a vampire, he'd burn to ash.

I pulled out my bowl and smoked until I saw the first hint of orange on the horizon.

It wouldn't be much longer. Little hints of pink had joined the bright swirls of orange. I was standing in the shadow of the shed's doorway, waiting to see what would happen when the sunlight hit the body. If Enrique didn't burn, I'd have to bury him before I left.

The sun's rays touched him, and the corpse's legs kicked like it was having a seizure. The random twitching continued for a few moments, then he stood. I couldn't let him escape, but what could I do without going into the sun to stop him?

His head turned from side to side, and Enrique shuffled toward the shed.

"Fuck," I hissed.

The sound was enough to snap Enrique out of his daze. His eyes swiveled until they locked onto me, and he charged forward like an angry bull. Something was different about him. His eyes were blank. Anything that was my friend was gone.

I wasn't going to let Enrique hurt me, and I sure as shit wasn't going to risk letting him hurt anyone else. There were hundreds of homes minutes from where we were. Leaving a hungry vampire here would be like dropping a zombie in a locked Golden Corral.

Running from the safety of the shed, I tackled Enrique to the ground. I was stronger than him, but he was like a wild animal fighting with everything he had to survive. It took all my strength to haul him farther away from the safety of the shed. So much for all my grand plans as a creature of the night. If I couldn't get him into the sun without endangering myself, I'd do what I had to.

There was no sound as the light washed over us like a tidal wave. It was like the world around us went silent as it waited to see what would happen next. The creature in my arms struggled as it tried to survive the sun, but I held him firm. It took all of my strength not to let him go, and when he burst into flames, it took determination. The burns on my hands began to heal as I shoved Enrique away from me and further into the light.

A single scream tore from his lips, and he burst into ash.

The wind scattered the ashes across the snow like a dirty cloud, and that was the last the world would see of Enrique Garcia.

The sun had me fully in its grips now. I wasn't burning alive. A glance at my hands confirmed they had healed. I felt weaker though like I'd pulled an all-nighter playing a new campaign of *Final Fantasy VII*.

I needed to rest, but so many questions buzzed in my mind that it was hard to power it down fully. The fact I could stand in the sun filled my head with even more questions.

Was I a vampire, or was I something else?

Going to Enrique's house was supposed to be the end of a chapter, but instead it looked like the beginning of a whole new book.

CHAPTER SEVEN

I felt the call of darkness approaching as I slept.

The moon was still high in the sky even though the last embers of daylight burned at the edges of the world. Winter was a time when darkness reigned supreme. It made a sick kind of sense that winter would be vampire season. If you could only come out in the dark, there wasn't a better time to be alive. Hell, most days were as dark as night with all the snow.

I'd slipped under the tarp to sleep in case the sun decided to nuke me anyway. I needed to play it safe until I figured out exactly what was happening. I felt weak like I'd come off a week of having the flu. I hadn't burst into flames in the sunlight, but it wasn't exactly forgiving.

Not only that, but I woke up hungry. As a human, that seldom happened to me. I was the kind of guy who normally skipped breakfast.

I thought about my future options to keep my brain from fixating on what feeding meant. I could stay in town and try to get to the bottom of this, but I wasn't ready. I didn't understand what was happening to me, let alone how to fight an experienced vampire.

What if Krista laughed when I put a stake through her heart? Not to mention that Rosa would ask questions when Enrique never showed up at their new house. If she called the police, they'd be looking for me, and I wanted to be long gone before that happened.

While honor demanded I stay and avenge my parents like some Viking blood feud, the logical part of my brain said start burning rubber like I left town yesterday. St. Charles and Geneva weren't exactly small cities, but hiding in them wouldn't be as easy as hiding in Chicago, or better yet, on the other side of the country. Hiding in a big city was the way to go, but the city presented another danger for a kid with no money.

My eyes adjusted as the last rays of sunlight faded. The world looked almost the same in the dark as if the sun were shining but with a few small quirks. It was almost like walking around with super-light sunglasses on.

I stepped out of the shed and stretched my limbs back to life. The entire time, I stared at the spot where Enrique burst into flames.

His shirt and boxers were almost nonexistent, but his jeans and boots were partly intact. It was almost like the sun made him internally combust. It didn't happen instantly, but once it started, there was no way to stop it. I'd been fine. I wondered if that was normal. It sure didn't feel normal.

Whoever heard of a vampire turning someone with a single bite? It didn't fit any of the lore I'd ever read, but neither did being able to walk in the sun. I wondered how much of what was happening applied only to me and how much applied to all vampires. There had to be a way to find real information out there.

I picked up the tattered jeans out of some morbid curiosity. The move drew my attention to a lump not far away. Enrique's wallet had fallen out, possibly while we scuffled. The leather on the outside was somewhat charred, but otherwise, it didn't look too bad.

I pulled out the cash and counted it a few times to be sure. Dude had four hundred bucks in twenties. He must have been out hustling that blueberry all day. I would have appreciated the grind if he weren't such a piece of shit. What he should have remembered were all the gangster movies we watched. The only ones who survived were the ones that got out early.

Enrique didn't get out soon enough.

Four hundred dollars was a lot of dough, but it wasn't enough to start a new life in another state. The only thing I had of my own to sell was the Jeep, and if I wanted to get rid of it quickly, I wouldn't be able to argue about the price. Not unless vampires could mind trick people like Palpatine did to Jar Jar. That was a thing, right?

Fuck, I didn't even know the basics.

There were times in life when it was easy to feel overwhelmed. Before now, those had mostly consisted of trying to balance work, school, and a social life. Now there was more riding on the choices I was making. When there was no safety net, I had to stay focused on what was most important without being sentimental. Getting rid of the Jeep was step one. Then I needed to get as far away from Illinois as I could.

I already knew I couldn't go to Tucson. It would be too easy for people to make that connection. Phoenix was bigger. It'd be easier to hide there and had no direct links to anyone we knew. It was the closest thing I could get to going home, and it was worth the risk.

Plus, what kind of self-respecting vampire lived in the desert? It was over a hundred degrees five months of the year, and the tap water tasted like shit. It didn't rain very often, so if cloud cover could get a vamp out during the day, it wouldn't happen in Arizona. That made it perfect for me. A potentially vampire-free zone made it the ideal place to hunker down and figure things out.

What I really needed was a mentor. Someone who knew the supernatural world and could help me navigate it. How I would find someone like that was a complete mystery. There was probably a chat group somewhere that could point me in the right direction but sorting through that sea of bullshit to find a diamond would be a waste of time. I needed to get out in the world and discover what I'd gotten myself into.

I couldn't do that while looking over my shoulder.

Enrique had already stripped most of my stuff out of the Jeep, but my tape collection was still intact. Yes, most of the world was listening to CDs already, but my ride had an old soul. Pink Floyd and Tom Petty, mixed with Nirvana and Stone Temple Pilots. My entire collection was still in the center console, but this wasn't the time to get nostalgic. Everything must go.

I already knew exactly where to get rid of the car. Slick Ricky was the only guy shady enough to bend the rules for a quick buck. His lot was officially called Ricky's Modern Imports, but the only thing modern or imported about the place was the car Ricky drove. Enrique worked there for a summer and said he spent most of his time spray painting chrome on the rims and doing half-assed repairs.

Ricky was the kind of person who wouldn't think too hard about handing a nineteen-year-old kid thousands of dollars in cash. As long as he believed he could get away with it. You had to look like a sucker but not a trap. If the deal was sweet enough, the greedy bastard might risk it, but I didn't want to push my luck.

I took one last look around the cemetery like it was a home I'd never see again. I would have much rather been in my room, grabbing some of my favorite things, but I couldn't risk going to the house. I would say my goodbye to St. Charles here. This was it. I was leaving.

The Wrangler roared to life, and I popped it in gear. Tonight I decided to put in my Days of the New tape. Those guys rocked, and if this was the last ride in my Jeep, I wanted it to feel spectacular. As I hit the road, the vibe felt as right as it would get.

I took the roundabout way back to town to come in from the opposite side of the cemetery's location. The last thing I wanted was to drive past our sandwich shop and get spotted.

Ricky's Modern Imports was lit up like a football stadium. There was no missing it or the giant billboard with Ricky's smug face smiling down on anyone dumb enough to drive on the lot. The slogan "We've got a deal for every budget" was plastered across the sign. They sure did, as long as you didn't mind paying an interest rate that would make a Vegas loan shark scoff in wonder.

Ricky didn't operate his business out of the kindness of his heart. He and others like him did it for cold hard cash and a lot of it. It made me furious since it felt rigged to keep anyone trying to get ahead trapped at the bottom.

Coasting onto the lot, I found a space in the front and put the Jeep in neutral before setting the brake. I drew a couple of deep breaths to get ready to deal with a pushy salesman. This wasn't the time or place to lose my temper. For this to work, I needed to make the transaction as clean as possible. Leaving a trail of bodies behind me was no way to make a clean getaway.

From here I was taking the train into the city and a Greyhound to Arizona. I'd pay in cash, and nobody on trains and buses cared who you were unless you made trouble.

Ricky walked out of his office with a smile. "You looking to trade up to something a little sportier?"

He was walking around my Jeep appraising its value for trade-in before I responded.

I kept a smile plastered on, even though this was the last thing I wanted to do. "I'm trying to unload it. My grandma needs surgery so we all have to pitch in where we can."

"I'm sorry to hear about that." Ricky didn't sound sorry. "I'm sure we can make a deal Grandma will approve of. Even with that stain on the seat." He motioned for me to follow him inside.

The Jeep was only a year old. I remember writing the check like I had any notion of how much twenty-one thousand dollars was. The money came from my grandma. When she died, she left me a little something, and my dad turned it into a little something more. The Jeep was my last connection to my family, but it would be too easy to track. I had to let it go.

Maybe the grandma line had been a mistake? It gave

Ricky more leverage than I would have liked, but it was the only thing I could think of that made sense. I'm sure he'd heard every lame excuse in the book a time or two. At the end of the day, it didn't matter why I was selling. His god was the dollar, and I was about to make it rain.

The door closed behind us, and Ricky pointed at the seat on the opposite side of his desk. "You own the Jeep outright?"

"I do." *Thanks, Grandma.* The woman was a stone-cold saint. Part of me wondered if she'd be mad about what I was doing, but I shrugged it off.

Granny was a lady who survived The Great Depression. She understood possessions were only things, and survival was more important than property. I'd never been forced to make decisions based purely on survival until now, but I was learning quickly.

"It's a '99?" When I nodded, Ricky continued typing on his computer. "Best I can do is five thousand."

I laughed.

Ricky was a bigger slimeball than I gave him credit for. "Try thirteen, and we might have something to talk about."

Ricky looked incredulous. "Thirteen? If I made those kinds of deals, this dealership would be closed. I could probably find a way to get you eight, but I'd have to move some things around."

This guy was something else. There was nothing to move around. The Jeep was damn near perfect. It even had a brand-new door. He could sell this thing for fifteen thousand tomorrow, and someone would probably thank him for it. Ricky didn't care about the state of the vehicle. He knew I was desperate and wanted to take advantage of me.

If I didn't get the price up soon, he'd probably start telling me stories about how his kids needed new braces.

Sitting across the desk from him almost made me sick.

"I'll take ten, but I want it in cash tonight." I placed the registration on the desk. "Tell me you're the guy who can make it happen."

By the smile on Ricky's face, I'd screwed up. "If you want cash, all I have is eight. Take it or leave it."

Eight thousand wasn't nearly enough, but as long as I could get him to handle all the details without me, it'd be worth it. "Eight in cash, and you handle all the paperwork yourself."

"Done." Ricky stood. "I'll be back in a minute."

It was crazy how fast this deal happened, but when you're taking advantage of a person it's probably better to conclude the transaction before they come to their senses. Can't have those pesky customers figuring out what you're doing and changing their minds before the paperwork is signed.

I will not eat Slick Ricky.

Who he was is exactly why I was here, but it didn't mean I had to enjoy getting screwed over.

"I really can't believe this." Ricky walked in, looking shocked. "I only had seven thousand in the safe."

His apologetic look made me want to smash his face in. Whoa, that was a little dark. Even if the condescending prick was trying to pull one over on me, it wasn't grounds to smash his head through his desk. If eating Slick Ricky wouldn't have put a huge "Dylan Was Here" sign on the dealership, I would have ended him in an instant. One thing I was quickly learning was that it didn't pay to piss off a hungry vampire. Tearing my eyes away from the gold chains on his neck took much more effort than it should have.

"Eight thousand." I slammed my hand down on his desk, and the corner snapped off.

Ricky stepped back and pulled another thousand out of his inner suit pocket. "Can't blame a guy for trying."

He tossed the extra bundle on the desk with the other seven. Eight thousand dollars in cash was right there. All I had to do was reach out and take it. The deal was horrible, and the Jeep was my baby. A person never gets rid of their first car lightly. It was full of wonderful memories, and I hated knowing it would be in Ricky's hands.

"Hey man, you only need to sign one sheet of paper for me, and I'll even throw in a little extra." Ricky fumbled out his wallet and tossed a couple hundred in cash out on the desk. "Just don't break anything else."

Seeing him scared brought me back from the brink. Holy shit, I'd been about to Hulk out on the guy despite telling myself not to eat him. There had to be something I could do to get my emotions under control, but I wasn't going to figure it out here.

I pulled out the keys, tossed them on the desk, and pocketed the money.

When all eight thousand was stuffed safely into my jacket, I signed the paper and picked up a single twenty from the extra cash Ricky dumped out. "Asshole tax."

It took everything I had not to crack up at the look on his face as I walked out of the office. Ricky thought he was about to die. It was crazy. I wasn't that guy. No one was afraid of me. I'd been in more fights in the last two days than in all of high school. Now I was tossing out one-liners like the guy who paid a surprise visit to Dabbler instead of the scared kid running down the stairs as fast as he could. Ricky must have been shitting bricks, but he could have also been calling the cops.

It was time to run.

Despite how the movies portrayed it, commuter trains didn't run twenty-four hours a day. The last train to Chicago left Geneva around ten. It meant there was a lot of ground to cover between where I was now and the station. If I wanted to make it on time, I would have to hustle or call a cab. The cabbie was another potential witness to my whereabouts, so I pulled up the collar on my coat and started walking.

The only other business I passed on the way back to town was the Pheasant Run Resort. At one point, it had been the crème de la crème, but now it was a mid-scale hotel with a fantastic brunch. Although, the heated indoor-outdoor pool and the waterfall pool by the fitness center were pretty spectacular. The golf course wasn't bad if you were into swinging the sticks.

Mostly, I snuck in to use the hot tub.

The mall and the high school were a few miles farther down the road. It was snowing again, but this was the real deal. It was cold as ice, crunching under my boots like I was walking on cubes instead of the powdery stuff. I looked at the snow and down at my feet with dread in my stomach. Was Detective Fraiser still alive under the ice? Was he like Enrique?

The thought put a chill in my bones that the weather hadn't been able to muster.

I couldn't leave town without checking. The story on the news would be outrageous. Live on WGN at nine: Man escapes from a pond and eats people. I'd be safe in Arizona, but innocent people might get hurt. The only way to put my mind at ease was to make a detour on the way to the train station.

It was Wednesday night, the week after Christmas, with sub-freezing temperatures and a snowstorm on the way. Not a real shocker that the mall was nearly empty, even though it was only eight o'clock. Any other week and the place would have been crawling with teenagers trying to escape the leftover holiday guests, but tonight no parent was signing up to leave the house so their kids could cruise the mall for a few hours.

The lot by the fountains in the back was the farthest away from the movie theater thus making it the employee parking zone. Most of the employees had already moved their cars closer to the buildings when they took their breaks, so the back lot had turned into a ghost town by the time I arrived. If anyone had found Fraiser, it wouldn't be this deserted.

I noted the lack of any yellow police tape or flashing lights. If somebody found an officer's car and it looked like there had been a struggle, there was no way the cops would have finished investigating. It made me wonder who Detective Fraiser was.

And who he worked for.

I kept my gaze moving over the snowy lot, ensuring I wasn't walking into a trap as I puzzled out the Detective Fraiser problem. My former best friend had allegedly called the police, but he could have called Sweeny instead. If Sweeny sent Fraiser, there was an actual lead to follow I could sink my teeth into.

The real problem was where Sweeny would lead me. If it was right back to Krista, I was in big trouble, or at least I could be. Vampire lore from movies might not be real, but getting close to Krista would be a mistake if there was a sire bond. Spending the rest of my undead life working for the lady who murdered my parents would suck all kinds of ass.

My boots crunched on the ice at the pond's edge, snapping me back into the moment. I'd decided. At least for now I'd be leaving. First, I had to ensure St. Charles wouldn't be ravaged by a vampire problem when the ice melted. Looking over the snow-covered ice toward the frozen fountain in the center, I wondered how I was supposed to lure a vampire out of a pond.

"Here, fishy, fishy!" I guessed Detective Fraiser's sense of humor was as good as Enrique's had been on the way to the cemetery.

I should have come better prepared, but when I unloaded the Jeep, I wasn't planning on a vampire throwdown. I needed a stick or a bat. Something I could tap the ice with to draw his attention.

Sunlight wouldn't help me end this fight, and I felt weak from not eating dinner yet. Getting into a fight without a weapon seemed like a bad idea. If Detective Fraiser was still alive, he'd be pissed off and hungry.

"Shit." I looked at the ice, knowing I should return when I had fully prepared to deal with the situation.

Instead, I took another shaky step out onto the surface. "Might not even be alive."

I'd never be that lucky.

"Here, vampy, vampy." I stomped on the ice. "Tasty humans for snackums."

Stomp, stomp, stomp. A loud *crack* echoed through the ice below my feet, freezing me in place. I looked down and realized the cracking sound wasn't coming from under my feet but closer to the pond's center.

"Did I do that?" My voice pitched higher, slipping into a Steve Urkel-like squeal faster than I would have liked.

If this were a family show, the vampire would hug you, but this was a horror story. My parents were dead, I'd killed two people, and things were only getting started. It would make a sick sense that mysterious Detective Fraiser would still be alive. It was how my week was going. Might as well get it over with.

I stomped on the ice again and yelled with bravado, "I don't have all night, you limp-dicked mother—"

Another crack sounded, and another. Looking down at my feet didn't show any fissures near me, but the entire pond felt like it was shaking as something tried to break through the surface.

Thump, thump, thump.

"Oh man, this isn't gonna be good." The ice burst upward, and a pale blue hand clawed at the surface.

Now that I knew the detective was alive, this seemed like the dumbest idea I'd ever had. Worse than going to Dabbler's apartment by a country mile. As Fraiser clawed free of the ice, I backed up, but there wasn't anywhere to run. The entire point of this was to stop him from attacking anyone else. My heart pounded like a racehorse on steroids. Every beat reminded me I was alive and wanted to stay that way.

What in the hell was I thinking?

I forced myself to stand firm as the detective climbed free of the ice. His eyes blazed with desire as he looked around wildly for something to eat. His clothes began to freeze as the wind rippled around us. A single snowflake landed on his nose, and his eyes focused on me. A low groan escaped his lips, and the detective shuffled forward. Fraiser was almost moving like a zombie. I wasn't sure what his deal was. Enrique had come at me fast. Maybe fear of the sun had driven my friend forward, and it had nothing to do with me.

"Hey, Chachi. You want a piece of me?" Not the kind of line that would win Actor of the Year, but it was sufficient to get the detective moving faster.

Fraiser lurched forward, and all I wanted was something heavy in my hand so I could bonk him over the head with it. The tension was killing me. Why wasn't he moving faster? *Dinner is right over here.*

Detective Bluehands lurched for me like a drunk trying to snatch his keys from the bartender at last call. It was easy enough to dodge him, and I kicked one of his feet as I passed, sending him sprawling. The detective went down in a heap. He moaned as he tried to stand. With his next meal so close, Fraiser wasn't willing to give up yet.

When fighting for your life, it never made sense to stop because you were winning. Every blow counted until you were safe. Instead of letting Fraiser get back to his feet, I jumped on his back forcing him back down. With the detective pinned underneath me, I tried to think of what to do next. It wasn't like I could hold him here until the sun came up.

I have to take out his heart.

"A weapon would come in really handy right about now," I bitched at myself for being the worst vampire hunter in history as the detective squirmed to get free.

Slamming his head into the ice seemed to calm him, but he hadn't given up his bid to escape. Headlights swung out across the pond and stopped on us. Out of all the malls in the area, you had to pick this one to shop at right fucking now? I couldn't get caught wrestling a vampire. I wasn't sure if the vampire fights had rules, but if they did, the first one was you probably didn't talk about it.

Tyler Durden would be proud.

"Hey, what's going on down there?" a man called from the pond's edge.

The detective snarled and dragged himself toward the new voice.

I slammed Fraiser's skull into the ice, then looked up and grunted. "Get back in your car and drive away."

"Listen buddy, whatever you're doing, stop it already. I'll go inside and call the cops." The late-night do-gooder sounded so certain he was the one in control of the situation.

The detective chose that moment to start bucking wildly. I slammed him into the ice again, but when I looked up, Johnny Do-Gooder was charging straight for us. He had a tire iron in his hand, and his expression said he wasn't afraid to use it. In any normal situation, this was the kind of guy I would have been happy to see rushing forward to help someone in distress, but this wasn't a normal situation. He should have walked away.

"I don't know what's going on here, but let him go!" He delivered the words with the same confident tone he'd used earlier. The raised tire iron was ready to break my skull open.

I slammed the detective to the ice again before pointing at Mr. Friendly. "Mind your own business."

To his credit, the man didn't hesitate. The tire iron came down in a wide sweeping arc straight at my head. Turning with the blow took some of the force out of it, but the guy hit me hard enough to knock me off the detective.

Were there bells ringing somewhere?

Detective Fraiser squirmed free and crawled toward the man.

"Hey buddy, you don't look so good." His voice still had a note of concern, so Mr. Nice Guy hadn't realized he was about to be dinner.

The detective had one hand around the man's ankle and pulled the leg closer to his mouth.

Mr. Save the Day had finally figured out things weren't right, and he was trying to use the tire iron to pry the detective's hand free. "Jesus, he tried to bite me."

The tire iron clattered onto the ice as Fraiser yanked the man's legs out from under him. So far, the detective hadn't been able to bite through his victim's thick winter pants, but now that he had him on the ground, it wouldn't take long for him to find a more accessible spot. My head was still swimming as I watched them struggle, but I made it to my feet.

I need the tire iron.

I found it after a few seconds of fumbling in the snow. Before I could turn, hungry slurping sounds followed a scream. Fraiser had latched onto Mr. Nice Guy's calf like the world's biggest leech. I ripped the detective free, tossing him onto his back. The tire iron came down in one fluid motion and slammed straight through his chest. Nothing happened.

Did the stake have to be wood or silver?

I pulled the tire iron free and looked in the hole it left. I'd never tried to stab someone in the heart before. Knowing where I put my hand during the anthem wasn't like trying to drive a weapon into someone's chest. Lifting the tire iron, I brought it down again and again until the detective burst into a cloud of flames.

"He bit me." The Good Samaritan sounded shocked. "That bastard bit me."

He should have been more concerned that his attacker had turned into a fireball, but now that he was injured, all he could think about was himself.

I was going to have to be extremely careful when I fed. I couldn't risk one of these vampires getting loose. I didn't know anything about them or why they seemed almost zombielike. I could contemplate all of this on the train, but something niggled the back of my brain. It was like I could hear another voice. It whispered that we deserved a little snack. Why deny ourselves the pleasure when it fell right into our lap?

One taste would take the edge off.

"Hey, what are you doing?" The man scuttled backward like a crab as I closed the distance between us. He wasn't fast enough.

I bit him, and delicious pure nectar from the gods exploded into my mouth. Then the gooey sweet liquid slid down my throat like I was hitting a beer bong. Instead of getting dizzy, I felt flush with power.

If another substance in the world made people feel as good as blood made me feel, it would have swept across the globe faster than a virus. It felt like I was eating every food I ever loved at once while having the most intense orgasm of my life. Feeding was that good, and I couldn't stop.

My hands shook as I let the body drop, and my rational thoughts regained control. I'd killed someone who didn't deserve it. Not only that, but by his actions, he'd been a pretty decent guy.

It also didn't seem like the detective's bite had turned him. I was pretty sure vampire cannibalism wasn't a thing. The Good Samaritan had still been human when I killed him.

"This really isn't my week." I bent and picked up the tire iron.

The man wasn't twitching like Enrique or coming after me like Detective Fraiser. He looked dead. I checked his pulse to make sure, and there was nothing there. What I was about to do didn't feel right, but I couldn't risk leaving another vampire behind. I brought the tire iron up and slammed it into his chest. The body burst into ash, leaving a dirty stain on the snow.

Looking at the spot where the body burst into flames, I tried not to blame myself too harshly. "Fuck!" I screamed it into the air. There was nothing I could do about it now, but I needed to figure this shit out. If I had to kill people, they wouldn't be people like the Good Samaritan. I made a promise to myself. Never again.

I trudged up the hill toward the man's car. The bright side was I didn't have to walk to the train station. A vehicle abandoned at the train station would make people think of several options besides murder. No one would look for me if they found it there. It wasn't a very glamorous line of thinking, but all I wanted to do was get the hell out of here and put as much distance between St. Charles and me as I could.

I needed some time and space to get a handle on things. There were a ton of questions I wanted answers to, but first I had to survive.

CHAPTER EIGHT

Waiting for the last train of the night in Geneva sucked.

There was an awning by the shops. Everyone was huddled under it, trying to avoid the worst of the weather. All of the businesses were closed. You couldn't get into the shop to buy a ticket. If you didn't have a pass, you had to buy your ticket on the train.

The weather didn't bother me, but these people deserved a shop where they could buy a cup of hot coffee. Sadly, there probably weren't enough customers or security to make it worth staying open. Everyone here looked like they had been partying or were knock-down-drag-out tired from working all day.

One woman let out a little cheer when the train came into view. When she saw me watching her, she quickly turned away. Looking down, I could see why. Dried blood splattered my coat. She probably didn't recognize what the stain was in the cheap fluorescent lighting, but the rips in the fabric wouldn't instill confidence. I tried to think of what would draw more attention, me in a long-sleeved T-shirt or a maroon-stained coat.

When the train stopped, I stripped off the bloody jacket and folded it over with the money inside.

There was heat on the train, but it wasn't warm enough for people to take off their coats. The commuters who had come together under the awning still huddled in groups around the train car. I found an empty seat on the second floor away from everyone else and tried to fade into the background. I hoped I wouldn't have to speak to anyone until the conductor came around. Most people bought tickets from the machine or had monthly passes.

I sat on my jacket so no one could see it. My shirt also had some stains on it. Mostly around the rip from where Enrique shot me. The black material hid the fact that it was blood, but the train was bright enough that the staining wouldn't go unnoticed.

"Did you lose your coat there, buddy?" The conductor had his hat tilted up, giving me his full attention.

Pulling Slick Ricky's twenty out of my pocket, I offered it to him. "My buddy thought it'd be hilarious to hide my jacket at the party. Then he couldn't find it when it was time to go."

I tucked my hands under my arms and shivered for effect.

"We've got a couple of things in the lost and found about to go to Goodwill. I'll grab you something." The conductor made change from his nifty steampunk-like coin belt, handed it to me, and disappeared down the steps.

It seemed like he bought my story and was getting me a jacket. There was always a chance he could be calling the cops who would pick me up at the next stop. Mostly I believed he was trying to help me out.

If the cops boarded the train, I'd run. I was pretty sure they couldn't catch me, but running like that for long might draw more attention than I wanted. It was better to play it safe. It'd cost me a hundred to catch a cab, but I'd spend it in a blink if it meant not getting caught by the police before reaching downtown. Cabbies had a way of not paying attention to things. It was a skill more people should master.

The farther we got from Geneva, the less chance there was that anyone would recognize me.

The conductor returned and held out a thick winter coat. "I think this will fit."

He had to be joking. The coat would fit all right, but I'd look like a six-year-old wearing their dad's jacket. The man who left this behind must have been monstrous. It wasn't the kind of thing someone misplaced. Still, it was better than looking out of place for not having one.

"Thank you." I took the coat and pulled it on without standing. "I feel better already. Should I leave this here when I go?"

He looked down at me with sad eyes, maybe imagining his son sitting where I was. "If you don't need it anymore, drop it off at your local donation station."

The conductor moved away from me, froze, then spun. He pulled a fully punched Subway card out of his wallet and handed it to me. "And get something to eat."

Before I could refuse, he was down the stairs and out of the train car. I wanted to tell him that anyone who ran an authentic deli wouldn't be caught dead in a Subway, but the gesture was so damn heartwarming all I could do was smile. It felt silly to keep the card for a sandwich I couldn't eat, but

I put it in my jeans for later. Since my definition of "Eat Fresh" had recently changed, maybe I'd give the card to the first person I saw who could use it.

Pay it forward.

The rest of the ride went by without incident. People shuffled in and out of the train at each stop, but soon enough, we were in the terminal in downtown Chicago. During the day, the station was a buzzing hive of madness. If you didn't know where you were going, it was easy to get on the wrong train and end up farther away from your destination than where you started. At night, the place was a ghost town.

As in Geneva, all the shops were closed. Even McDonald's had pulled down the metal gate in front of their store. Our train was the only one debarking at the moment, and there were probably only thirty of us moving toward the front doors. The place was so deserted there didn't even seem to be security. During the day, you couldn't toss a cigarette butt without hitting an officer.

I stepped out into the Chicago night and smiled as I remembered coming here a few months previously for the Taste of Chicago and the fireworks. It was such a cool time to be down by the lakefront. It was like a carnival, but all the rides were the best restaurants in the city. Patrons bought tickets and exchanged them for food at any of the booths. Pizza, sausages, and desserts that made even the lactose tolerant cringe with worry.

They closed the streets after the fireworks show so people could walk back to the train station. There simply wasn't enough room on the sidewalks for so many people. It felt like leaving a game at Soldier Field except half the damn state was there instead of only Bears fans. Enrique and I got drunk as skunks and saw a crazy fight on the train ride home.

As fun as that was, the city had a different kind of beauty when it felt empty.

It took me a few moments to get oriented. Then I started walking. The nice thing about a large urban center was that most transportation hubs were near each other. It didn't take long to get anywhere in the city from the train station.

Cabs, buses, and the "L" all ran pretty much all the time depending on where you were. Catching a cab from the airport would always be easier than flagging one down in Cabrini Green. It wasn't even the Candyman's fault. I looked over my shoulder, happy not to see a hook-wielding killer standing there.

Sweets to the sweet.

The streets were almost deserted. Most of the others exiting the train station went to the well-lit parking garage across the street. Being alone at this time of night in downtown Chicago wasn't advisable. There might not be as much crime in the big city as TV shows depicted, but there was enough that making yourself an easy target was a bad idea.

With my newfound strength and speed, I wasn't too worried about running into trouble. My giant coat made me look more homeless than wealthy so the smart criminals wouldn't chance it. Why risk robbing someone who has nothing? It was a pretty good disguise for someone carrying around eighty-four hundred bucks and some change.

Sneaky was my new middle name.

The few people who followed me peeled off in different directions, and now I was alone. It was kind of a cool feeling. The farther I moved from the train station, the more it felt like I had the entire city to myself. All I needed was some epic music playing, and it would have felt like a scene from a post-apocalyptic book. A lone figure walking the empty city streets at night with snow swirling around him.

"Time to pick up the pace." With no one watching, I began to run.

One thing they don't tell you is that running in the city draws far more attention to you than walking. Cops wonder what you've done. People looking out their windows take note to see if something interesting is about to happen. As soon as someone starts to sprint, it's like the world is waiting to see what the rest of the story was going to be. At night, with no one else around in my giant coat, I probably looked suspicious as hell.

Please ignore the man in the oversized jacket. Nothing to see here.

A smile lit up my face as the ground flew beneath my feet. I took shortcuts I never would have dared to try before. I was a creature of the night, and this was my element.

If the damn coat wasn't so bulky, I'd really turn up the speed and see what I could do. Tripping over the coat would ruin the mystique I was trying to build, so I settled for a half-decent jog. At vampire speeds, I probably looked like an Olympian.

Ducking into an alley between two large warehouses, I dodged a trash can, leapt over a cat, and continued toward the bus station. Walter Payton would have been proud. The only thing missing was someone for me to stiff-arm. Twirling in a three-sixty, I jumped over a broken bottle and raced past a giant dumpster.

Something swung at me from the shadows and slammed into my chest. I hit the ground hard, smacking my head against the asphalt. My lungs burned, and some of my ribs might have been cracked. Each breath felt like I was sucking on shards of glass. Two men walked out from behind the dumpster. One of them was holding a splintered two-by-four in his hands.

"You got him good, Bert!" His partner tittered.

Bert shoved him behind the trash can hard enough he hit the building. "Of course, I did, Ratman. 'Course I did." He looked at the broken board in his hand, tossed it aside, and stared down at me with an almost bashful expression. "Sorry about that friend, but you were moving pretty quick there."

"A man moving like that has something to hide," Ratman squealed. "Right, Bert?"

Bert pointed at Ratman, tapped the side of his nose, and grinned. "Exactly my thoughts, Rat. So, what do you have for us, my Christmas goose? What kind of goodies are you hiding under that big coat?"

My breath was coming easier, and a rib snapped back into place. A short scream escaped me.

Bert's fist slammed into my face. "That's enough of that."

Laughter wasn't the response he expected, but it was the one he got. I was Tyler Fucking Durden. Only my nose was already healed from where Bert broke it moments before. I couldn't drip blood all over his face like Brad Pitt did in the basement of the bar, but I could still scare the shit out of him. Laughter bubbled out of me like poison. This should have been the most terrifying moment of my life, but I was in full control.

They just hadn't figured it out yet.

"What's wrong with him?" Ratman peered out from behind the dumpster.

Bert ripped my coat open, looking like he'd had enough

of the crazy but wasn't willing to leave empty-handed. "Who cares?"

"You know, it's not very nice to hit people." The words came out of my mouth, but it felt like I was listening to them instead of directing the conversation.

My face exploded in pain again. When my eyes focused, Bert was holding out his hand to his friend like he was waiting for something. I laughed again. What was he going to do, shoot me? The joke was on Bert. Shooting me didn't work very well for the last two guys who tried it. I kept laughing, a gurgling stream of glee in the darkness. It felt good to let out some of the emotion I'd bottled up, even if it wasn't in the healthiest way.

"Maybe we should go?" Ratman looked longingly down the alley like he was waiting for the chance to run.

Bert kept his palm flat and level, fully expecting his orders to be carried out. "Give me the knife."

Ratman produced a stiletto from his coat and placed it in Bert's hand. "Be quick about it. I don't like this."

It was the kind of knife only used for one purpose. You couldn't do much with a stiletto except open letters and stab people. It was a single blade pointed at the tip made for shoving in between the gaps in plate mail armor. Or, in this case, apparently helpless teenagers who shouldn't have been out late at night.

The smile returned to Bert's eyes as he lifted the blade. "Are you going to tell me what you're hiding, or do I have to cut it out of you, little goose?"

His smile wilted when I matched it with a manic version that showed my teeth. I must have been one hell of a sight, face dripping with blood, grinning like an idiot. I certainly felt ridiculous, but I wasn't in complete control anymore.

Something else was taking over, something monstrous. The laughter began again, and Bert stabbed me.

The look on his face when I grabbed him around the throat and pulled him toward my mouth was priceless. Bert's knife was still buried in my stomach. He pulled the blade out and slid it back in a few more times. Blood bubbled between my mouth and his neck. It was hard to drink so much while the darkness mocked the stupidity of the feed bag's futility. I hissed as Bert's blade punctured a lung, but I didn't stop feeding.

The killer inside me was hungry.

Bert's life ebbed away and I pushed his lifeless body to the side. "Didn't your mother tell you not to play with knives?" Bert couldn't respond. His glassy eyes stared back at me.

Fresh blood rushed through my veins, and I felt alive in a way I never had before my turning. It was like living in a world where anything was possible. Only the loss of control tempered the raw pleasure.

I couldn't go around feeding on everyone I got into a tussle with. That would eventually lead to me getting caught. The last place I wanted to end up was in some billionaire's lab being experimented on so he could live longer.

No one puts Dylan in a box, baby!

Ratman took off running, and I let him go. The thrill of the chase was something I hadn't experienced before, but the dark presence was calling to take control again. It wanted to hunt and kill, and God help me, but I wanted to let it out. I was tired of being trampled on and abused. It was time to take back control.

Or maybe it was time to give some up.

I stepped over Bert's lifeless body and stripped off my outerwear. There was a crate by the trashcan the men had used to play cards. I knocked their game off the top and set my coat down. I took the jacket with money and placed it inside the coat to keep it safe.

Now I had to deal with Bert's body. I didn't have anything to shove through his chest, so I tried something new. I took his head in my hands and smashed it into the side of the dumpster with all the strength I could muster. His skull burst apart like one of Gallagher's watermelons. Gore sprayed across the alley, and the body burst into flames.

It seemed like there were lots of ways to kill young vampires.

All of a sudden, I didn't feel quite so indestructible, but I wasn't back in full control. Ratman was still sprinting down the alley, and I couldn't let him get away. Not if I wanted to sneak out of the city. Leaving a witness was a bad idea. Even with nobody to corroborate his story, someone would start looking for me.

I scented the air like an apex predator stalking its prey. There was a faint scent of sewage and blood. I zeroed in on Ratman. He had the right instinct.

It was a shame he didn't act on it sooner.

He ran with everything he had, but he might as well have been in slow motion. Part of him sensed me coming, and he glanced over his shoulder. I sped up and jumped onto the wall.

Three awkward steps on the side of the building later, I flew toward him as he completed his turn. Before he could squawk, I had my teeth buried in his throat. The blood flowed, and I sucked it down in thick delicious slurps.

Ratman went limp in my arms, and I pushed his lifeless body to the ground. I stared up at the sky and screamed into the night in triumph. The darkness inside me wanted more, but first it wanted to make sure Ratman never rose from the dead. The heel of my boot came down on Ratman's skull, and there was a wet splash against the leg of my jeans.

"Fuck." Making a mess of my only pair of pants snapped me back into full control.

I didn't want to think about what would happen if I completely gave in to the darkness. I wanted to get out of here. Running away from murder scenes seemed to be a theme for me lately. The only good news was the complete lack of evidence in the alley.

I ran back to my coat and picked it up. For the first time, I was thankful for its ridiculous size. It would cover up the worst of the mess. I'd grab some new clothes and a shower at the first truck stop I found.

It was an oddly practical assessment after what happened. Maybe I was distancing myself from these two kills because it felt like someone else had done it for me. That was a bag of worms I'd have to dig into at some point, but now wasn't the right time, despite all my questions.

What in the fuck even happened? Who was the voice in the back of my head? Was I losing my shit?

It was too much to deal with right now. All I had to do was get out of here, get on a bus, and relax until Phoenix. Then, I would be home free.

I buttoned my coat, stepped out onto the sidewalk, and looked around. The streets were as deserted as they were when I entered the alley. No one appeared to be watching, but I walked down the street hunched against the cold I couldn't feel to blend in. A few quick turns put me back on the main road and heading in the right direction.

A bright blue light glowed on the horizon and I made out the "G" in white lettering around the edge of the bus station. Salvation was at hand, and it came in the form of cheap affordable cross-country transportation.

CHAPTER NINE

I was still riding the pleasure wave when the Greyhound terminal came into view.

The giant neon dog lit the night above the building like the arches of heaven calling weary travelers home. Buses were lined up in neat rows waiting for the heavy load of passengers in the morning. The station's only traffic was those making pit stops before continuing to other parts of the country.

The wheels of commerce never stopped spinning.

The inside of the cavernous station was almost empty. Some passengers slept with bags clutched to their chests. Others listened to CD players or drank cheap coffee from the vending machine. The cups with the playing cards were always a dead giveaway about the quality of coffee an establishment provided.

Not a single one of them looked up to see the new arrival. This was my kind of place.

I'd used some snow to clean the blood off my face and hands on the way to the station. Before I scared the ticket lady half to death, I decided to hit the bathroom for a proper washing. I kept my head covered with my hood, trying to hide my features until I saw how I looked.

A man was waiting by the bathroom doors. He didn't look like security but had that same kind of aggressive stance. *Thump, thump, thump.* His heart rate sounded fast. What could have him so worked up this late at night?

A woman exited the bathroom, and he grabbed her arm. "What do you think you're doing, making me wait like that?"

She tried to yank her arm free but couldn't. "Cut it out, Paul. You're hurting me."

"You're going to get a lot worse if you don't shut the fuck up, Cynthia. I'm about done with you." Paul gave her arm one last squeeze to ensure she got the message.

Oh man, I needed to take a serious chill pill. I couldn't take my eyes off him even though I knew killing him in the middle of the station would be a huge problem. *I will not kill Paul before buying my ticket.* If I repeated the phrase enough, I might mean it.

The dark presence in my head wondered how the station would look bathed in blood. It purred for the chance to be set free. Images of the people I walked past to get to the bathroom flashed through my mind. It wanted all of them.

All you have to do is let go.

Who the fuck was talking inside my head? The images fell away, and the voice quieted. I was losing my shit. The last seventy-two hours had been a complete tailspin, but I couldn't afford to crack this close to freedom. I needed to take baby steps. Baby steps to the bathroom. Baby steps to the ticket counter. Baby steps onto the bus. Everything would be better when I was on the road.

One small step at a time.

A shoulder slammed into mine. "Watcha looking at, weirdo?"

"Paul," the woman pleaded.

I will not eat Paul before buying my ticket. Give me the strength to deal with the shit I have to and the courage not to turn this place into a Jackson Pollock painting. I didn't turn and murder Paul like he was begging for. Instead, I kept my head down and walked into the bathroom without saying a word. If he followed me inside, I wouldn't be responsible for what happened.

The door closed behind me, and I was alone.

The water did a lot better job of washing off the blood than the snow had. When I looked into the mirror, I gasped. There was blood smeared on my chin and neck. The stuff covered half of my T-shirt. Not the kind of thing that would go unnoticed for long. All it would need was one person taking an interest and pointing me out to the police.

Screw that noise.

I stripped off my big jacket and tossed it aside, along with the bundle of cash wrapped in Enrique's old coat. The tap water was lukewarm at best, but it was enough to clean my shirt and get the blood off my face and chest. Who knew feeding on blood would be so damned messy? I spent the next five minutes drying the shirt under the hand dryers. It wasn't perfectly dry, but it wasn't soaking wet, so I put it back on.

I pulled Enrique's four hundred in twenties from my stash, tucked them into my jeans, and bundled the rest into the old jacket. Looking a good deal cleaner than I had when I walked into the bathroom, I put on the oversized coat.

I felt pretty good about how I'd handled the whole Paul situation. There was hope for me yet. All I had to do was keep working the baby steps. Buy the ticket, get out of here, and start a new life. It wasn't that complicated. People moved to new cities and started over all the time.

One day I'd be back.

The woman behind the bulletproof glass watched a tiny six-inch screen TV. She looked up as I approached but without much interest. Her name tag read Betty.

"Where you going, sugar?" Her tone reminded me of my mom.

It took a second to pull myself back into the moment. "Phoenix, Arizona."

"You have family out there or something?" She sounded concerned but checked the ticket prices without hesitation.

It dawned on me that I probably looked a little young to travel out of state in the middle of the night. "Yeah, my uncle lives there. He's an electrician. Invited me out to spend the year apprenticing."

Betty glanced at me but kept typing. "I've got a couple of things I can do for you. We've got a bus leaving in an hour for Indianapolis.

"From there, I can get you to Albuquerque and finally to Phoenix. Trip takes about forty-eight hours, and it'll cost you a hundred and fifty-two dollars unless you've got extra bags. Or we could look for cheaper options with more stops."

Pulling out my cash, I counted off a hundred and sixty bucks and passed it through the slot at the bottom of the window. "Just me. My Dad went down with all my stuff a couple of weeks ago. Told me to stay here and enjoy some time with my friends before leaving."

Betty quickly made change and slid the bills under the partition. "You get down there safe and do your dad proud. You hear?"

"Yes, ma'am." There was no other answer to give.

I pocketed my ticket, found an empty seat, and waited for them to make the call. This was it. I was almost out of Illinois. In less than an hour, I'd be rolling.

I couldn't wait to put Fraiser, Enrique, and the two stick-up artists behind me for good. It would give me the time to focus on figuring out what I was and how to control the darkness growing inside me. There was a future out there for me. It was going to be a little less traditional.

The Path to Greatness was flexible and could be adjusted as needed.

The stop in Indianapolis only lasted an hour.

I got off the bus because everyone else did, but I didn't have to go to the bathroom or stretch. Even with being cramped in the uncomfortable seats for hours, my body felt fine. I returned to the bus before everyone else, claimed my spot in the middle by the window, and pretended to fall asleep.

Paul got on the bus, pushing Cynthia in front of him. "Just wait until we get there. I'm going to make you pay for all this stress you've been causing."

When she started to complain, there was a sharp *crack*. The bus driver looked in the mirror and noticed I wasn't sleeping. He started to get up, and I shook my head.

It wasn't worth it for him to get involved. He'd get hurt. If Paul hurt him, I'd drain him on the spot. I couldn't risk the confrontation despite everything inside me dying to show him the error of his ways.

Cynthia was crying now, and the bastard was already cooing to her about how he'd never do it again. How it was her fault he got so worked up all the time. Why did she always make him so fucking angry? I could see her in my mind's eye, cuddling back into him now like all was forgiven, and the cycle would continue.

My fangs dropped, and I let out a little hiss of pain.

This wasn't the time to let the beast out of the cage. I had to keep it cool. Paul would get his one day, but I wasn't going to be the one to give it to him. Leaving a trail of missing people along my escape route wasn't exactly the kind of thing I could afford to do. Krista could have friends everywhere. They could be watching the news looking for stories that would help track me down.

Fear did the trick to get my emotions under control. All I had to do was ride out this trip, and I'd have the time to figure out things in peace. When we reached Phoenix, I could disappear. The bus driver must have shared my sense of discretion because he sat and kept his eyes forward.

Ten minutes later we were back on the road.

We reached Albuquerque in the middle of the night.

Unlike the last time we stopped, this time I was antsy. The hunger had started to build again. It had been an entire day since I'd eaten, and the sun had bled away most of my strength. I remembered watching the sunrise and thought if this were the day I burst into flames, the passengers would have one hell of a story to tell their grandchildren.

It didn't happen.

For some reason, I was immune to the sun's rays. I didn't know how or why, but minus the hangover feeling daylight caused, it was damn useful. When the darkness returned, the hangover drifted away. I felt better almost instantly, more like myself than I'd ever been after a Friday night drinking with Enrique. The worst part about the sun wasn't my loss of strength. It was that it left me so damn hungry.

An empty stomach meant I needed to feed, or the darkness would do it for me.

When we stopped again, I joined the queue getting off the bus. This time, I wanted the freedom to stretch my legs. Unlike most of the depots I'd been through, the Albuquerque station was rocking even at one in the morning. All the overhead lights were on, and the restaurant and gift shop were open. They also had bathrooms with showers you paid for by the minute, but it was clean, and the door had a lock, so that was something.

Before a shower would do me any good, I needed new clothes. I headed to the gift shop and expected to find a bunch of touristy bullshit. You know the stuff I'm talking about. "My Dad went to Albuquerque, and all I got was this shirt" kind of stuff. Instead, there was a wall full of Levi's jeans, rugged-looking work shirts, coats, and two styles of work boots. Steel-toed, and "I don't mind not having toes if something goes wrong."

It was the easiest shopping I'd ever done.

I bought a pair of jeans, boots, a thick hoodie, and a T-shirt, then threw in socks and boxers plus some cheap sunglasses. The fluorescent lights outside were so bright they screwed with my vision. Normally only posers wore sunglasses after dark, but under these lights it was necessary.

"How do the showers work?" I made small talk with the lady behind the cash register as I handed over a couple of hundred-dollar bills.

The light sparkled off Rachel's name tag as she ran a pen over the corner of the bills. When the ink turned gold, she put them in the register. She looked at me, hesitating before making change as if how she broke down the bills might matter for the shower.

"There's a five-dollar fee to open the door. That includes the shower for three minutes. If you want longer, you need to feed more dollar bills into the dispenser. We have a single pack of shampoo, conditioner, and some body wash if you need them."

"Make sure I get a few fives back, and that's a yes on the soap and shampoo." Damn, I was an easy mark.

It probably wouldn't take a genius to figure out that someone wearing a gigantic jacket who'd been on a bus for almost two days without a change of clothes might need a shower. Rachel counted out my change and handed it to me with a smile. She must have worked here for a while to not even bat an eye at the weird kid in the giant sleeping bag-like coat rocking the sunglasses he bought like a rock star.

I bet she had some awesome stories.

Rachel smiled. "Give me a moment to bag everything up."

She put the boots at the bottom of the bag with the hoodie on top of them. Then everything else went in. She flashed the package of shampoo and soap at me before tossing them in the bag so I could see they were in there. She set the bag on the counter.

"If you need anything else before your bus leaves, you know where to find me." Rachel sounded hopeful that I'd come back.

Must have been my vampire magnetism because even I knew I was a little ripe.

There was no way she was flirting with me. The fact I'd thought so showed how much I had to learn about women. She was doing her job, probably hoping for a few more sales if she got commissions. It was good old-fashioned customer service.

"I will." Grinning to cover up any misunderstanding, I gave her a cheery wave as I turned and walked into Paul.

"Watch where you're going, penis breath." He slammed his shoulder into me as he pushed past.

Not the most original guy in the world.

Cynthia followed in his wake like a tugboat trying to right the ship. "Sorry."

"Don't apologize to the weirdo. He walked into me." Paul grabbed her arm and yanked her out the door and into the parking lot.

Rachel and I watched the couple walk around the side of the building until they were out of sight and shared a sad look. I had to remind myself that eating people was wrong. Paul might be total shit, but he needed to be in jail, not in the morgue. It wasn't my job to be judge and jury. That was what cops and the district attorney were for. I left the shop and headed for the showers.

I located an empty shower stall inside the bathroom and slipped my five into the door before stepping inside. There were two meters for cash in the room—one for the shower and one for the door. The three minutes of shower time came with fifteen minutes in the room. I slipped an extra five in each slot to buy some time and stripped out of my clothes.

I tossed most of my old gear in the garbage but kept Enrique's coat with the cash stuffed inside and the big jacket the conductor had given me. The jacket would be too warm for Arizona, but the conductor had asked me to donate it, so it was coming with. I left my new clothes in the bag and turned on the hot water.

While the water heated up, I removed all the tags from my new clothes. Steam filled the room, and I turned down the hot water before stepping into the first shower I'd had in days.

Was there anything more refreshing than a shower when you felt dirty?

Under the nozzle was where I did my best thinking. Some people liked to exercise or sit on the porcelain throne while thinking, but not this guy. I always took a shower if I needed to work out a problem or was feeling down. The first few minutes went by sitting under the nozzle and enjoying the feeling. Then it was time to scrub.

Blood was an easy thing to clean when wet, but it was a real bitch to get off when it dried. It was under my nails and behind my ears. I'd even managed to get some in my nose. All of it washed off, and despite my conscience trying to guilt me into feeling bad about what I'd done, I didn't feel all that guilty.

Mess with the bull, and you'll get the horns.

It wasn't like I was out there killing willy-nilly. There was only one death I felt remotely bad about—the Good Samaritan. The detective had bitten him, but I never gave him a chance. I'd been doing better since then. Everyone on the bus was still alive. Even Paul, the woman-beating super-douche.

The goal would be never to kill anyone like the Good Samaritan again, but I wasn't going to roll over and take abuse because I could heal. I'd done that for years behind the counter at the shop. I was through with letting people walk all over me.

It was time to take control of my life.

When the water stopped, I felt like a brand-new man. Once dressed in my new gear, I opened the door only to find Paul standing there.

I started to push past him. "It's all yours."

"I know it is." He kneed me in the gut and shoved me back into the bathroom. "Let's get a look at the rest of that cash you've been flashing around."

My stomach ached from where his knee slammed into it. I could have sworn I gave myself a pep talk about not taking shit, but here I was on the floor not even a minute later. Paul was fucking with the wrong guy right now.

The dull ache in my stomach wasn't only from the blow.

I flipped back to my feet and stared into Paul's eyes. "Not the best idea you've ever had." I brushed off the front of my new hoodie. "This is your one shot to turn and walk away."

I don't know who I thought I was. Delivering ultimatums wasn't my style. I was more likely to apologize even though someone bumped into me first. A little kindness was all it normally took to get people to leave me alone.

Paul didn't share the same philosophy. He pushed into the room and pulled the door closed behind him.

"Nowhere to go now, freak." He smiled and flipped open

a four-inch pocketknife. "Give me the cash, and you can walk away."

My smile caught him off-guard, but Paul never hesitated.

He jammed the knife into my side and pressed his face close to mine, grinning in triumph. It lasted until my hand clamped down on his wrist. He tried to pull back, but I held it in place even though his knife was still in me. I broke his arm with a squeeze, wrenched his neck to the side, and drained him. My strength returned. The pit in my stomach was satisfied. The knife came out with a sucking sound, and I dropped it in the trash as the wound healed instantly.

There was no blood on the outside of my jacket, only a new hole. The inside of my hoodie and my brand-new shirt were a mess. Not to mention my mouth. I washed the blood off my face and tried not to think about the corpse on the floor behind me.

"Fuck." This wasn't part of the plan.

Cynthia would be puzzled when Paul didn't show up, but she would be better off. I bent and pulled out Paul's wallet. I also slipped off his rings and necklace.

The gold I dumped into the trash. I could have saved it, but if Cynthia started throwing out accusations, I didn't want any of the creep's stuff on me. There was fifteen bucks in Paul's wallet, not even enough for a decent meal for the both of them.

I tossed the wallet in the trash with the rest of his crap. My new clothes had already suffered enough, so exploding his head against the wall was out of the question. It took me a few seconds to find his knife, then I rolled up my sleeve and began cutting. The blade snapped against his sternum, but it managed to break the bone. I slipped my hand inside his chest and squeezed his heart. The body burst into flames almost instantly.

Paul's fifteen dollars went into the machine. Two fives for the room and one for the water. I picked up what remained of Paul's clothes and tossed them in the trash with the rest of his shit. Then I used the shower to clean up everything I could, including my hand. A few minutes in the mirror was all it took to ensure I was clean. Then I was out of the room.

The world could rest easier with one less asshole in it.

Cynthia was waiting outside the bathroom. "Have you seen Paul?" She looked like she was about to have a breakdown.

I turned and looked around the station, trying to come up with an excuse that would stop her from going inside and looking for him. "I saw him hop in a Corvette with some blonde chick on the other side of the station."

"Are you sure?" Her face was a mask of rejection and suspicion. "He said he was going to look for you."

"Some guys will do anything to get out of breaking up." I shrugged as if ditching your girlfriend at the bus station was an everyday occurrence.

The bus driver climbed off the bus and shouted, "We're leaving in two minutes. Get back on the bus."

Cynthia still didn't look too sure. She looked between the bus and station and back at me with mounting desperation. "That bastard! He promised it'd be different this time."

When the tears started, I took that as my cue to get the hell out of there. I climbed onto the bus, found my seat, and pretended to go to sleep. She might be heartbroken now, but hopefully Cynthia would be better off in the long run.

Any man who smacked a woman around wasn't worth a pile of dog shit. This was her shot at a brand-new life.

Hope she makes the most of it.

The bus started rolling, and I smiled at all the commotion outside. We were leaving, but ten other buses had pulled in, and two more followed us to the freeway. If anyone was following me, they would have their work cut out for them. It was nice knowing that things were finally starting to go my way again.

I nuzzled deeper into my seat and started thinking about everything I had to do when we reached Phoenix. Finding a place to live and getting a job were at the top of the list. Then there was the whole vampire thing. I was still wrapping my head around the change, but it was time to get serious about making plans and figuring out what I was.

There would be a lot of trial and error along the way, but it was exciting. I felt like Spiderman when he first discovered his powers. Great tragedy shaped my life, but I would emerge stronger from it. This was my time to be extraordinary.

First I had to survive.

CHAPTER TEN

My first month or so in Arizona went relatively well. No one from Illinois showed up on my doorstep, and Cynthia hadn't dragged the Phoenix police into the matter of her missing boyfriend. Even if she did, finding some rando who disappeared in another state wouldn't be a priority for them. With the giant jacket and sunglasses I'd worn when leaving the bus in Phoenix, I doubt the police would be able to pull usable camera footage from the depot.

It was funny how life worked out. Sure, I had to eat people to stay alive, but at least I wasn't piling bodies in the street. The fact my bite turned the people I fed on into vampires as soon as I drained them was useful in that regard.

I thought I could figure out how to feed on someone without killing them, but once I started, I couldn't stop. Now it was all about finding the right people to feed on. God knows finding a shitty human was easier than trying to buy the bagged stuff.

It turned out human blood was super regulated and

controlled. Who would have thought scoring a bag of blood would be harder than getting a gram of heroin? The list of people willing to risk their job to help some weirdo with what they assumed was a blood fetish was infinitesimally small. Not even a few hundred bucks would grease those wheels.

Breaking into a blood bank was also off the table. The hospital was the only place with more cameras than the gas station. It was crazy how digital security has grown over the last couple of years. The cost of security cameras had come down enough that more people were using them. Some places even bought fake ones and mounted them. The idea that someone was always watching was enough to make most people do the right thing.

It wouldn't be long before cameras were so affordable everyone had one. Teenagers worldwide should rebel now, before video evidence of their escapades existed.

Parents of the future were going to have things so easy.

Home security was something only rich people could afford when I was younger. The cops were still going to schools and passing out poison stickers to put on the cleaning products instead of getting kids to sign up for D.A.R.E.

I'd always thought D.A.R.E. was a sneaky way to get kids' fingerprints in the system. What kind of fourth-grader is already screwing around with drugs? It was funny they came at you super early on, then you didn't hear the drug messaging again until you were a senior in high school. Then they delivered abstinence speeches and horror stories instead of discussing responsible drinking and getting a ride. Those probably would have been smarter since most kids thought they were invincible.

And I thought everyone over age ten saw *Footloose*.

With the hospitals and blood banks out as far as suppliers went, I thought about paying someone for their blood, but who in the hell would be up for that? There was also the matter of starting the "I want your blood" conversation with a random person. It wasn't something you could jump right into. With the bagged stuff firmly off the table, I'd resorted to working with the criminal underground.

AOL chat rooms were as handy for luring predators out as they were for the actual predators acquiring victims. There were all kinds of shitty people in the world. It was amazing what pretending to be a twelve-year-old boy on the Internet would reveal about people. Most of my diet was pedophiles. I was making the world a safer place for children everywhere one bite at a time.

When I couldn't catch a pedophile, I looked for the worst person I could find. Anything to help me ease the sting of guilt I felt each time I took a life. I'd never been prone to violence as a human, and now my body count made Ted Bundy look like a beginner. Not that comparing myself to one of the vilest people ever to walk the planet was flattering. It was factual.

Feeding kept the crazy at bay.

As long as I avoided the sun, I could go days without feeding, but one morning of sunlight meant I needed to eat that night. If I didn't keep myself properly fed, the voice in the back of my head got stronger. Death, mayhem, and carnage were some of its favorite words. There was a constant struggle for control, but the easiest way to win was to keep my belly full and stay out of the sun.

Staying away from daylight also had other advantages.

My strength and speed never decreased when I stayed

nocturnal. I was a hundred and ninety pounds and about six feet tall. Most of my body was lean, but I wasn't exactly packing on the muscle like a professional athlete.

When it came to working out, I didn't. Before becoming a vampire, I couldn't bench press my body weight. Now I could do one-armed push-ups for as long as I wanted.

That strength made being a bouncer at The Tasty Lamb much easier.

We weren't a biker bar, but our crowd tended to wear more leather than ASU gear. Coming from Tucson by way of Illinois, I could appreciate the lack of Sun Devil apparel a little more than the average bouncer. Go Wildcats!

This deep in enemy territory, it paid to avoid angering the locals so I smiled and cheered when appropriate to keep the peace. There were enough members of our clientele who wanted a shot at toppling the bouncer. I didn't need to pour gasoline on the fire.

There was always one thing you could count on in a room full of drunk alpha males. One of them would be looking for a fight.

It was a slow night working the door at the bar—not a big surprise since it was one in the morning on a Wednesday. Normally I'd take off if things were dead and use the extra time to find my next meal. Not much use for a bouncer when the staff inside outnumbered the customers.

Only the dedicated and the regulars who had days off in the middle of the week were knocking them back tonight. I opened the door to peek inside. It was as empty as the last time I checked.

Despite the lack of customers, I couldn't shake the feeling that something bad was about to happen and I needed to be here. The last few nights at the bar, I'd felt like someone was watching me at the door. Knowing there might be people looking for me always had me feeling paranoid, but lately it was more than that. I had to remind myself to calm down. If there was a witness to my crimes, they could never validate their story. My best defense was always going to be a lack of evidence.

I drew a few deep breaths and scanned the parking lot. Nothing, like the last ten times I'd looked. I was on edge and needed to relax. No one was coming for me. Nobody cared. Even the voice in the back of my mind was silent. It was nice not to feel like Dr. Dylan and Mr. Bloodsucker for a little while.

Tiffany poked her head out the door. "Hey, I'm leaving in thirty. Want to walk me home?"

Fuck yeah, I wanted to walk her home. I liked everything about the girl. She was five-foot-five and spunky as all get out in an "I'm going to kick your ass" way. She had raven black hair and wore enough black eyeliner to make one of those Emo kids jealous. All I wanted to do was eat her up, which was part of the problem.

She was so hot that she made my fangs pop out.

"I don't think that would be such a good idea." I looked down at the ground.

The sound of her sweet laughter filled the air. "Get hold of yourself, studly. There's been some kind of stalker on the news. Two women have died."

She stepped outside and lit a cigarette. "Of course, the cops don't know dick. Working a bunch of leads, my ass." She ground out the smoke on the side of the door before tossing it in the trash, then smiled at me, flashing the most beautiful green eyes. "Do me a solid, and I'll owe you one."

How could I say no?

"Of course, I'll walk you home." I bowed low. "Just don't get any ideas about luring me inside. I bite."

Tiffany looked me over and nodded. "I bet you do."

Ripping the door open, she shouted inside. "Josh, I'm not going to need that cab after all. I talked Studly Davidson out here into walking me home."

The door swung shut as Tiffany entered the bar, cutting off the rest of their conversation.

I walked through the empty parking lot and out to the street. The road was clear in both directions. Most people were at home tucked into bed, enjoying their sleep. My slumber would be coming soon. I needed to be back home and inside with the blackout curtains in place before the sun came up.

Otherwise, I'd need to start tomorrow by finding someone to feed on.

Trying to find bad guys to snack on all the time wasn't easy. There was no database for normal people to look up murderers and rapists so they could take them out. The cops tended to frown on vigilante justice. That was why they always tried to catch Batman instead of letting him clean up the city.

Finding the right person took time. I'd been lucky so far, but I searched for my next target every night. Hungry or not, it was nice to know where my next meal was coming from.

Maybe the cops would like me better than Batman. I never left them a mess to clean up.

The street was still empty in both directions, but the night's calmness didn't do anything to ease my tension. My apartment was closer to the freeway, so I'd grown used to the sounds of daytime traffic as I slept. Not hearing a car running or a police siren felt out of place in the city. Even at one a.m. on Wednesday, something was going on. Tonight, it was like the entire city punched out early.

Tiffany walked out the door a few minutes later, bundled up in an oversized hoodie and wearing a cute little backpack. She held her arm out for me to take it and met my eyes with fierce determination. "Let's do this."

She thought something might happen. I was on edge, so I was inclined to follow her down that particular rabbit hole. Not that we'd have to worry. Even if someone attacked us, I could handle it. There was no reason for her to be afraid, and if she released the death grip on my arm, all would be right in the world.

I lifted my arm, and Tiffany went up with it. We both laughed, and her grip eased enough to return circulation.

"Don't worry. Nothing is going to happen to you when you're with me." It was the truth.

I didn't have a lot of friends in this world. The ones I had now were priceless.

"After seeing you toss the Delgado brothers out of the bar, I'm a believer." She leaned into me, seeking warmth I couldn't provide.

"Those douchebags. They had it coming." With the way they came at me, the two idiots were lucky I didn't drain them.

"Yeah, but the last guy who tried to throw them out ended up with thirty-two stitches and a broken arm." Tiffany sized me up as though trying to figure out a puzzle. "And he was way bigger than you."

I lifted a finger and scolded, "You know it's not nice when you tell a man someone else's is bigger than theirs."

Tiffany held her fingers about two inches apart. "If the shoe fits."

We laughed and continued walking down the street arm-in-arm. Her apartment complex was about a mile closer to the bar than mine in the same direction. We moved from the main thoroughfare onto the side streets. Tiffany's calm slipped away as the streetlights faded in the distance.

Thankfully, I could see well enough for both of us.

The streets in this neighborhood had even less traffic than the occasional car that passed us on the main street. Large pine trees lined the sides of the road, and it felt weird seeing big, lush trees in the desert. People had a lot of misconceptions about the West. It wasn't all dust and pretty sunsets.

We had pretty sunrises too.

Tiffany's apartment complex came into view. With home in sight, some of the tension dropped from her shoulders. "Thanks again for doing this."

"It's on my way. I'd be happy to walk you home until the cops catch the guy." It was the right thing to do.

I'd never be able to forgive myself if something happened to her because I was too lazy to spend a few minutes seeing her safely to her door.

Tiffany grinned like a big sister, and I knew I'd missed the mark by a mile when implying something else. It was nice to have someone to talk to again. We moved off the sidewalk and into the parking lot. Some of the lights were out, but that was nothing new for this part of town. The complex had missed the memo that a killer was on the loose.

The large tree toward the back of the property blocked

out the light, leaving this side of the apartment complex in almost complete darkness. Only one apartment had a light on outside, but that wasn't unusual for these buildings. I'd been to these apartments a few times with Miguel, who worked in the kitchen. The dude had Sunday Ticket, and it was the only way I could watch Da Bears without going to the bar. I wasn't physically in Chicago anymore, but part of me would always live in the Midwest.

"I think I can handle it from here." Tiffany pulled free and opened her arms for a hug.

The hug felt amazing. "My mom would never forgive me if I didn't see you to the door. No funny business, I swear."

She thought about it for a second and peered into the darkness. "Let's go."

I trailed behind Tiffany, and when we made it to her building, I stayed out in the courtyard while she opened the door. The last thing I wanted was for her to feel crowded. I received the message about being friend-zoned and would forever act accordingly. When I heard the lock turn, I knew I'd done my good deed for the day.

When I lifted my hand for a friendly wave, something plowed into my exposed ribs, and I flew through the air. It was like I'd been hit by a truck instead of a person.

The bad thing about big trees is that they aren't very forgiving when you smash into them.

"Dylan?" Tiffany called in a voice torn between pissed off and concerned. "You said no funny business."

"Get inside!" I screamed as I pushed myself up.

My body began to heal as I ran for the door. It was good my pain receptors shut off when things got bad because I felt my arm snap together in a few different places as I moved. Only one thing I knew was capable of that kind of power.

A fucking vampire.

Why was there one here now? Had it come for me? Tiffany's door slammed shut, and the lock turned. The vamp slammed into the door, and the hinges shuddered. A few more good hits and he'd be through it. I sliced the pie around the corner as I approached in fast forward.

The door creaked like it was about to break, and seeing the vampire, I knew why. He was six-two and a buck eighty with a big bushy beard. The bastard was all lean, ropey muscle. He might have stood a chance if I hadn't been feeding properly. Instead, I grabbed him around the waist and tossed him casually away from the door like an older brother guarding his room against a sibling invasion.

The vamp didn't give two shits about me. He wanted Tiffany and was already walking back toward the door. Blood stained his shirt, and his fangs glistened in the moonlight.

So much for no vampires in the desert.

Bushbeard the Vamp looked at the closed door longingly. Then, as if sensing any hope of an easy meal was gone, he turned and ran. There was no way in hell I was letting that fanger go.

Not only did he throw me into a tree hard enough to break an arm, but he also went after my friend. *Not fucking cool, Vampy, not cool at all.* The vampire ran at full speed, but I was faster. A man leapt out of my way as I barreled around the corner. He was wearing all black and held a camera.

I could deal with him later. Right now, I had more important things to do.

Across the street was another man in black. This one

had a walkie-talkie and a camera. The vampire didn't care about being filmed. He was hungry and saw an easy target.

The vamp turned and beelined for the second man. The stranger in black saw the change in direction and didn't hesitate. He dropped his camera and sprinted away as fast as his legs could carry him. It was like he knew what was coming after him, and his only chance to live was to be a gazelle in a sea of leopards.

Death nipped at his heels, but salvation was coming.

I kicked the vampire's ankle like a middle school bully making him trip over his own feet. He hit the ground hard but had enough grace to flip over and right himself again before I could close the distance. We faced each other, both trying to decide what to do next.

Despite the fact I'd killed my share of vampires I'd never really been in a fight. Smashing unconscious vampires' heads into things or dragging them into the sun wasn't exactly a battle built on sportsmanship, and bouncing humans out of bars was more about restraint than actual talent.

I had no idea how it would go when matched against a vampire who was almost as strong and fast as I was. My first guess was that restraint was the last thing I needed. Instead of waiting for the fanger to attack, I charged forward recklessly. Who was going to stop me?

This fucker had tried to kill Tiffany. He wasn't going to live long enough to see the sun.

The vampire was the kind of fighter I used to be—a bad one. He threw punches I saw coming from a mile away. Bouncing taught me a few tricks, and I put them to use.

I let a clumsy blow slide off my shoulder and rocked him with an uppercut. As the vampire stumbled backward,

I ran forward and slammed both feet into his chest, sending him crashing into a parked car. Glass tinkled across the ground as the vampire tried to pull himself free of the wreckage.

The two-foot kick to the chest was a badass power move, but it left me exposed.

Thankfully, the vamp hadn't been expecting it. His getting stuck in the car gave me time to recover. The car didn't fare so well. The person who owned this vehicle was going to be pissed. *Hope they have good insurance.*

The doors squealed as the vampire wrenched himself free. Blood seeped from his mouth, but the wounds on his body were starting to heal. I wasn't going to give him a chance. I punched him in the chest over and over. My punches flew at such a rapid pace that the vamp couldn't counterattack and had trouble blocking. I lost count of how many blows I landed, but the vampire stubbornly kept his feet. His recent feed was probably the only thing saving him.

"Just end it already," one of the men in black said from behind me. He sounded disgusted.

The second man in black pulled a wooden stake from his coat and grinned. "Maybe he doesn't know how."

I slammed the vampire into the car, aware that the alarm would draw unwanted attention. I glanced at the men and realized they looked enough alike to be brothers. The stakes in their hands told me they also knew about the supernatural. They both looked intrigued by me, but neither appeared very friendly. They were probably trying to figure out who or what I was.

Fangs started to struggle, so I plunged the stake into his heart. The vampire—and the wooden stake—burst into flames. There was a little clinking sound as the tip of the stake fell to the ground and bounced.

"It's the silver tip that makes it so effective," one of the men stated as he bent to retrieve the silver point from under the car.

The other man watched me with wary eyes. "Would you mind telling us how you chased him down like that?"

Would I mind? Fuck no, I'd been dying to tell someone about myself. But I didn't know these guys. They could be ready to whisk me off to some government-run black site. It was bad enough these two weirdos knew about vampires and had seen my strength and speed, but now they wanted to know all about me. How could I trust them? As much as I wanted to spill my guts to them and beg for their help, I turned and ran away.

Sure, it could have been my chance to get some answers finally, but it also could have been my trip to a government box where they ran experiments on me. There probably wasn't a billionaire in this country who didn't think they were extra special snowflakes who deserved to live forever. They weren't going to get that gift from me.

I ran.

Greg

"Saul, did you see that guy?" I looked at my brother in wonder.

He frowned as he stared at the dented car and rolled around the silver stake tip in his hand. "Greg, I'm not sure he was a guy."

I tugged on Saul's jacket and pulled him away from the wrecked vehicle toward our car. Once my older brother's brain started working, he forgot about everything else. I didn't want to spend the rest of the night answering questions in the police department. The first and most important part of a Watcher's job was to remain unseen. Getting caught by the police would have us both in Dad's office on the receiving end of another lecture.

I didn't know about Saul, but I'd had enough of Van Helsing's lectures to last a lifetime.

Now that we'd dealt with the fledgling, our night was only getting started. There was paperwork to deal with and videos to submit to the archives. Then we'd have to look into the young man we'd met. He didn't move like a human but didn't act like a vampire. A stronger vamp wouldn't have hesitated. It would have ended the fledgling without a second thought.

You could kill a young vampire in a multitude of ways that didn't work on older ones. Enough damage to the body and they died as if you'd staked them. It took a fledgling vampire at least ten years to move out of the survival phase and have enough of its human memories restored to function properly. During that gestation period, their bodies changed.

The bones and skin hardened. Not Terminator hard, at least not that anyone had ever recorded, but enough that things like regular knives and small caliber bullets became almost meaningless. No one in the Helsing Society knew what a master vampire could do. We'd never gotten close enough to one to record their abilities in a meaningful way. Everyone who tangled with a master had died. Every single one. Even our champions.

There hadn't been a champion in generations.

"I'll call headquarters and put a team on the woman." I looked at Saul for confirmation.

He looked thoughtful as he slid into the car's passenger seat. "That's a good idea. Maybe she can lead us back to him." He shook his head in disbelief as he thought about what we'd witnessed. "Did you see what he did? Going toe-to-toe with a vampire. It's unheard of."

"It was a fledgling, Saul." I put the car in drive and pulled out. "It's been done before."

It wasn't exactly an honest answer. Part of me was too jealous to admit some kid took down a vampire by himself when it took us an entire team of people. Even then, we still lost members in the trenches. That's why our dad stopped most of the missions. Sure, we rid the world of a few fledglings a year, but we all wanted to do more. We wanted to take the fight to the vamps.

Saul clenched his fists. "Yes, when we've had a champion with the gift. We haven't had a true Van Helsing in over a century."

I thought about it for a moment. Saul was right. Every attempt by our group of Watchers to fight back en masse met with disaster.

The Helsing name wasn't only our family. It was our duty. When a champion was born, we'd be able to turn the tables on the vampires. Until that day, it was our job to chronicle the activities of the supernatural world. We survived by watching and biding our time.

Our great-grandfather was the last true champion. Everyone thought the next would be our father, but the ancient magic skipped him as it had all the others. When he had two sons, he always said it would be one of us. It hadn't happened yet, and our window for being selected was quickly closing.

There had never been a champion over thirty-five who was blessed with the gifts to fight. If it didn't happen for us soon, it wouldn't happen, period. Until there was one worthy of our family's legacy, the power would remain dormant. Meanwhile, we watched, we waited, and we hoped that one day soon the warrior would rise.

It wasn't the scared teenager we'd faced down. He was something else entirely.

"He might not be a Helsing, but he was fighting a vampire. It has to mean something." I was grasping at straws but wanted to fight back against the darkness instead of watching.

Saul leaned back in his seat, already planning our next steps. "Whoever he is, we need to find him. If he's something that needs to be dealt with, we have to know."

"He might not be human, but the kid saved my ass. Not only that, but he killed one of them. When dad reads the reports, he's going to shit." Looked like we were getting a lecture even without the police intervention.

Maybe this was the thing that would get us out there fighting again.

"What do you want to do, storm a nest behind this kid?" Saul patted my shoulder. "Remember what happened to Thomas?"

How could I forget? I was the one leading the raid. It was only a fledgling. It should have been easy. Fucking thing got the drop on us from the rafters. By the time I stabbed it in the heart, Sean had a broken leg. It had shattered Aaron's arm and snapped his collarbone like a Thanksgiving wishbone.

They were the lucky ones because Thomas was dead. Saul watched the whole thing, frozen by fear. I only lived because the fledgling was too busy feeding on our friend to see the stake coming. I hated fucking vampires, but I was never scared of them.

Saul was, and a Helsing should never be scared.

My older brother was right in one regard. It was foolish for me to have convinced the others to go after a fledgling without the benefit of a champion. In all of our history and lore, we only found true success in the war against the vampires when we had a Helsing champion.

We might not be able to fight back, but we might have found the one person who could. "This kid could change everything, Saul."

I wanted desperately to believe we finally had an ally in the fight against darkness.

Saul grabbed a pack of Camel Red Lights and pulled out a cigarette. "First, we have to find him. Then we have to make sure he's not one of them or something worse."

I'd never thought there could be something worse for Phoenix than a vampire. The werewolves stayed out of the city, and the witches ruled most of Flagstaff. This was vampire territory, and they didn't like unannounced visitors. If this kid was from out of town, he might have started a shit storm. Normally, a few vamps taking each other out was a good thing, but if this was a nest war, a lot of innocent people would die.

If the kid wasn't only human, what was he?

Part of me screamed that it didn't matter what he was. When Saul handed the kid the stake, he didn't hesitate. Killing a vampire said a lot about which side of right and wrong a person stood on. I also knew this wasn't his first time facing a vampire. The kid knew exactly what he was doing. I hated puzzles, and I was going to crack this one.

I wanted to fight back, and this kid was the key.

"This could change everything." I felt like this was one of those moments that would change everything.

Saul took a deep drag on the cigarette. "Or it could change nothing at all."

Being the older, more responsible one must have been a real bummer.

CHAPTER ELEVEN

Dylan

Didn't people know mornings were for sleeping?

The pounding on my front door wouldn't stop until I answered it. If it was the cops, they didn't have enough evidence of wrongdoing to kick the door in. I pulled on a pair of flannel pants and a hoodie and went to the door. If I opened it right, I might be able to avoid the sun completely.

The knocking began again.

"Hold the fuck on. I'm coming!" Not very elegant, but the pounding stopped.

When the door opened, I was surprised to find Tiffany with a giant cloth bag in her arms. "Get out of the way. I'm freezing my tits off."

She pushed into my apartment carrying a mountain of food. The kitchen was a whirlwind of activity before I closed the door.

"It's dark in here. Why don't you open some windows?"

Tiffany opened the empty cabinets. "How do you live like this? Not a paper plate or a plastic fork in sight."

When you didn't eat food, there wasn't a real need for flatware. "I like to eat out."

"Not today." Tiffany had things in the oven that already smelled divine. "Today I'm going to thank you for chasing that guy off. Hope you like a spicy breakfast."

Oh shit. Oh shit. Oh shit.

How would I get out of this without sounding like a giant asshole? This situation underlined why I shouldn't get close to people. I didn't have plates or silverware. What would Tiffany think when she opened the fridge, and I didn't even have a bottle of ketchup? If I was going to make my life work long-term, I needed to enhance my cover. I was sure Target would have dishes that didn't cost a fortune.

I wasn't opening all of the windows fast enough, so Tiffany did it for me. "Seriously, it's like a cave in here."

"I was trying to hibernate." I pulled up my hood, but the sun would eventually get me.

Tiffany returned to the kitchen. "This is going to take a few minutes. Why don't you take a shower?"

In other words, I was going to be in the way.

It wasn't a bad idea. There was still dried blood on my knuckles from last night. I stripped off my clothes and grabbed a few clean things out of the dresser drawer. Three steps into the hallway, I realized I was buck naked, and I didn't want Tiffany to think I was some super creeper.

The oven made a noise, and I ran into the bathroom, slamming the door behind me. This was a nightmare. She was out there acting like a mom, and I was walking around like an overeager first-timer at a swinger party.

I was safe in the bathroom now, and with the shower going, she wouldn't sense my panic. I only had to worry about how she'd react when I tried eating her food and not the fact I flashed her my package. I had no idea what would happen when I tried to eat, but I also didn't know how to get out of it. If I had a bad reaction, I'd have to leave. Where in the hell would I go?

I heard California was kind of nice.

The warm water didn't take away my worry about eating, but it washed the blood off my hands and arms. Under the dried blood was brand-new skin. It was like my knuckles hadn't spent the evening turning that vampire's ribs into paste. I hadn't had time to think about the two men. Were they onto me? Were they watching me now?

I needed some weed. I was starting to sound paranoid. No way those two older guys could have run fast enough to catch up to me. They had to be over thirty, and I was topping out at a speed that would make an Olympic sprinter blush. There was a better than even chance I was clear of any trouble.

Well, not from the woman in the kitchen.

Tiffany seemed to think I was a hero. Maybe the two guys would too. It wasn't out of the realm of possibility. They looked as shocked by what I'd done as I was. Where did they get a silver-tipped stake? I was sure they didn't pop those off the rack at Walmart. The better question might have been, how would I get my hands on a couple of those bad boys?

Then there was the vampire issue. My time in the desert had been mostly vampire-free until now. I must have been naïve to think it would stay that way forever. Life was starting to get complicated again.

I killed the hot water and grabbed a towel. It was time to find out what happened when I tried to eat human food. Dressed and ready to rock, I opened the door, and the scents hit me right away. It was like I'd stepped into heaven. My apartment had never smelled this good. The only way I could put it into words was it smelled like grandma cooking in the kitchen when I was a kid.

I was salivating. *That had to be a good sign, right?* I went into the kitchen. "Smells fantastic." I meant every word.

Tiffany looked a little flustered. "It's going to get interesting when we eat with no silverware, but we'll make do." She thrust a giant serving spoon into my hands. "Use the lid of the dish as a plate."

There was bacon, English muffins, orange juice, and fluffy scrambled eggs with cheese. It was a veritable feast. She even made silver dollar pancakes.

I loaded my plate. The smells brought all kinds of memories with them. Food featured in some of the best moments of my childhood. Eating was a celebration of life, and I wanted to try everything Tiffany had cooked.

I sat at the table and stared at my food. For all my enthusiasm, I didn't know where to start. Maybe with something small. Tiffany watched me, waiting for my reaction when I tried the first bite. Hopefully, I didn't toss the bacon onto the table with a stomach full of blood.

Was my hand shaking?

The salty bacon exploded in my mouth. It was like Christmas when you got something extraordinary from Santa for the first time. *God, I missed food.* Why hadn't I tried eating normal food? Life would be almost perfect if I could go back to eating regular food. The second strip of bacon went down twice as fast. Then I shoveled silver dollar pancakes into a puddle of syrup and ate them whole.

When I looked up, Tiffany was grinning from ear to ear. "What? It's that good."

"I hoped you would like it." She looked around. "The next time you save my life, I expect you to have forks and proper dishes."

I stopped shoveling food into my mouth so I could respond. "If you keep feeding me like this, I'll save your life every day. As for the dishes, I'll get some this weekend."

"What happened last night? I heard you scream, then that guy was banging on my door. I thought he was going to knock it off the hinges."

I shoved my empty makeshift plate away and told her a version of the story where he hit me from behind. Tiffany knew I'd screamed to save her and chased the guy off, so I left those details the same. I didn't mention the other two guys or the fact the killer had been a vampire.

"I don't think he'll be back, but I'd still like to walk you home tonight." I was dead serious.

She had questions. That much was obvious, but Tiffany also had the self-restraint not to ask them, and I liked her all the more for it.

She smiled. "I'd like that, but after last night, Mom is going to pick me up."

"Tell her I'm pissed she took my job." I smiled warmly. "That was seriously the best thing I've ever eaten."

I wasn't lying. Food beats blood in the taste department, hands down, every time.

I missed the pure bliss when I tapped the vein, and I had no idea if human food would power me up. There was always a chance I could have some severe side effects later, but I felt pretty good right now.

My stomach gurgled, and I thought it might be time to usher Tiffany outside. The sun streaming in through the windows finished bleeding away all the extra power I'd been holding onto, and I was starting to feel a little hungover.

Tiffany was already up and loading the leftovers into some zip-top bags. She stored them in the refrigerator. The kitchen was still a mess, but I had to draw the line when she started cleaning.

"The chef never does the dishes in my house. I'll take care of that stuff." I took the sponge out of her hands. "Thank you for breakfast."

She pulled me into a hug. "Thanks for saving my ass."

She had her coat back on in a flash and was at the door. "See you at work tonight?"

Damn, the woman was like a tornado, but I liked it when a storm left me well-fed. "I'll be there."

I opened the door for her. My slippers weren't hard-soled for outside, but I stepped into the sun. I still loved the feeling of the sun's warmth on my skin, and since my powers were already gone, I might as well bask in it for a few moments. Later I would have to feed to regain my power. If there were vampires in Phoenix, I didn't want to meet them feeling almost as helpless as a human.

"See you tonight." I waved as she walked down the stairs and waited until she was in her car.

"That's enough of that." I walked back inside and closed all the curtains.

The sun might be nice in small amounts, but I didn't want to push my luck. There was always the chance if I stayed in it long enough, I'd end up as crispy as Enrique. The experiment wasn't worth the risk. I burped and was pleasantly surprised that it tasted like food instead of the copper tang of blood.

Tiffany hadn't made nearly as big of a mess as I thought. Most of the items she'd brought with her she must have cooked at home. It still took me fifteen minutes to get everything back in order. With that done, I felt better. There was something about a clean house and a full belly that made a man feel good. My stomach grumbled again, and I sat to watch TV. Maybe I could take a nap before work.

I let the mindless sounds on the tube wash over me as I thought about the implications of being able to eat real food. If it meant I didn't have to eat people, this might be a way I could survive without being a killer. It might mean going back to regular old me for all of eternity. I wasn't sure if I wanted to do that.

Saul

"He was standing in the sun? You're sure of it." I nodded at Greg and covered the phone with my hand so the person on the other end of the line wouldn't hear. "He walks in the sun," I stage-whispered to my brother.

Greg still looked excited about the implications of working with our new friend. I was trying to decide if the fact he walked in the sun made him any better than the vamps. He could be a creature we hadn't chronicled yet, or he could have been the first werewolf to return to the Valley since the Squaw Peak Massacre of the '80s. The kid could even be a warlock. The one thing I knew for sure was that he wasn't simply a human with incredible skills.

That made a partnership with him risky.

Greg looked up from the computer screen. "We received confirmation from the other branches. He's not a Helsing. At least not one tied to any of our official records."

I hung up the phone and sat across from my brother. "We know he walks in the sun and is strong enough to take down a fledgling. How do we know we can trust him?"

Greg smiled as he realized I was still on board with his foolish plan.

"How does he know he can trust us?" Greg didn't look worried about getting him on our side. "The way you build trust is by earning it."

The simple fact was I wanted to work with the young man, whose name we'd learned was Dylan, but there were red flags. We didn't know anything about the kid that went further back than a month. That was where his trail went cold. The only thing we'd been able to find in our Internet and other searches around the time of his arrival was a story out of Illinois about a kid who had gone missing. No picture accompanied the article.

There were reasons to be cautious, but the more I thought about it, the more it made sense to take the risk. If he could kill vampires, whatever retaining his services cost us would be worth it. He was our first real chance to fight back against the vampires since our great-grandfather died. We were tired of waiting. It was time to make the bloodsuckers pay.

"What do you think it costs to buy a vampire hunter these days?" The real question was how much money we could take without Dad noticing.

Greg met my eyes, and I could already tell he wasn't happy. I leaned forward as I spoke. "If it's a question of trust, we can't pay him off like a mercenary. We have to bring him in close.

"If our future relies on this young man, we have to do more than send him into danger with the promise of a little money. He deserves better than that, and we can do better. We could make him part of the family business. There is precedent for it."

Greg laughed. "We can't force him to marry someone. Even if we might have some volunteers for the assignment."

I could name at least four women who would call dibs immediately. Of course, Greg was right. We couldn't tell him he had to pick. This wasn't a fiefdom, and we weren't his lords. At the end of this, I hoped he would be our partner.

Greg pushed the book aside and wiped tears from his eyes as he finished chuckling at the thought of the young man fighting off hordes of competitive female suitors. "Guess we'll make him an honorary member."

I tapped my finger against the book, thinking of our Order's history. There were many examples of extraordinary men and women added to the Helsing Society. Some of them married in, but we recruited others for their innovation.

Ebony St. Clair invented the silver-tipped stake. John Foreman created our newest set of armor. Each was a full-blooded family member with the tattoo to prove it, and neither of them was born a Helsing.

Bringing in the right people from the outside was key to the Helsing Society's survival, but was Dylan the right person to join us? There was a lot of anger in him. The young man could have killed the vampire at any time but beat it to a pulp first. Not to mention he didn't have a stake let alone any silver. What kind of nutter hunted a vampire without a stake?

Might as well ask one to meet for lunch.

I tapped the book again, smiling as I thought about another bloodsucker meeting the sun. "Maybe it's time we properly introduced ourselves."

Greg grinned and nodded as he stood, then froze. "What are we going to tell Dad?"

Shit. That was the real problem. Greg and I might have been ready to lead our society in a new direction, but Dad was old-school. He took the words of our forefathers to heart in a way we didn't understand. All our lore said we should watch and wait until a new champion was born among us. Then we would lead the fight against the vampires and have the chance to eradicate them.

Our grandparents waited. Our parents waited. Now, we waited. It had been so long since we had a champion that people were losing faith. Half of our members were ready to fight regardless of the rules. We'd watched as vampires killed without hesitation—women, children, the young and old. We saw it all, and we did nothing.

Dad called it our test. One that every generation failed. The lore was littered with stories of Helsings battling against the forces of darkness, only to be broken and destroyed. Our champion was the one who gave our order strength. The original Helsing killed the vampire known as Dracula, but he always knew there were others. He spent the rest of his life ensuring there would be a legacy of champions willing to continue his life's work. That was our mission, our purpose.

To finally end the vampire scourge.

Knowing you were at the bottom of the food chain like a seal with a great white shark was a horrible feeling. In that dynamic, there was no question of what the seal should do when faced with the apex predator. The seal got the fuck out of there. It's what any rational human being would do with vampires, too. Instead, we were talking about fighting back and doing it without a champion. It was madness. Facing down more than a fledgling was a death sentence.

Then there was Dylan.

He walked during the day, and he ate human food. If he wasn't a human, he was damn near close enough for me. We might not have a champion, but maybe he could be the spear's tip until one emerged.

All the Helsing Society needed was a little help to get the ball rolling. We knew where all the nocturnal action took place. We just didn't have the power to do anything about it.

Chronicling the deaths instead of stopping them was eating away at us.

Greg and I were ready to take the final step last night when the vampire threw Dylan into the tree. The kid hit hard enough to break multiple bones but pushed himself back up. Then he chased the vampire down on foot, saving my ass. That alone was enough to make me want to talk to him. I wondered how he knew so little of our world. The kid was a mystery, and I hated a riddle I couldn't solve.

As for what we would tell Dad, my vote was for not very fucking much.

"Maybe we should go and talk to the kid first. You know, feel him out before we bring Dad into things." It sounded reasonable enough as I said it.

Greg always liked the taste of trouble. "I'll grab my coat and a few more stakes."

Were we really going to do this?

"I'll get the car and meet you out front." Yep, we were doing it.

Greg ran out of the room. I watched the empty doorway for a second, feeling like a kid again. This was how it felt when the world lay at your feet, and all you had to do was pick a direction to succeed. We'd done our time watching and spent our hours reading the histories. It was our turn to make history.

The vampires were through using Phoenix as their hunting grounds. The Helsing Society would stamp them out of existence.

With a little help from a new friend.

CHAPTER TWELVE

"Oh, dear God!" My stomach rumbled, and I ran to the bathroom like someone had slipped a laxative into my coffee. Maybe human food wasn't such a great idea after all. Sure, it tasted amazing and wasn't necessarily making me sick, but it ran right through me. It was like the time I went to Mexico and drank the water. Three hours after eating, I was shitting like a dog who ate half a tray of lasagna.

And the *smell*.

It was like something died inside me and slowly leaked out as it decomposed. Guess that was what happened when you hadn't shit in a month. If I was going to keep eating people food, I needed to invest in a heavy-duty air filtration system. Maybe upgrade the toilet too.

The latest convulsion passed, and I sagged against the seat. "What I *really* need is something self-cleaning."

There was no way I was giving up human food. It was too tasty. If the price of not having to feed on people was that I wrecked a few bathrooms along the way, so be it.

I still couldn't believe I hadn't tried this until now. Food always smelled so good, but I assumed I'd get sick. Not having someone I could ask questions about the supernatural sucked.

Maybe I shouldn't have run from those guys last night. They were old enough to be friends with my dad, but it didn't mean they were out to get me. They didn't dress like cops, and neither of them was willing to fight the vampire.

They looked more like burglars from a bad '80s movie. It wasn't their clothes that got my attention, but the fact they were already staking out Tiffany's neighborhood before the attack. They could have followed her to me if they knew where she lived. The doorbell rang, and it almost scared the shit out of me.

At least I was in the right place.

I wrinkled my nose against the stench, which lingered despite my courtesy flush for myself. I did my best to ignore it as I finished and washed my hands. I hoped Tiffany hadn't changed her mind about the status of our relationship. Hero or not, one whiff of the bathroom would convince her to run screaming from the apartment. I sealed the bathroom door behind me and left the vent fan on.

The kitchen still smelled delicious. Despite my recent bathroom woes, I wanted to eat more. Sadly, there wasn't enough time before work to have another IBS meltdown. More grub would have to wait.

I made it to the door and glanced out the peephole. My worst fears were confirmed. The two guys from last night stood on my porch. I needed to have a better daylight escape plan.

With no other option before me, I opened the door. "Can I help you, gentlemen?"

The men smiled, and I wondered if I was about to be invited to join a cult.

"I think we might be able to help each other." The first man extended his hand. "My name is Saul, and this is my brother, Greg."

Greg tipped his cap. "It's nice to see you again."

At least they were being honest about last night. Honesty earned a little courtesy in my book. "Please, come in."

I moved aside, noting both men tensed as they entered. "I'm afraid I don't have anything to offer you but bottled water."

Greg sat at the table and scanned my spartan furnishings. "Nice place you have here."

The place was a dump. Greg knew it, I knew it, the whole damn world knew it. You didn't make light of it unless you were poking fun or trying to butter me up. The smiles led me to believe it was the latter, but I'd toss them back outside if they were fucking with me. "If you'd like to move in, I'm sure they have other units."

Saul sat at the table too and removed his gloves. "What were you going to do to that vampire without a stake?"

The question caught me off-guard. We'd gone from some bullshit pleasantries to the heart of the matter. The truth was, I hadn't thought when I attacked the vampire. I was angry. Pissed that he hit me and tried to kill Tiffany. I wanted some payback.

There was only one honest answer, and I decided to roll with it. "I probably would have smashed his head in."

"You can do that?" Greg gaped at me.

I shrugged and sipped my water. "Under the right circumstances." Those being that I had fed and hadn't been in the sun recently.

Saul tapped the table. "And those would be?"

I realized I was telling these men a lot about myself, and they hadn't told me anything yet.

"Listen, guys, thanks for stopping by unannounced and everything, but I've got work later, so we're going to have to wrap this up." I learned a long time ago that nothing in this world is free. If these two wanted more information, they would have to pay for it with some of their own.

I pointed at the door. "If you don't mind."

Saul didn't move an inch. "We're here to talk about vampires. I think you'll be interested in what we have to say."

"Then maybe you should start talking instead of asking so many questions," I snapped. I was tired of chasing the carrot.

Greg tapped his brother on the arm. "I like him."

Saul glared daggers at him, and I almost laughed. I kind of liked these guys. They seemed all right. They knew more about vampires than I did, but I wasn't getting sucked into a one-sided relationship. This was a tit-for-tat zone. If you wanted to play, you had to pay.

"Maybe we shouldn't have come." Saul looked like someone had tossed him under the bus.

"Now that we're here, I like him even more. The fact he doesn't like you is a bonus." Greg's eyes twinkled with the friendly mischief of a brother enjoying himself a bit too much at his sibling's expense.

Saul looked flustered but continued. "We are members of a society dedicated to the eradication of the vampire race."

Even being a vampire, hearing someone say it aloud made me realize how crazy this was. It wasn't like you could put "vampire hunter" on a job application. Might as well tell them you spent your summers chasing Bigfoot.

"No shit." How I managed to keep a straight face, I'll never know.

It wasn't a great response, but I needed to make sure these guys weren't some Internet crazies trying to get information from me. I knew vampires existed. So did they. What they didn't know was that I was one of them. *Kind of.* It almost sounded like they were trying to give me a job when they should have been trying to stab me with one of those fancy silver-tipped stakes.

"No shit." Greg deadpanned before smiling brightly. "The truth is, we'd like your help."

"You see, for all our knowledge, we don't have a lot of practical application." Saul was warming up to me. "We need someone who can fight a vampire without instantly dying."

Greg nodded. "With your help, we might be able to shift the balance back in the human race's favor."

"You guys came here to ask me to hunt vampires with you?" I loved the idea of hunting down vampires. It would give me the skills to catch up with Krista and end her. What I didn't love about the arrangement was hiding who I was from actual vampire hunters. It wouldn't only be these two. By the sounds of it, there were many more people dedicated to eradicating people like me.

Anything I learned from them would be huge, but it was a big gamble. Was it worth the risk? Maybe I'd join them until I could learn more about myself. Then I'd have a real decision to make. Guess I'd cross that bridge when I got there. There was no point in living if you planned everything down to the last detail. At that point, you were checking things off a list.

Saul gave me a moment to digest the information and nodded. "The job would come with some perks." He looked around. "Mainly some better living conditions."

Greg pinched his nose. "I think there might be a sewer line problem."

That motherfucker.

It took everything I had not to crack up. It was like when someone ripped a silent fart in the room and waited for it to wash over everyone without saying a word. At first everyone looked around, but accusations soon flew. I didn't want to answer questions about my stinky shit, so I decided to move this along.

"I'm working at The Tasty Lamb tonight. I get off at two-thirty. If you guys want to talk more, I'd be happy to chat." I was dying to get in but didn't want to sound too eager about joining their little club.

Greg stood and extended his hand. "I'll have the team put something together for us. There are at least five other fledglings in the city we could deal with."

This time I nodded like I knew what a fledgling was. "I'll see you later."

Saul pulled his gloves on. "This city could use someone like you. Together, we can shape a better future for humankind."

More like I could learn as much as possible and get the fuck out of Dodge. "The Tasty Lamb, two-thirty."

I ushered them both outside and sagged against the closed door once they'd left. What had I gotten myself into? In the space of a day, I'd gone from anonymous to working with some kind of secret society that fought vampires. My mind spun so hard that it felt like I'd spent the last twenty-four hours drinking every shot in sight. I was going to be a vampire hunter.

My gut gurgled again, loud enough that the brothers would have heard it if they'd still been here. Maybe I should write a book. I'd call it *All Vampire Hunters Shit* by Dylan McCormick. I ran to the bathroom like the wind.

I was distracted at work all night.

Being out in the sun and not feeding made bouncing heads a harder chore than usual. Like any alphas when the herd sensed something was off, more of them wanted to take their shot at the title. After the fourth fight of the night, I broke a guy's wrist. That seemed to be enough for everyone to get back to normal.

"Put some ice on it," I shouted into the parking lot as the car sped away.

I was nervous about the pending meeting and my lack of blood.

All the restraint I'd built keeping the darkness at bay was gone by the time the sun had set. The voice was telling me what I needed to do. It reminded me of how the bar full of humans would make a tasty snack. The voice was the panhandler who wouldn't give up. It was driving me nuts.

The voice quieted when outside and away from the people, but I only knew one way to silence it completely, which wasn't going to happen right now. Eating regular human food might have done the trick, but I couldn't risk eating with Saul and Greg on the way. I didn't want our first vampire hunt to fail because I shit myself. I'd dig into those leftovers after I got home. Hopefully, the food would help take the edge off the pit in my stomach.

The criminals of Phoenix could rest easy until tomorrow.

Over the next hour, the bar began to clear. It was still a weekday, so few patrons made it until two o'clock. As Tiffany had said, her mom waited in the parking lot so she wouldn't need an escort home. A van pulled up on the street, and it could have only been Greg and Saul. The van had a creeper vibe that said stalkers inside, but it was practical enough to get a job done.

I stuck my head inside and waved at Tiffany behind the bar. "I'm out."

"You're working tomorrow, right?" She smiled. "Can you bring those dishes back with you?"

I tipped an imaginary cap. "It would be my honor."

I closed the door and waved at Tiffany's mother as I walked past. She didn't return it. Who could blame her? By now she'd seen the smashed car at their complex and the fear on her daughter's face when she told the story about the psycho banging on her door. While she might not tell the police who was responsible for smashing the car, Tiffany's mom certainly wouldn't encourage her to spend more time with me than she had to.

It was safer for both of us that way.

The Helsing brothers got out of the van and walked across the street. I waved at them and motioned to the side of the parking lot. Two or three cars there would block some of the wind for them. Despite Arizona having a reputation for being hot, it dipped into the low forties quite often in the winter. With the right amount of wind, it felt like being back in St. Charles.

Now wasn't the time to think of home. "What's up, guys?"

Saul looked excited as he nudged Greg with his shoulder. "What would you say to a trial?"

"First, I'd have to be arrested for something." Smartass was my default response these days.

Greg chuckled. "What my brother means is we know where another fledgling is. If you could take it out, we'd be able to pay you."

That was pretty vague. I'd been a part of enough shady deals to know you get the terms upfront so there weren't any misunderstandings.

I liked Greg and Saul. The last thing I wanted was to eat them because they tried to screw me over. It would come down to the offer. If it was enough, I'd take the bait. Otherwise, they could hit the bricks.

It was time to find out what was on the table.

"What, you send me places, and I kill stuff for money? Like a bounty hunter?" These guys might have been reaching. I was no legendary warrior.

Saul looked offended. "We hope you'll join the order. Each member gets a small monthly stipend, and we'd create a bonus structure for the jobs we all agreed deserve your special brand of attention."

"I'd be a part of the decision-making process?" Joining up with Team Helsing started to sound like the right option.

Greg glanced at Saul with a hint of annoyance. "First we need to know what we saw last night wasn't a fluke."

"I'm supposed to trust you two have my best interest at heart? What happens when you decide this experiment is over? I get fired?" I didn't have to think about this stuff when my parents were around, but I was on my own now, and stability mattered.

I didn't want to be the first homeless vampire in Phoenix.

Saul looked like he was thinking it over, and Greg looked like someone had filled his mouth with Lemonheads. It wasn't that I didn't need to learn more about vampires or that hunting them down didn't sound rewarding enough. I needed to ensure they were as invested in me as I would be in them.

"Some kind of signing bonus, then." Saul smiled. "A little something you can keep squirreled away if things don't work out."

Greg looked at his brother. "A champion would never."

"He's a new kind of champion." Saul was still smiling. "Until the Helsing Society has one of its own, he's our best bet at stopping vampires."

Greg looked me over like I was a piece of beef. "It better be worth it." He stomped back to the van.

Saul wore a "what are you going to do" expression. "I think a hundred thousand dollars would be a nice nest egg. Pass this audition, and we will change your life."

He'd set the bait, and I fell for it hook, line, and sinker.

It was a lot of money, more than I'd make in four years at the bar. That kind of cash should have made me suspicious, but it only made me wonder how big their organization was. They found me quick enough after only seeing me for a moment, and they were also keeping track of multiple vampires. I wasn't sure why they called them fledglings unless they meant these were newly turned vampires. It never dawned on me that the vampires could have ranks.

I still had so much to learn. At the very least their organization sounded big enough to have the funds to deliver.

"If I go with you tonight and pass your test, I get to keep the hundred grand regardless of whether I join or not?" I asked it like a question, but I meant it to come out as a statement.

I was trying to set some boundaries. The truth was, I wanted to be all in, but I couldn't afford to be reckless.

Saul nodded. "To see what you can do." His eyes were full of wonder when he continued. "It's not like I'll have to pay if you're full of shit."

Because I'd be dead.

How many people could say they had a job interview quite like this? Make it, and you are a member of an ancient secret society. Lose, and not only is membership revoked, but your life is forfeit. *High stakes.* Was it worth it for a chance to find out more about myself? I thought it was, and there was no telling if I'd ever get another opportunity for something like this.

I looked from Saul to the van and back. "Are we leaving right now?"

"Unless that's going to be a problem." Saul sounded like he was starting to have doubts.

Was it a problem?

I guess that depended on how strong the vampire was and whether or not I could sneak up on him. Not being anywhere near full strength had me worried about the outcome of a fair fight. A hundred thousand dollars wouldn't do me any good if I got my head ripped off. It wasn't like I could ask the guys to pull over so I could grab a snack. If they wanted to go right now, I would have to do this without powering up.

At least I didn't have to worry about shitting myself.

A smile spread as I thought about the fearless vampire hunter ducking into the corner of a warehouse to take a dump.

Nothing to see here.

Saul took my smile as a good sign and extended his hand. "Deal?"

"Deal."

In for a penny, in for a pound.

He pulled me into a fierce hug and dragged me toward the van. "We'll fill you in on all the details on the way. Get you outfitted with some gear."

"Wait." I stopped. "I get cool gadgets?"

Saul's smile told me he was excited to explain something he loved to the new guy. "You have no idea."

"Should have led with the fact I get to be Batman." I clapped his back. "Could have saved yourself a hundred thousand dollars."

Saul laughed. "If you can do what I think you can, it's the bargain of a lifetime."

I stepped into the back of the van and closed the swinging panel door. This was it. I was going to hunt my first vampire with two members of the Helsing Society. I was about to learn the truth about vampires and what I was. When I had the knowledge and was strong enough, Krista would have a bad day.

When I knew the truth, I was coming for her.

CHAPTER THIRTEEN

Saul

Dylan was a damn sharp kid.

I watched him as we drove. If I'd had the guts to do what this kid was doing now, maybe I would have been the champion. I shoved the jealousy down and focused on the fact we were finally fighting back.

It was wrong of me to keep thinking of him as a kid. A young man was more appropriate, maybe even a man outright. He was working and living on his own. If there was a clearer marker of adulthood, I didn't know one. Unlike our new friend, who was making his own way, I'd been born into the family business.

Dad, or as the other members of the society called him, Van Helsing, was the leader of our order. He was a direct descendant of Van Helsing's daughter, but the Van in his name was a title. Dad's real name was Peter Harrold Cooper. It didn't get more middle America than that.

Naming me Saul must have been very adventurous for him.

Dylan was about six feet tall, with broad shoulders. He looked like a kid who would play safety on a football team, or he could have been a linebacker with a few more pounds. He wasn't intimidating but had a quiet presence that spoke of calm confidence.

That sense of calm would serve him well in the coming years. Fighting against the supernatural wasn't for the faint of heart. We'd tried it once and utterly failed. Greg and I swore we'd never do it again, but with Dylan, things were different. If he was strong enough to battle a vampire face-to-face, we stood a real shot at turning the tide. The untouchable would soon learn how the rest of us felt.

It would be glorious.

Separating my desire for this to work from the facts took some doing. I wanted this partnership to be successful, but I also wanted to ensure I wasn't sending Dylan to his death. The fledgling from last night was evidence enough that he could succeed, but what if he didn't? I'd have to live with sending a young man to die. Maybe this was a bad idea?

Greg took his time driving, trying not to draw attention to the van. Dylan looked me over, probably wondering when I'd start filling him in on the details. His continued sense of calm gave me the nudge I needed to get started.

Pulling a small chest out from below the seats, I set it on the floor between us and opened the lid. "In here, we have a selection of weapons. Silver-tipped stakes. Knives with silver embedded in the blades. You're going to love our newest invention."

I tapped an aluminum can. "Guns that shoot paintballs

filled with holy water and colloidal silver. We haven't found any indication that holy water does a thing, but we have more than a few priests in the society, so why not?"

Picking up a small paintball gun, I loaded it and passed it to Dylan. "The balls won't do much more than piss off an older vampire, but against a fledgling they're a damn good distraction if you don't have anything else to slow them down."

I pointed at the other side of the chest to draw his attention away from the weapon. "Here, we've got some harnesses and stuff for the gear and a bulletproof vest."

"A bulletproof vest?" Dylan picked it up and held it out at arm's length. "Don't you think that's a little much?"

"Not if you don't want your guts on the floor, kid," Greg called over his shoulder.

"You're right. The vest won't do much to stop an angry vampire." I tapped it to draw attention to it and away from Greg. "Sometimes a fledgling will acquire human help, and they normally carry guns."

Dylan shrugged like someone shooting him wasn't a big deal. There was something up with this young man. What kind of kid wasn't scared of a gun? I reached into the chest and loaded silver-tipped stakes into a bandolier he could wear around his chest. Everything was going to work out. Dylan could handle it. I knew he could.

We were about to put a little shine on the Van Helsing name.

Dylan

Now that I was in the van and Saul was holding a bulletproof vest in his hand, I wondered what kind of trouble they were sending me into.

I wanted to laugh at his comment about the human help having guns. I'd been pumped full of more bullets than I could count, and none of them slowed me down. Instead, I shrugged. It made me feel better that Saul was concerned enough about my safety to offer me the vest. At least I knew they were trying to look out for me.

The vest would be smart for a few reasons. If someone shot me, I'd probably feed off them, and if the brothers saw me, I'd be in for a world of problems. It'd also be hard for me to explain bullet holes in my clothes and no injuries. The last thing I wanted them to do was to dig further into my past.

"Do you think this fledgling has help?" I asked to give Saul something to think about besides my reaction.

The older guy was a little too sharp for me. Whenever he watched me, I felt like he was trying to figure out my secret. This was such a batshit crazy idea. I was about to join a society dedicated to wiping out things like me. My mind spun, and I drew a deep breath to calm down. Saul looked like he was considering calling the whole thing off. I had to pull myself together. This was my shot at getting the information I needed to live a long and healthy eternity.

I had to take it.

Greg called from the front of the van, "We don't think he has help. All our Watchers on the building have only reported a single fledgling at this location."

Stripping down to my T-shirt, I pulled on the vest and tightened it. "Where are we going?"

"You're going to love this." Greg pulled onto the I-10.

"Old industrial plant. It's got these huge silos, and he's hiding in them or the warehouse between them."

Saul handed me the bandolier of stakes. "Put these on before your jacket."

A few minutes later I had three knives, two pockets full of silver paintballs, and a chest full of stakes. I felt like one of the Frog Brothers or Charlie Brewster. It was my time to take the fight to the forces of evil, which was cool. Who else got the chance to gear up like this except a secret agent? Even a secret agent man wouldn't know the truths I'd recently uncovered. I was Bond. James Bond. Double O negative.

I snorted.

"Something funny?" Saul closed the chest and pulled out a map of the buildings.

I felt like a kid who got busted for talking in class and wanted to redirect the teacher's attention. "No idea exactly where the fledgling is on the property?"

"Not this time." Greg sounded a little put out at not having more to go on. "This was strictly long-range reconnaissance. Getting our people too close to the action means they don't come back."

For the first time, it dawned on me how terrifying this must be for them. I remembered how helpless I'd been when Krista attacked me. I wouldn't wish that feeling on anyone. It took courage to go up against someone when you knew they could rip you apart in an instant. These two men were braver than I'd ever been, and I wasn't going to let them down tonight. This vampire was going to die.

Saul looked at the map. "My guess is he's nested in the warehouse. The silos should be empty. That said, I'd probably clear one of the silos first so you know for sure, and there is somewhere to retreat if things get dicey."

So, I was going in unprepared and alone.

"Guys, if this is going to work out in the future, we need to do better than he might be in a building somewhere. Your job is the intel. Mine is the hunting." I didn't have to tell them their half of the job looked a little sparse.

Greg turned off the freeway and down a side road. "You're right. Next time we'll have more to go on."

"We'll pick the target together and review intel before we strike." Saul sounded thrilled by the prospect.

The brothers wanted to make this work. Would they if they knew what I was? I guessed I'd go from being their pet hunter to being on the hit list real quick. I couldn't afford to have the vampires and the Helsing Society looking for me. I needed to get whatever information I could from them and break off our relationship before I got caught.

Saul's phone rang, and he switched it off. "Dad," he told Greg and put the phone down.

Greg groaned when his phone rang. "Oh, shit. Now he's calling me."

"Don't fucking answer it." Saul's face was white as a sheet.

Greg waved him off and pulled to the side of the road as he answered. "Dad, what's up?"

Saul looked like I had drained him.

"Oh, you know Saul. We're on a stakeout, and he wanted to be prepared." Greg pulled the phone away from his ear and mimicked saying blah, blah, blah with his hand. "Yes, we'll bring everything back."

Greg hung up. "You'd think we'd never left the house before."

"Still thinks we're fifteen," Saul agreed.

I laughed. It was funny how you'd think life would change when you got older but watching how the brothers dealt with their father reminded me of being at home.

I looked at Saul with a Cheshire Cat smile. "Never met a man more scared of his dad than a vampire."

Saul smiled and tousled my hair like I was his kid cousin. "You're a cheeky fucker."

"Don't you forget it." I stared into the darkness, scanning the empty lot.

"I almost forgot." Saul pulled out a small leather briefcase. "One hundred thousand dollars."

Greg glanced at me in the rearview mirror. "Don't go spending that all in one place. Not until we can fudge up some tax records for you."

The Helsing Society had proven they were the real deal. Now it was my turn to live up to the bargain. Greg drove for another fifteen minutes and pulled into a vacant lot. "The silos are a mile and half down the road."

"If we get any closer, we risk detection." Saul powered his phone back on and handed it to me. "From here on out, it's just you. If you need help, call Greg. He's speed dial number three."

Greg looked wounded. "Number three."

"It's not the order that matters. It's making the list." I pocketed the phone and opened the van door. "See you soon."

"Dylan." Greg looked worried. "If you get in over your head, run. We'll come up with a better plan next time."

Saul nodded. "I'd rather try again than have to send someone to pick up your body."

"Not exactly the world's greatest pep talk, guys." I

grinned at them. "For the size of the bonus, I'm willing to let it slide."

Before they could say a word, I closed the door. They might not think I was taking this seriously, but nothing was more important to me than this moment. Tonight was my "in." After this, I'd learn everything there was to know about vampires and how to stop them.

Saul's phone rang, and I dismissed the call. It took me three minutes to figure out how to put the phone on silent. The only problem was I hit so many buttons that everything was in French. What was the French word for Greg? Oh well, I wasn't planning on running into trouble. I looked at the van and ran for the silos in the distance.

Greg

"It's Dad again." I showed my screen to Saul.

Snatching the phone out of my hand, Saul turned it off. "Don't fucking answer it. We've got work to do."

"He's just going to keep calling." Dad wasn't one to give up because he failed the first time.

Saul snorted. "Unless he tracks us down, there is nothing to worry about." He handed me a night vision scope. "Now, keep your eye out for anything that could hurt Dylan."

The phone rang again, and we both looked at it like it was alive. "I thought you turned it off."

"I did." Saul didn't sound so certain.

I hit the answer button. "Dad?"

After the yelling stopped, I muted the phone and glanced at Saul. "He's not happy."

We both cracked up.

Dad was one of those Type A, never stop working guys. It was his identity. If he didn't have two jobs and three projects at the same time, he felt worthless. Never was there a man so determined to fill his life with the completion of tasks as our dad. He blew his top when he thought we were out screwing around, possibly losing a hundred thousand dollars for no reason. It was glorious when Dad lost it—as long as he wasn't directing the impending explosion at you.

Saul was right. I shouldn't have answered the phone.

"We'll see you in the morning!" I said as he started another tirade. I tapped the End button, tossed the phone on the center console, and stepped out of the van. "Let's get closer and see if we can help our new friend."

Saul tossed me a stake. "For protection."

"Now you sound like Morgan. 'We don't want to have an accident, do we?'" The look on my brother's face as I described my latest escapade was priceless.

Saul hopped out of the van and closed the door. "You're a dog."

"If you only knew the half of it." I put my arm around Saul's shoulders, edging him away from the van as the phone in the console started glowing again.

This was the first step into a bright new future.

CHAPTER FOURTEEN

Dylan

It felt like I was playing *Goldeneye*.

Instead of being loaded with cool gadgets and a gun, I had silver-tipped stakes and a burning desire to go to the bathroom. Maybe that was a normal reaction when someone felt nervous, but it didn't feel normal. I felt like the kid standing in the corner, grabbing his crotch, and shuffling from foot to foot because he didn't know where the bathroom was.

I guess it was better than pissing myself.

Maybe it was something primal. I'd never been a hunter before the change. Since I turned, I'd mainly hunted humans who were weaker than me and killed their asses before they completely turned vampire. I'd been hopped up on blood when I killed the fledgling last night. Tonight, I was almost as weak as the day Krista turned me.

Now that the hunt was on for a real target, I wondered

what I'd find there. Bodies of his victims or piles of trinkets he'd pulled off the bodies? There was no way to know without going inside. I would have told the brothers to fuck off if I were still human, but I wasn't anymore. I could do this.

The money was a hell of a motivator.

When invested wisely and not touched for, say, two hundred years or so, one hundred thousand dollars was the kind of money that could secure my future. I guessed I had all the time in the world to let it grow. The less I spent, the more lavish my future would be.

All those stock splits and reinvested dividends had to work out for someone, right? Why not this immortal? If I was going to live forever, it better be with a taste of the good life. My stomach grumbled, and I looked at it like it was a traitor.

Now isn't the time, I mentally whispered to my gut like it would obey my commands. It was a mistake to come out here without eating first. Even a good old Wendy's hamburger would have done the trick.

I didn't know why, but having a square burger on a round bun always made it better for me somehow. It was also the best combo to satisfy my fry and burger quality test. Some places had great burgers, and others had great fries. At Wendy's both were pretty good, and that was a win in my book.

If I worked fast enough, I might be able to kill the fledgling before I had to shit.

I knelt behind a bush and looked over the empty lot leading to the silos, thinking about food more than another vampire. I was so damn hungry I couldn't stop my mind from wandering.

How was it that Burger King had served fries worse than a grade school cafeteria for my entire life and no one had called them out on it yet? In and Out Burger had the same cut on their fries, but they were so much better, and they had a Double-Double with cheese. Watch the fuck out.

Ugh, I needed to stop. I'd drink blood to end the damn cravings. Forcing the thoughts of tasty burgers and strawberry shakes out of my mind, I focused on the mission.

Nothing was moving. I might as well have been back in the cemetery in St. Charles. The two silos loomed over the space like gigantic tits with the warehouse a small jeweled necklace between them. It wasn't much of a jewel now. Time, vandals, or the fledgling had broken most of the windows, and something had ripped off the garage doors. One of them was still hanging in its frame like someone drove through it, and the door got wedged in place.

In short, Greg and Saul didn't bring me to the nicest place.

Even homeless people would stay away from a building like this. I'd never been inside an actual haunted house before, but if there ever was a building that could qualify, it was this damn place. Kids might use this kind of abandoned property as a hideout or to smoke a little weed before riding their bikes back home. Some smart college kids might be able to pull off a silo party.

No one was partying tonight, not even the crickets.

I moved closer to the silos. Saul was right about one thing. It would pay large dividends to ensure one was empty before going to the warehouse. Then I could move forward when I was sure the hunter wouldn't become the hunted. All I had to do was take care of one fledgling vampire. How hard could it be?

There was nothing but open ground between me and the silo on the right. Once I moved, I needed to cover the distance in a hurry or risk the fledgling seeing me through the warehouse's shattered windows.

I pulled one of the stakes free from the bandolier and sprinted across the open space looking for any sign of movement in the warehouse. A tremor ran through the cracked pavement as I thundered across it. The weight of the wooden stake in my hand was reassuring.

Nothing to see here. Move along.

My heart was pounding when I reached the silo. With my back pressed against the building, I waited for the hammering to stop while desperately listening for the sound of running feet.

A breeze moved through the open structure, and there was a rustle as a plastic bag drifted along the ground. There were no gunshots, no cries for help. If the fledgling had anyone here to help, they were staying quiet.

Being able to see in the dark made this journey so much easier than if I needed a flashlight. If Saul or Greg were standing here, they would have looked into the pitch-black interior with no idea whether or not there was a man with a gun waiting inside. Not unless they wanted to give away their position.

Me? I sat in the dark watching the guard as he stared out the open door. I thanked my lucky stars he hadn't seen me run across the parking lot.

As far as I knew, vampires didn't use guns, especially fledglings. If this one was old enough to have helpers, it was stronger than Greg and Saul knew. This vampire was already more powerful than anything I'd encountered before. This wasn't an ideal situation. I was underfed and weak.

My body quieted, and I heard the gentle heartbeat of the man in the warehouse. So, he was a human with a gun. I would have gotten the hell out of there as fast as possible when I was human. As a vampire, a single human didn't pose much of a threat.

This time I couldn't run away.

Everything I needed to know about the future was on the line. My first instinct was to keep up with my Double O negative theme, but it wasn't practical to search for another entrance to the silos when I'd leave an enemy behind me. I'd taken bullets before, but I had a vest to take the hit for me this time.

The real problem was my clothes. I couldn't afford to keep buying new clothes. Even shopping at Target was getting pricey. If taking on men with guns would be a regular thing, I needed to talk to the guys about a clothing budget.

I'd hunted enough low-level losers to know most bad guys weren't the brightest. There was a chance I could avoid getting shot if I played my cards right. I picked up a broken piece of asphalt and tossed it into the silo on the guy's right. He spun toward the noise, and I charged forward. The gun went off three or four times before I sank my teeth into him, but he faced away from me, so the bullets hit the side of the silo.

Stealth wasn't on the table anymore, so I drained him and drove a stake through his heart. His body burst into ash, and his gun and most of his clothes fell into a smoking pile on the floor. I looked at the weapon and realized I hadn't taken the gun for the silver paintballs. The Brothers Helsing were right. Next time we needed to come better prepared.

I backed into the shadows, leaving the smoldering remains where they were. My mind was already figuring out how I'd explain the blood on my face when I returned to the van. Whatever I told them needed to be good enough. Either they would believe it, or I'd have to grab the money and run for it.

A hundred thousand dollars in startup money was better than what I brought to Arizona. It was enough to start a new life anywhere. If I wanted to disappear, it was my best chance.

But only if I couldn't talk my way out of it.

Two people ran from the warehouse to the silo. I wasn't sure how I knew it was two, only that their footsteps sounded different. One of the men was heavier than the other one. All of my senses were heightened from feeding, and I was already moving faster than I had been minutes before. The other two men had flashlights and swept wide beams of light through the silo as they looked for the source of the commotion.

"Yo, Stevie! Where you at?"

A second voice called, "Come on, jagoff, stop fucking around."

Saul's and Greg's information was getting worse by the moment. I hadn't found a vampire yet, and now two more humans were in the room. They'd soon discover the pile of ashes. Shit was going to get wild.

"Hey, what the fuck is that on the ground?" The first light shone on a smoldering boot.

The second light swiveled in the same direction. "Holy shit, that's his coat." He knelt next to the pile. "And his gun."

The first light moved from the boot into the shadows, then hit the ground and spun in a slow circle. At least that's what it would look like to anyone watching. I snatched the guy from behind so cleanly he couldn't scream. Then we were deep in the silo's darkness.

I drained him while his friend checked the smoldering clothes for any clue about what happened. I got the impression they'd never seen a vampire killed before so they had no idea what to make of everything. It wouldn't take long for the last guy to realize his buddy was gone, but if he looked now, he'd find another smoking pile.

Circling the last guard was easy enough. I didn't feel bad when I snuck up on him from behind. Most people probably couldn't kill a man with his back turned, but I had no problem with it. He was a traitor to all of humankind, and for what? The chance to live here. This place was worse than Dabbler's.

All the guards were dead and drained. I had staked them, and all that remained of the three men were half-burned clothes and a trio of handguns.

There was nothing left to discover in the silo, so I went to the warehouse. With each step, I tried to open my senses. I'd heard the two men running forward. Maybe I could sense something else.

I was riding a wave of ecstasy so high there was a new connection to the universe opening up in the world around me. Everything felt like it was going to work out. I'd found dinner, and if there was a fledgling inside, our strength should at least be comparable. A fight between myself and a vampire would no longer be a one-sided affair.

This was my night to shine, my moment.

I felt two men behind me when I stepped inside the

warehouse door. How they entered the silo without my knowing, I wasn't sure. Unless they were vampires. Then it all made sense. What didn't make sense was how off Saul's and Greg's information was. What in the hell had they been thinking?

I turned to face the new threat, trying not to freak the fuck out. "Fellas, I'm sure we can work something out that doesn't involve you ending up like the help."

"The master wants a word with you." A new voice spoke from behind me. "Something to do with dispatching his men."

Great, now there was a third crew member, and he could talk.

This was where having a partner would have come in handy. Doing things solo was all well and good, but when shit hit the fan, there was no backup plan. These three vampires had me dead to rights. One of them was talking. I hadn't seen that out of fledglings yet, only noncoherent babble if they spoke.

"If it's all the same to you, I think I'd like to skip meeting the master." Master was a term that should have died in the Dark Ages.

The vampire blocking the doorway grinned pleasantly. "It wasn't a request."

I wouldn't be able to smartass my way out of this one. I needed to act before they realized I might be dumb enough to resist. My mind was full of fancy fight scenes from my favorite movies. I knew somebody scripted all those moves, but I'd imagined myself fighting through those tight spots so many times. This was like *Syphon Filter*, but I had two pockets full of paintballs instead of a gun.

"Well, when you put it like that." I let the silver-tipped stake fall from my fingers and clatter on the concrete floor.

The leader of their group lifted his chin. "I kind of hoped you'd resist." He turned and walked away like I was of no importance.

With a snap of his fingers, the two fledglings closed on me. I didn't know how close the master was, and I didn't want to find out. I was powered up enough to take out the vamps in the rear, but the one in front had me worried. I was in trouble if he was stronger than anyone I'd encountered besides Krista and Ivan. That particular meeting didn't work out so well for me.

I needed to return to the van before this spiraled any further out of control.

I slipped my hands into my pockets and grabbed a double handful of paintballs. "One more question before we go."

He turned, and I let the paintballs fly.

The current Van Helsing

"Mr. Helsing, they still aren't answering either line," Johnson reported as she looked over the equipment in the back of the van.

I watched the dots on the screen, wondering what possessed my two idiot sons to go to the silos. For the last two months, the area was strictly off-limits for a reason. One of my agents almost got killed, and she'd been a mile away from the place. The tracker showed Saul was inside the damn warehouse. If we didn't get there soon, he was going to die.

I wasn't going to lose one of my sons.

"Johnson, tell the men to get ready." Grabbing the double-barreled shotgun off the rack, I loaded the weapon with silver-coated buckshot.

Silver couldn't kill a vampire outright, but it made their day a living hell. Pump a vamp full of enough silver bullets, and you could get close enough to stake them. Then it was *sayonara*, bloodsucker. Nothing left but a cloud of ash.

Just the way I liked it.

There was a reason we didn't fight the vampires. We couldn't win. Not in any meaningful way. All they had to do was start biting humans en masse, and we would never be able to stop the spread. They were like a virus, but every good virus knows killing its host is a no-no. Vampires needed us to live, but we didn't need them. One day we'd shed the vampiric curse, and the world would be as it should.

I dreamed of the day our champion would appear and lead us to glory.

For years, I thought it would be Saul. Maybe he was trying to prove something to me by going to the silos. He should have been smarter than that. He knew we needed a champion. Until we had the power to take on a master, there was no point in fighting.

My boys weren't the only ones who learned that lesson the hard way. Every generation had a few members who thought, "to hell with champions. We'll bring down the vamps ourselves."

I certainly had.

Killing fledglings with a trained squad and the right

weapons wasn't rocket science. The problem was that fledglings had sires, and their sires had masters somewhere up the chain. They didn't like it when they lost soldiers, and eventually something nastier showed up to fix the problem. In my case, it was a master who wiped out my entire team and let me go to taste the stench of my guilty conscience.

My boys had already made the same mistake, and I thought they would have learned from it. They fucking hadn't learned a damn thing. Now I would have to put members of the Helsing Society at risk to save their idiot asses. It would have been more practical to let them die, but no father would abandon their children because they were in danger. It was my job to protect them, my job to save them.

Even if they were no-good knuckleheads.

"Sir, teams two and three are ready," Cochran called.

I peered into the van. Team one consisted of two of my oldest friends and me along with Cochran and Johnson. All of us wore state-of-the-art vests and thigh protection. The two support staff had custom-built rapid-fire paintball guns and extra cartridges, whereas the boys and I had shotguns.

Teams with the paintballs would lay down a wide range of covering fire. We'd use the shotguns to knock the vamps down and stun them until someone could end the bloodsuckers with a stake. It was a dangerous game, and us coming out on top hinged on not getting overwhelmed.

If this was a true nest, there was a chance none of us would make it out alive.

Johnson announced, "Teams two and three are right behind us, and the backup squad is pulling up to Greg's van."

I opened my comlink to all three teams. "Operation

Hustler is a go. Keep your wits about you and stay together. When we've secured the targets, we bail. No hero shit. Everyone comes home alive."

All sixteen team members replied in the affirmative.

The van slid to a halt, and it was time to go. Johnson killed the interior lights, and we slipped on our night vision goggles. I opened the door and jumped out of the van. If Greg and Saul were in there, we would find them. My boys might be stupid, but I wasn't offering them up as snacks.

Plus, it was the perfect excuse to finally go hunting.

Dylan

I'd always wondered how they made Pizza the Hutt in *Spaceballs*. Now I knew.

All you had to do to make a vampire look like a pizza was cover him in colloidal silver suspended in holy water. His screams were loud enough that his two fledgling helpers froze in their tracks. It wasn't smart to hesitate when your life was on the line. I grabbed one of the fledglings and turned him to ash before they realized I wouldn't do what they said.

Not very smart.

The second fledgling had a little more fight in him. We circled each other while his boss kept trying to rip the silver out of his face. The fledgling missed his chance to jump in before I was armed, but now that I had a stake in my hand, I was ready for him.

There was a noise outside the warehouse. It sounded like a van. No, it was more than one.

Vampiric hearing was cool as fuck.

Since the boys weren't expecting backup, the arrival of vehicles could spell trouble for me if I was caught inside with the vampires. It was time to get the fuck out of here like those kids in the *Blair Witch Project* should have done. I threw my stake at the fledgling, and it hit him in the chest and bounced harmlessly away.

I laughed at the result. I don't know what I'd expected, but it certainly wasn't that. If this were a movie, my slick moves would have worked.

The fledgling smiled, and I grabbed the knife from the sheath on my hip and plunged it into his heart in one smooth motion. His smile disappeared in a rush of brilliant crimson fire as ashes fell around me.

Time was running out. It was time to deal with the screamer.

I crouched to pick up my fallen stake. The vampire wasn't screaming anymore and looked downright pissed off about the entire situation. The silver hadn't killed him, but taking that kind of beating would have sapped some of his strength.

We stared at each other in a stalemate of epic proportions. The vans drew closer. I had to make my move.

I lunged forward, and the pale bloodsucking bastard turned to run. I was riding crazy high from draining the three security guards, so it didn't take me long to catch him from behind. He might as well have been moving at human speed. I shoved a stake into his chest, and nothing happened. He hissed and began shredding my chest with his claws.

Wait, when did vampires get claws?

If the vampire's heart wasn't where it should be, it was

probably still somewhere. I managed to pin one of his arms, which gave me enough room to plunge the stake in again. When it didn't work, I thrust again and again like I was playing Whac-A-Mole. I hit something on the right side of his chest, and the vampire froze.

His heart was on the wrong side of his chest. Bet that had saved his ass in a fight or two, but not tonight. The vehicles outside screeched to a halt as the body burst into flames. I heard doors opening and footsteps running toward the silo. They had the entrance covered, so I raced deeper into the warehouse. I didn't know who was out there, but I'd met my vampire and bad guys quota for the night and then some.

I was out of there as soon as I could reach one of the broken windows.

The new arrivals moved into the warehouse in a well-coordinated team. With every turn I made, I realized they were following me. None of them could see me. There was too much broken machinery left inside. How were they tracking me?

It had to be Saul's fucking phone. I tossed the cheap thing aside like it was poison and used my new strength to leap up the machinery and out of sight. I hunkered down and waited for the chance to run.

A group of three men with shotguns circled the phone.

"It's his phone, but where is Saul?" a man with salt and pepper hair sticking up between the straps of his night vision goggles asked the other two.

A voice drifted out of the darkness. "Van Helsing, you have made a catastrophic error coming to my home."

"Retreat!" the leader screamed at the top of his lungs.

Their group fell into formation and moved back toward

the exit as they scanned the warehouse. The first of them died so quickly they didn't have the chance to scream. The master was here, and it was time for me not to be. I didn't hesitate. I didn't think about helping. I just ran. This was my first taste of real fear since becoming a vampire.

I didn't like it one bit.

CHAPTER FIFTEEN

Saul

"Was that Dad?" Greg asked as three vans raced past us.

I was already running toward the silos. "Go and get the van."

If Dad was here, something was wrong, and I'd sent Dylan into way more trouble than he'd expected. How was it that our first mission ended up in worst-case scenario territory? Was God's plan to relentlessly punish us until a champion emerged? It seemed grossly unfair. The vampires didn't have to play by the same rules. They could kill us without discrimination. They were at the top of the food chain, the apex predators.

My dad was heading straight for them.

He must have tracked my phone somehow and thought I was in the building. It was stupid of me not to come prepared with a prepaid phone for Dylan. Instead, Greg and I had rushed into this because of what we'd seen the night before. It was stupid and reckless, and now it wasn't only

Dylan I'd put in harm's way. In our eagerness to get a win, we'd missed the mark. My only hope was to get them all out before anyone got hurt.

The vans screeched to a halt outside the warehouse, and I screamed and waved my arms over my head. I must have been too far away, or they were too damn focused and pumped full of adrenaline to hear me. The Helsing Society piled out of the vans like we did in training and moved toward the silo Dylan was in.

I stopped shouting and ran for everything I was worth. This was my fault. I had to stop it. The teams disappeared inside the silo, and fear pushed me forward faster than I'd ever run. Clearing the remaining distance to the vans in less than two minutes, I yanked open one of the doors and grabbed a paintball gun off the back wall.

"Hands up, fanger!" I looked up into the muzzle of Johnson's nine-millimeter.

I tried to be disarming. "You're even more beautiful when you're angry!"

Sadly, she didn't fall for my charms but lowered the gun.

"You're supposed to be inside." She looked at the computer screen in front of her.

I finished loading the paintball gun and stuffed my pockets full of extra canisters of ammo. "Sound the retreat. Get everyone out of there, now!"

Johnson picked up her microphone. "I've got eyes on the package. Time to exfil. Van, are you there?"

She looked at me, confused. "There's something wrong with comms."

"Keep trying!" I sprinted toward the building. The sound of a shotgun firing made my feet fly like the wind. If I was going to spend more time in the field, I needed to get in better shape. The whole hunting thing involved a lot more running than being a Watcher.

I was learning the hard way that planning wasn't my strong suit.

Dylan

Saul ran into the building, and it was pure madness.

The fact that I chased him back into the silo after making it out alive was doubly so. That didn't stop me from relentlessly charging forward. I was faster than him, but he had one hell of a head start. Panic must have taken a few seconds off his forty time because he had disappeared into one of the silos before I made it back to the parking lot.

I had to get him out of there. Without Saul, I might never know the truth.

Saul ran to protect his family. I ran to save my chance of learning what I was. We both had so much to lose, but we didn't have to. The master was only another vampire, after all. With enough firepower and me on the scene, there had to be something we could do to stop him.

The inside of the silos hadn't changed much. It was still dark and cavernous. Voices screamed at the entrance to the warehouse, and Saul's footsteps headed in that direction. I heard his heart jackhammering. It was like following the motion sensors from *Aliens*. All I had to do was keep running, and my senses would guide me to the right place.

"Get out of here!" Saul roared at the others.

People turned and ran as soon as he gave the order. With a few of their members dead, getting them moving didn't take much convincing. They ran past me. A few of them pelted me with paintballs before they saw my vest. My skin was itchy and uncomfortable where the silver sprayed it, but it didn't burn me like it had the vampires.

Saul's voice boomed from deeper inside the warehouse, and that got my feet moving again. I used my jacket to wipe my face and hands and tossed it aside as I picked up the pace. I raced past three more piles of ash and smiled. The master was down a few key employees, and I'd helped make that happen on my first night. Despite how catastrophically bad the mission was going, I wondered how much the three of us could accomplish with better intel.

Greg was right. We could take the fight to them.

We needed to talk about a few things if they wanted me to keep going. "Like my clothes budget," I muttered as I thought about everything I had to replace.

The costs were growing by the minute.

A grin twitched at the corners of my mouth despite the danger I rushed into. It probably wasn't the right time for a joke, but humor had always been my escape when things turned dark. Laughter was the best medicine.

The last unorganized stragglers sprinted past me without stopping. A few looked at me quizzically, wondering who I was and why I wore some of their gear. None of them cared enough to stop and ask.

The last six people who passed me were injured and helping each other. There were two broken arms, one broken leg, and one woman with a dislocated jaw. The two healthy members of their group covered their retreat. I was surprised that no vampires were pursuing them, and I wasn't sure if that was a good sign. The master could have been trying to lure Saul farther inside.

Shotgun blasts rang out, and Saul's heartbeat went into overdrive. "Dad!"

Fuck.

There would be no dragging him out of here if his dad was ahead. I saw his back as Saul rushed recklessly forward. I'd be next to him in a few seconds. I didn't want to scare the shit out of him and take a stake to the chest, and anything I said now might freak him out. The man was already operating on pure panic.

"Saul," I called and ducked behind a pipe.

Paintballs splattered the area I'd vacated moments before. "Dylan."

"Yes." I stepped out with my hands up so he could see it was me, and I was unarmed. "We have to get out of here."

Saul shook his head. "Not without my dad."

"Then let's make this quick." I took the lead and ran at a pace Saul could match.

Despite cleaning it, I couldn't be sure I got all the blood off my face. The last thing I wanted was for him to get a good look at me in the dark. The shotgun blasts up ahead slowed and stopped. A scream and a sickening crash echoed as a body slammed into something hard. It reminded me of when I heard someone get hit by a car. They didn't walk away, and I doubted whoever got crunched here would be better off.

One last scream cut off abruptly and silence ensued. I rounded the last corner well before Saul and froze. A man stood in the center of the wide-open space with bodies strewn at his feet. This must have been the master.

I'd expected a monster, something ten feet tall with talons sharper than a werewolf. Instead, I confronted a man who was maybe five-foot-seven and a buck sixty-five. His brown hair was cut short and parted on the side. If anything, he was average in almost every way.

He wore a nice suit, but it wasn't flashy enough to grab your attention. I would have said he was Hispanic if you put me on the spot, but it wasn't like I had time to do a background check.

One man was still alive.

The man kneeling in front of the master with the vampire's hand wrapped around his throat must have been Saul's father. Rivulets of blood dripped from where his nails had broken the flesh. Van Helsing stared at the master with pure loathing in his eyes. His face said it all. He didn't care if he lived or died. All he wanted to do was take the master down with him.

Saul opened fire. The master didn't flinch as the paintballs slammed into him. He hissed in annoyance as he turned his attention to us. The skin on his hands didn't sizzle as he wiped the liquid off his face with a handkerchief. He smiled like he'd received an unexpected bonus after he cleaned himself off.

The motherfucker wasn't worried. This was going to be trouble.

"One of the sons. What an unexpected delight." He lifted Saul's father with one hand as if he were light as a feather and looked at him straight in the eyes. "When I finish draining you, I will extinguish your entire family line."

"Fuck you!" Saul's father spat in the master's face.

If nothing else Van Helsing had massive balls. The kind they sang songs about. In the face of certain death, all Saul's father cared about was not giving the master an ounce of satisfaction. He was also trying to buy us some time. He held a silver knife behind his back and was about to use it.

"No!" Saul ran forward as his dad plunged the blade in.

This was madness. The master was too strong for us. This was a fight we weren't prepared for and couldn't win. The only thing that would happen if we tried to save Saul's father is we would all die. I'd run away in Illinois, and it would pain me to do it again, but we had to live so we could fight another day.

I grabbed Saul around the waist as the master began to feed on his father. Lifting the man onto my shoulder, I ran in the other direction. The idiot pounded on my back, trying to get me to put him down, but I kept running. What in the fuck had these guys been thinking? This wasn't a single fledgling. This was a massacre. Three vans were already pulling away outside, but one still idled in the parking lot.

God, I loved vampiric hearing.

The master laughed, and his voice echoed off the silo's walls. Saul stopped struggling, and the extra balance allowed me to pick up the pace. We made it out of the silo. I tossed Saul into the van like a sack of dog food, then jumped in. Greg's eyes were wide as saucers as I slammed the door shut.

I pounded on the ceiling with my fist and yelled, "Go. Go. Go!"

The van's tires squealed, and we fishtailed for a second. Then the rear tires caught, and we were rolling. The engine revved as Greg gunned it.

I moved to the van's back window and peered out.

"You left him there." Saul was working himself into a tizzy.

I ignored Saul as he glared daggers at me and watched behind us, looking for any signs of the vampire. A moment later, the master burst from the silo and chased us. We had to be doing fifty miles an hour, and he was gaining ground. It was an incredible display of power. I would have been in complete awe if the fanger wasn't coming to kill us all.

"You need to go faster, Greg." I pushed Saul back down into the seat as he tried to stand to confront me.

We had more important things to deal with.

Greg glanced in the side mirror. "Holy shit."

The van's engine thrummed as we accelerated, but Saul was good and angry now and didn't give two shits if we all might die in a few moments. "You let him kill my dad."

Greg's shoulders sagged, but he didn't let off the gas. "Dad's dead?"

"Yes! And this monster let it happen." Saul took a wild swing at me, and I batted it aside, holding him in place with ease.

This had gone far enough.

"I know you're angry that I saved your life, but this wasn't my fault." I pushed him down and moved away. "One fucking fledgling, you said. I took down three guards, two fledglings, and a vampire who could talk."

I pointed at him to ensure he understood the gravity of his reconnaissance failure. "Not to mention the fact there was a master."

It was my turn to get angry, but I needed to relax before my fangs popped out. My vest and shirt were in tatters, but I didn't have a scratch. That and I'd picked up Saul like a football and ran out of the building with him like it was nothing.

It wouldn't take the brothers long to realize I wasn't some kid. The only thing keeping them from making the connection now was their father's death.

I didn't want to be a dumping ground for Saul's grief, but I didn't want to antagonize the man any further. I was still coming to grips with my loss. It made it much easier to sympathize with him. I knew exactly what he wanted. Revenge. I wanted it too.

"Wait, there was a master?" Greg slowed the van and took a hard right despite the red light. Then he floored it.

Saul looked like he was in enough control of himself not to attack me again, so I looked back out the window. I didn't see anyone chasing us. "I think we're clear, but don't slow down yet."

Killers caught up with you when you slowed down.

Saul's face paled as the enormity of what happened in the warehouse settled over him. "The silver didn't hurt him."

"And he knew who you were." I sat opposite Saul, my heart aching for his grief. "The master must have been trying to lure you in. He knew he was under surveillance."

Saul sank further into his seat. "I'm going to be chronicled as the son who got Van Helsing killed."

We pulled onto the freeway, and Greg slowed enough to avoid attention. "Yes, everyone is going to know we fucked up. Who cares? The real question is how we are going to fix it?"

"I don't think we can." Saul pushed the briefcase toward me. "I'm sorry we can't do more."

"Greg, drop Dylan off at home. We have to deal with a shit storm when we get back to base." Saul gave me a sad smile. "Thank you for saving me."

The way his voice broke when he said it, I knew our time together was over before it started. Tears streamed down my face at the thought of losing out on this opportunity, but I had the money. If nothing else, life would get easier as I figured things out on my own, but I had to find a way to leave the door open for a return.

I wanted into the Helsing Society, and I wanted them to know how I felt. "I'd still like to help. You know where to find me when you're ready."

I wanted to beg him not to end our relationship like this. I still needed answers. The Helsing Society would be my best chance to get them. I hoped that in time, Saul would bring me back into the fold. I had the money to get away and start a new life wherever I wanted, but all I wanted was to stay here and search for the truth about myself.

Despite everything that went down and the fact there might be a master looking for me, I wasn't ready to move on. No one would link a vampire hunter back to a bouncer working at some shit hole-in-the-wall bar as long as Saul and Greg kept their mouths shut. I needed to get strong enough to take out Krista. Then the world could do what it wanted with me.

Before I died, I was taking that bitch with me.

We sat in total silence until the van stopped at my apartment complex.

I opened the van's door and looked back into Saul's haunted eyes. "Thank you for finding me. I hope to see you again soon."

Saul's eyes hinted at the fire I'd seen on our ride to the silos. "Teaching the failings of our history is the best way to make sure we don't make the same mistakes again. There may still be something we can teach each other."

Greg's expression as he looked over his shoulder was as dejected as his brother's. "Stay safe."

"I'll do my best." I held up the briefcase. "This will help."

I stepped out of the van, and the door closed behind me.

Before I could turn, Greg punched the gas, and they were gone. My first shot at real answers, and it was gone in less than a day. I wondered how old you had to be before the disappointments didn't sting as much.

On the plus side, I had tangled with a master and was still alive. I bet there weren't too many people on Earth who could say the same thing.

Sometimes it paid to be happy about the small things in life, but I was also a hundred thousand dollars richer.

That wasn't small change.

Despite the hope the brothers left me with, I didn't see Saul again for five years. When he did track me down, it wasn't to offer me another briefcase of money but another job.

Getting older was a funny thing. Sometimes your mind played tricks on you, and other times, the harsh truth was all too clear. It took five years to hear from the man and another five working together before he truly trusted me. Fifteen years later, Saul was like my grandpa—if Grandpa left you little red envelopes with information on monsters that needed to die.

We'd become close over the years, almost like family. He was helping me track down Krista, and I was learning everything I could to take down the master. The next time we found him, we'd be ready. Together, we could accomplish anything.

Those vamps would never see us coming.

CHAPTER SIXTEEN

2025

There was a red envelope on the dining room table.

How did Saul always know exactly where I'd be? The old bastard still had a knack for finding out everything he shouldn't have been able to. It was probably why he'd stayed alive for so long after being named the new Van Helsing. Everything changed for us that night, and Saul vowed that they would never be taken by surprise again.

By now, one of his Watchers would have reported my return to the apartment. I wouldn't get out of whatever task he assigned me without consequences, mainly in the form of a lecture about responsibility. It was easier to do what he asked, even if it cut into my *Madden* time. Justin Fields was on the cover this year, and I wanted to get in a few seasons before things got competitive online. While every part of me wanted to hit the couch, vape some Herbal Sciences, and torch a few peeps online, I was pretty sure I'd be heading back out before I got the chance.

That was our deal.

Saul kept tabs and hunted down leads on ways I could hurt Krista's business, and I helped him with the occasional problem Greg's Templars couldn't handle on their own. By now, I was sure Saul knew what I was, but if he didn't have a clue that I wasn't strictly human, the fact that I'd stopped aging in my late twenties would have been a dead giveaway. He was probably a little jealous because he looked every day of his fifty-seven years while I could still head over to Tempe and have beers with college kids if I wanted to.

For a while, I'd been worried I would grow old and die despite my vampiric traits, but then I cruised into my forties looking like I'd bagged my first big promotion after graduating college. I was old enough not to get hassled about my age when I went out but young enough to get into places older people wouldn't be able to. It was a great balance. It was too bad more people couldn't stay twenty-seven-ish forever.

As I plucked the envelope from the table, it was hard not to appreciate the attention to detail Saul put into his craft. The envelope's card stock was world-class, and experience told me the paper inside would match. When everything around us felt like it was getting cheaper in quality by the second, it was nice to know some people still valued quality over the largest profit margin possible.

Part of me wondered how over the last twenty-five years, we'd gone from businesses wanting to produce products with the highest quality standards to trying to make the lowest cost product a consumer would still spend their hard-earned money to purchase. The name of the game today was profit above everything else. It was hard to watch, but Saul was different. This paper had class, like the man himself.

His immaculate penmanship flowed across the page.

If I could always count on Saul for something, it was that he'd never do anything half-assed. The old dog had a certain sense of style the younger generations couldn't replicate. I inspected the note, rubbing the thick woven paper between my fingers. It was easy enough to imagine him at a desk surrounded by candlelight, writing this with an inkwell and quill. If anyone asked why he didn't send a text, he'd give them a ten-minute dissertation on why doing things the right way mattered.

He was right. Nothing was more important than how you handled yourself. There was this weird reasoning that it was fine to treat people like shit as long as the attackers thought they were in the right. My dad always told me how you treated your employees mattered as much as how you treated the customers. If you treated your employees with dignity and respect, the rest took care of itself.

Unless someone like Sweeny paid them more to stay away.

I'd been so angry back then, and I still was although it had settled from a blaze to carefully banked coals. It took me a long time to understand why my dad didn't sell, but if your values evaporated when things got tough, they didn't mean anything. My dad was the kind of guy who never backed down from what was right, even in the face of adversity. I didn't know if I'd ever be as good a person as he was, but I knew I'd get to live long enough to try.

Hopefully, he'd be proud of his vampire son.

Most people were glad the old ways were dead, but that seemed to be more about outdated ideas and events from the past. No one wanted us back in the 1400s. War loomed around every corner as the world shrank, and everyone in power scrambled to hold onto as much of the map as possible. Today, it wasn't only the common folk who wanted to avoid war. The vampires wanted it too.

Nuclear bombs tended to reduce the food supply drastically.

People often romanticized history, but no one wanted to relive *The Pacific*. There was a difference between a wonderfully cinematic story and the horrors of living it. Nothing about an army descending on your town to wipe it from the face of the Earth was romantic.

It was a different world than when the original Van Helsing fought his first vampire. In many ways, time made us better as people. More conscious of others' feelings and concerns.

It also made us easier prey.

Nothing made the "tasty snacks" simple to catch, even when half of the human race was overweight. Most people blamed the government for how all cheap food was incredibly unhealthy. They piled on equal rancor that work-life balance had gotten so out of whack some people didn't have the time to cook for themselves. The government shouldered the blame for a lot, but I always put the cheap high-calorie foods on the vamps.

Who wanted to do all that running?

I chuckled, and Fluffy gave me the side-eye as she stirred from her spot on the coffee table. It was time to stop waxing poetic over the feel of fancy paper and discover what kind of mess Saul was dragging us into this time. So much for a night of *Madden* and vape. It was time to get to work.

Dylan,

I'm sorry to call on you again so soon, but the Helsing Society needs your help. There was a fledgling attack two nights ago. Greg's Templars have taken care of most of them, but one of the fledglings escaped. They haven't had any luck tracking it down. I need you to find it and put it down before it kills anyone else.

Come and see me when you finish. I have some new information for you.

Saul

Upon reviewing the location he circled on the enclosed map, it was easy to see why Saul was worried. The attacks were close enough to downtown Phoenix that if a fledgling was roaming free, there wouldn't be a shortage of people to feed on. That meant many dead bodies, which made the police ask questions. What kind of vampire would be reckless enough to sire a fledgling and set it free?

This wasn't like twenty-five years ago. Everyone had access to a camera these days. Leaving one of the newly turned to wander on its own was a big mistake. A fledgling only cared about one thing, and that was its next meal. They weren't smart enough to do anything but feed.

The hunger in the newly turned was insatiable. They needed blood and lots of it. That was how they completed the transition. Without enough blood in the early stages of development, a fledgling regressed into a zombielike state.

We called the dumb ones revenants. Fledglings who received enough blood slowly gained back more of who they were as humans. They were less zombie and more like the talker I turned into Pizza the Hutt with a double handful of Saul's paintballs.

I wasn't sure this was a fledgling attack. The vamps had

taken to turning humans in controlled environments. They didn't want one of their progeny to make the news for eating people. We had to put it down quickly if it was a wayward fledgling. If it killed someone while I was looking, I'd have Saul find its sire and put them down too.

Rest easy, Phoenicians. Dylan McCormick is on the case.

Phoenix was the city I chose to call home, and it received my protection by default. If vampires weren't interested in cleaning up after themselves, I took them off the board. This city was too big to have a vampire war on its hands. If the werewolves thought the vamp population was expanding, there was no telling what they'd do. Twenty-five years of experience with the supernatural taught me that things could always get more complicated.

Sometimes I felt like Cypher from *The Matrix*. I just wanted to get plugged back in.

Not that it was an option. No one could go back in time. At least not yet. My parents were the only things that made me look to the past. If they were here with me now, I wouldn't change a thing. Being a half-vamp was pretty damn cool, even with all the fighting.

Maybe because of the fighting.

For one thing, I could eat human food. I didn't lose my vampire advantages if I did. I only got the worst case of the shits three hours later. Still, being able to enjoy a hamburger and some Ben and Jerry's was something other vampires couldn't do. I could also walk in the sweet, glorious sun. That hadn't changed after all these years. If the other vamps knew, they'd be so damn jealous.

Not that I walked around in daylight very often. The sun's rays still stripped away my strength. The longer I was exposed to it, the harder the reset.

That was when the voice returned. Every time I thought I'd fed long enough to bury the voice for good, it always came back. It was easy to forget I had a silent partner until I hadn't eaten for a few days and the whispers began.

No amount of human food on the planet worked to shut the voice up. Only sweet, sweet blood took the edge off. It was a delicate balance, like being a diabetic.

At least I didn't have a master to answer to.

There was one rule in vampire society, and it was like the dark side of the Force. There was a master, and there were those they controlled. No middle ground existed. The strong dominated the weak.

It was a constant struggle for supremacy until they controlled every vampire in the nest. Then the nests fought to control other nests until they created territories ruled by the elders. In many ways, the vampires had regressed as a society while humans grew.

The only upside to the fangers was that they didn't believe in politics and didn't run those mind-numbing TV ads we all had to suffer through every election cycle. That didn't mean the bloodsuckers and I would become BFFs anytime soon. The only kind of vampire I enjoyed was the one at the end of my stake.

In all my years of doing this, I'd never met a vampire who thought of humans as anything more than food and playthings. I taught them what it was like to feel fear in the night. To remember what being prey was like.

I was William Wallace, taking his revenge.

Tapping Saul's card against my chin, I looked at my dry herb vaporizer and shook my head. Somehow, he always knew where I was and when I got stoned. Meeting up with Saul after smoking was like hot boxing in the garage and having your parents come home. There was nothing quite like seeing your dad appear in a cloud of smoke with a look on his face that said he was an inch away from ending your life. It was easier not to do the crime in the first place and avoid all the drama.

I wanted to load up a bowl of Runtz by Herbal Sciences, but I tossed the letter on the table and prepared instead. The vaporizer on the table didn't give two shits about where I was going, but the imp who sat on the edge of the coffee table did.

Fluffy flew into the air. "Where is he sending us this time?"

It was cute. She was starting to think of us as a team. I didn't know you could form one when one person didn't have a choice in the matter, but apparently, it was possible. Not that I hadn't grown to love my little sidekick, but having an imp attach itself to you was a little much. That and the little she-devil was always smoking my weed.

Fluffy flew into the study and landed on the desk. Her claws tore long jagged streaks in the leather inlay. I looked at the desk and sighed, and she snapped her fingers. The leather knit back together as shiny as new.

"Enough of the sighs. I want to know where we're going." The imp grinned, but all I saw were a million razor-sharp teeth. "Come on, don't hold out on me."

There was no shaking Fluffy once she wanted to tag along. It didn't matter where I went. Even if I took a plane, the Fluffster was by my side in a day. Instead of bemoaning the fact I'd saved an occultist with no money and an active summoning circle, I decided to make friends with her. At least I thought it was "her." Imps didn't have sexual organs or hair, at least not on the outside. Mostly what I noticed when looking at Fluffy were the wings, the big Dobby-like eyes, and the mouth of razor-sharp teeth.

Did I mention her teeth?

Our relationship sounded like the start of a bad joke. A half-breed and an imp walk into a bar...

Despite the joke sucking, I laughed and answered Fluffy's question. "We need to head downtown." I grabbed my bulletproof vest and slipped my jacket back on. "And we are not going shopping."

Fluffy grinned. Two rows of razor-sharp teeth gleamed in the light. "Can we at least walk around?"

If you'd asked me a year ago, I would have told you the chance of a demon liking the shopping and restaurant area downtown was as absurd as a donkey on roller skates. I would have been wrong.

Fluffy loved the malls and anything like them. She basked in all the despair driven by capitalism. Nothing made the imp happier than a declined card or someone getting jealous when their friends bought a pair of shoes they couldn't afford. It was like those emotions topped off her magical tank.

It was good that we weren't in DC, or Fluffy might have had the juice to take over the world.

"I promise to let you do your thing, but first we have to work. Saul's counting on us." I looked at Fluffy and pointed a silver-tipped stake at her like an accusatory finger. "I need you to be on your best behavior until then. We don't want another incident."

The demon launched into the air with her wings beating furiously. "I'll have you know that I saved your ass during the popsicle incident."

"I wish you'd stop calling it that. It sounds like you had

to pull a popsicle out of my ass instead of us killing a den full of fledglings in a popsicle factory." I rolled my eyes. *Demons. What's a guy gonna do?*

I knew Fluffy was trying to get a rise out of me, so I let the dreaded popsicle incident slide off my back like water off a duck. "You remember it your way, and I'll remember mine."

The imp tittered.

One of these days, I would meet a lady, Fluffy would bring up the popsicle incident, and the woman would run screaming from my apartment. At least I'd always have my imp for company.

"Let's not forget about the times you almost got me killed. Like in Vegas, Santa Fe, and Denver, but my favorite is probably Tucson." I rubbed the spot on my chest where a vampire shoved a tire iron through it.

Fluffy landed, looking sulky. "It was a flesh wound."

She sounded sorry enough, and there was nothing worse than a sulky imp. "Are the terms of the deal acceptable?"

If there was one thing demons loved, it was a deal.

Fluffy flew in a few lazy arcs before landing on my shoulder. "I want ten minutes of 'me' time before we go."

"Done."

Fluffy found a stray roll of Lifesavers on the desk, plucked a green one free, tossed it on the floor, and ate a red one. "Then your terms are acceptable."

It was hard to look into those dark eyes, knowing they'd seen things I never wanted to imagine, but I did it anyway. "What are the rules you have to follow?"

With Fluffy, it always paid to clarify.

Tucking her wings back, Fluffy stood tall like a soldier in morning formation. "Stay out of the way. Stay quiet. Repeat steps one and two if there are any questions." She saluted me like a general.

I snapped my ankles together and returned her salute. "Perfect, soldier. I appreciate your dedication to this unit's continued success."

"Fuck off." Fluffy lit a cigarette.

Where the demon got the cigarettes, I'd never know. "No cancer sticks in the house." I plucked the cig free, snuffed it, and tossed it in the trash. "We've talked about this."

"Fine, but I want eleven minutes." Fluffy crossed her arms and glared at me with determination.

It never paid to argue with a demon, even if it was an itty-bitty one. "Eleven minutes, but not a minute longer."

Fluffy launched herself up and flew circles around me in excitement. "Missed a strap," the little demon cried in glee as she pulled it tight.

Gasping for air, I swatted at the flying rat. "I've got it."

The rest of my gear was in place, and the last thing I needed was my magical hoodie. Misty had outdone herself when she created the enchanted item. Walking around the city in a bulletproof hoodie was much easier than a vest.

Getting shot still hurt, even if the pain was fleeting. If I had to describe how getting shot felt to anyone, I would have said it was like a parent stepping on a stray Lego at three in the morning. It hurt way more than it should have and it was best to avoid it whenever possible.

I left the study, looked around the apartment to ensure I didn't miss any other surprises, and headed for the door. "Fluffy, let's roll."

"You got it, boss." The imp landed on my shoulder. "I love the mall."

CHAPTER SEVENTEEN

Griff

"Griff, this is Detective Franco. Can you tell him what you told me?" Officer Brody's eyes said, "You better tell him the same load of bullshit you told me, or there will be trouble."

Man, I hated the fuzz.

Taking a job at the Gas-N-Sip was supposed to be less stressful than my last gig, and it should have been doubly tasty with the extra pay for working overnight. Fewer customers, more money, that was how they sold the job offer. The gig should have been a win-win, but shit like this kept happening to me. I couldn't catch a break. I was over it.

Where were my God damned cigarettes?

They were in my pocket. Right where they were last four times I checked. Only this time, I needed one bad. Screw these cops. They could get my story later if they couldn't handle a little smoke. Like after a twelve-pack and a shot of something stronger. One thing was certain. I'd never step inside the Gas-N-Sip again unless it was for some beer.

Minimum wage wasn't worth all this hassle.

Officer Brody touched my shoulder and pulled back when I jumped. "Can you explain what happened to the detective?"

"I'll fucking tell him. Just get those ugly cop shoes off my nuts for a second." Not exactly what you should say to an officer of the law, but my nerves were too jangled to care.

Ugh, I felt itchy all over. That feeling when you find a bug crawling on you, and even though you killed the little bastard, you can't shake the sensation that one of its little friends also decided to call you home. I didn't know what to say to the detective that I hadn't already told the officers. Talking about the incident again wasn't going to make me feel any better.

I lit my smoke and looked at the destroyed storefront. Maybe I was lucky to be alive. A few pulls on the cigarette took the edge off, but I wanted to get the hell out of there. If that meant telling the story again, I'd do it, but so help me God, I was taking a case of beer with me when I left. They could dock my last check if they cared enough about it.

Looking up, I met Detective Franco's eyes. "You ready for this? Because I'm only going to tell this story one more time. Then I'm fucking outta here."

"I decide when you go home." Detectives could be real pricks that way.

It wasn't like I hadn't played this game before. The detective was in for a real treat. "You know, the bump on my head is really starting to hurt. We'll have to talk after I see a doctor."

"You're the only witness." Detective Franco sighed like the fact he had to clean up this mess was my problem.

My hand shook when I brought the cigarette to my lips.

"Like I said, buckle up, buttercup. I'm about to let her rip. Then I'm going to dip. So, get out your pen and take some notes."

"Officer, did you check the security footage?" Detective Franco was looking for any way to avoid dealing with me.

He was grasping at straws.

"I did, but the guy ripped out the entire system." Officer Brody looked at me. "Any cloud storage?"

I pointed at what remained of the mini-mart. "Have you seen this place? You're lucky the camera works."

"But not so lucky with the footage, huh?" Franco glared at me.

The bad cop routine was almost enough to make me laugh. "Tough break, big guy." I flicked my cigarette into the half-destroyed store. "I guess you'll have to take my word for it."

"Spit it out already." Detective Franco clicked his pen a few times to let me know he was ready to roll.

The need to light another cigarette had me fidgeting with my lighter. "Like I told Officer Brody, I work the night shift because there are fewer customers."

"Down here, they'd be almost nonexistent," Brody chimed in.

The look on my face at being interrupted was enough to silence him. "Like I said, talking to people isn't my favorite thing in the world, so I work at night."

"Seriously, not again." I watched the man shambling toward the door on camera one and wished I was allowed to lock them during my shift.

Big "I Own the Place" Willy said never lock the doors.

It was easy for Bigs to say shit like that because he worked during the day when everything was just peachy. He even gave the cops free coffee during his shift, so the place normally had at least one cop car in the lot. At night, when Bigs cut off the free drinks, the police found other places to do their paperwork. I normally spent the entire night in the store alone, stocking shelves and cleaning.

Just the way I liked it.

They say stereotyping people is wrong, but I'd been held at gunpoint twice. I wasn't fucking around when someone sketchy walked toward the store. As soon as they got close, I had my hand on Stacey, and it didn't leave her well-worn curves until the offending party had paid for their merchandise.

Oh, sweet, sweet Stacey.

Stacey was my double-barreled twelve-gauge shotgun. I'd sawed off the barrel to make a devastating short-range weapon. One blast from Stacey would spray Mr. Methareno across the wall like an extra in a *Rambo* movie. The gun was my pride and joy—a tool to make a man think twice before acting a fool.

Stacey didn't play stupid games.

Normally it took a lot for me to deem someone sketchy enough to grab Stacey, but this guy had weirdo rolling off him in waves. The last thing I needed was another psycho ruining one of the displays because he was all cranked out. Dealing with this kind of shit wasn't in my job description. Not without a serious raise on the table.

Stacey felt good as I tightened my grip around her. She gave me the courage to say things I'd never have the balls to without the shotgun to back me up. Stuff like get the fuck out of my store. Only tonight I would head off the problem at the door.

Fuck Big Willy. Who has a name like that anyway?

I moved around the counter and ran toward the front door so I could lock it. The loser's shuffle must have picked up speed because he was at the entrance before I could flip the lock closed. The junkie tried pushing the door open, even though I was standing right in front of it. The fact I could smell him through the mostly closed door didn't say much for his chances of having currency in his pockets. I shoved the door, so the stink of decay would stay outside where it belonged, but the door slid farther inward.

The guy was stronger than I was, and it wasn't even close.

When my feet slid, I abandoned the door and brought up Stacey. "Hey, mister! It's time for you to get the fuck out of here!"

I'd never fired a gun at a person unless the person-shaped targets at the range counted. My hope had always been that the weapon would be a significant enough deterrent to scare people away. It always worked in the past. In an insane world, it was better to have some power when the devil came knocking. I also didn't want to face a murder rap, so I had to make sure he heard me.

"Get out of the fucking store!" My voice cracked at the end. Confrontation wasn't my strong suit.

The man's head snapped up when I screamed, and his eyes focused on me like he'd noticed I was there for the first time. "Grrrraaah."

Oh, shit, this guy had zonked himself out of his mind on something. He couldn't even form words anymore. What was up with all these junkies? Last week some asshole smeared shit all over the bathroom walls. If you want to get into shit painting, do it somewhere I don't have to clean it up. Whatever happened to simple principles like keeping the crap in the shitter?

I quickly realized it was time to get a new damn job. The Gas-N-Sip wasn't fulfilling me as a person anymore.

"Hey man, if you've got cash and need something, tell me what it is, and I'll get it for you." I eyed his muddy boots for a second. "It'll save me from having to mop."

He lurched toward me but didn't say a word.

"Listen, dude. I'll use this if I have to!" I shook Stacey in his face to ensure he saw the shotgun.

He had bloodshot eyes, and drool leaked out of his mouth like my dog Brewster when I grabbed the bag of treats. Homie was into it in a bad way. Why did I always have to deal with this shit? Why couldn't rabid bums attack when Big Willy was working and the cops were here? I knew one thing for damn sure. I would quit this chicken shit job in the morning.

Willy could take his fifteen an hour and shove it.

It wasn't my job to go to jail over a few insured snacks. I lowered the gun thinking how dumb it was to point it at him in the first place. If he made a big enough mess, it'd be Willy's job to clean it up. Serve the bastard right. I did my best to pretend he wasn't right behind me and headed back around the counter. Willy was going to throw a shit fit, but I'd tell him to send my final check to my address.

"Listen, bro. Do whatever you're going to do." I didn't hear anything as I rounded the corner, but I glimpsed the security cameras.

The crazy bastard was coming right for me with his arms outstretched like a zombie. There was no time to shoot, but I turned my body enough that he only grabbed my shirt. Then I flew through the air. The people in movies never looked as hurt as I felt after landing ten feet away against the beer cooler in the back.

Meth made this guy as strong as The Rock playing a superhero. It was lucky for me that I managed to hold on to Stacey. His strength didn't mean shit to her. She was all woman!

Jesus, he's almost on me.

There was no time to think. All I could do was raise my gun, and Stacey did her thing. I fucking blew the guy's guts across the store. The shot tore a considerable chunk out of his side and blew one of his arms off at the elbow. I stared at the scene in wonder for a moment. Then it hit me all at once. I was responsible for turning a human into splatter art.

I puked.

Popping Stacey open, I reloaded the shotgun and moved forward. Reloading the weapon felt ludicrous. I mean, no one could have lived through that, but it was how those fake militia guys at the range taught me to do things. So that's what I did. I kept Stacey pointed at the man as I inched forward. The body jerked, and I almost fired again.

Holy shit, he was still alive.

"I'm calling an ambulance, buddy. You're going to be fine." I picked up the phone and looked at the guts sprayed across the wall and didn't understand how it was possible.

Worst. Day. Ever.

Setting Stacey down, I grabbed the phone and dialed nine-one-one.

"Emergency Dispatch, how can I help you?" The voice was calm and assertive, filling me with confidence.

"Hey, I'm at the Gas-N-Sip on Twentieth Ave and Van Buren. I just shot someone. They need help."

"You just shot someone?" Furious typing filled the line. "Officers have been dispatched to your location. Are there any other victims? Are you in any danger?"

In danger? I laughed. Only if that fucker could regrow an arm. I looked at the store windows that had blown out into the parking lot and the Jeep at the gas pump. My nervous laughter died. I'd killed someone. Firing Stacey wasn't nearly as thrilling as I thought it would be.

"Everything is fine now. I'm going to leave my weapon on the counter and wait outside for the officers. I don't have any other weapons." I looked at Stacey and back at the guy on the floor, but he wasn't there.

What in the fuck? The dispatcher was still talking, but I put the phone down and inched around the counter. Where in the fuck could he be? Why didn't I bring Stacey?

Oh shit.

My gaze followed the smeared blood trail on the floor as it wrapped around the counter. I knew what it meant, but I didn't want to admit it could be real. I didn't want to face the danger that waited right behind me. I was all alone. The fucker had one arm and no guts. How much trouble could he be?

A hand clamped down on my shoulder, the grip tight enough to make me cry out in pain. The dude turned me slowly, and I had to go with the motion or risk something breaking. It didn't make sense. No one should be this strong. Especially not some tweaker with one arm and no guts. The stump of his elbow bumped against me a few times like he hadn't realized the arm was gone.

"Help!" I screamed at the top of my lungs, but who would help me?

The cops were probably five minutes away, and no one else was down here except the guy in the Jeep. If I were him, I would have bolted as soon as Stacey went off. I punched the arm holding me down. I fucking clawed at it, but nothing worked. It was like the thing was steel instead of flesh and blood.

He leaned forward when my knees hit the floor and snapped viciously at me. His face didn't move when my fist crashed into it. Instead, it drew closer to my neck.

"Hey man, if you're hungry, let me buy you a Hot Pocket." It was a desperate and foolish ploy.

It didn't work.

If the man had both arms, I probably would have been dead already. I certainly wouldn't have lived long enough to see something explode from the junkie's chest. It was like the scene from *Alien* when the monster burst out of that guy's chest, but instead of an extraterrestrial, it was a metal-tipped stake. The hand on my shoulder went slack, and the tip of the stake began to glow.

"A wooden fucking stake." I looked at the weapon sticking out of the junkie's chest and hoped its wielder had saved me.

With the way this day was going, it couldn't get much worse.

"Let me get this straight, Griff." Detective Franco looked torn between laughing at me and calling all his buddies so they could listen to my story. "You shoot a guy. He gets up and attacks you, and some mystery man shoves a wooden stake through his heart and disappears from the scene. Did I hear that right?"

"Don't forget, they took the body." Officer Brody was being one helpful motherfucker tonight.

If anyone knew how it sounded, it was me. How was it possible to kill someone and have their blood and guts all over the place with no body to be found? No way was I gonna tell them the damn junkie burst into ashes. They already thought I was crazy. They'd have to figure that shit out on their own.

God, I needed something stronger than a cigarette right now.

All I could do was show them the bruise on my shoulder as evidence my story wasn't a pure fabrication. No way I could have done that to myself. They could do what they wanted with it. I didn't care. I was through with this place.

"Laugh if you want to, but the guy squeezed me hard enough with one hand that he damn near snapped my collarbone." I stripped off my shirt so Detective Franco could see the perfectly shaped handprint.

I shook my head, pulled my shirt on, and lit another cigarette. "That's my story, and I'm sticking to it."

"Officer Brody, take this guy over to Banner. Get him a psych eval." Detective Franco was already talking about me like I wasn't there.

I stood and looked into the detective's eyes. "I'll tell you what your science guys will find. It's going to be exactly what I told you, down to the last detail. Then I want an apology."

"Brody, let's find out what the doctors think." Detective

Franco walked over to the broken glass and shouted questions at one of the crime scene techs.

"Guy's a real winner." I looked into the mini-mart, wondering who would pay for my visit to the looney.

Officer Brody laughed. "You should see him when there is a body."

CHAPTER EIGHTEEN

Dylan

It turned out downtown was a total bust.

Driving around the more populated destinations hadn't revealed anything. Fluffy and I had taken to the streets on foot, completing a semi-thorough search of the shops and exteriors of the buildings for hours—big fat zippo. The police scanner on my phone hadn't picked up anything more interesting than a handful of shoplifters and a DUI or two.

I was getting frustrated, and Fluffy's good mood wasn't helping the situation. She'd loved our extended time downtown, but I was in a rut.

There was a time when I thought being a vampire hunter would be the best job on Earth. People would worship me as the hero of all humankind. In reality, I was more like Sam and Dean, with better accommodations and a way cooler ride. You couldn't off-road a '67 Impala through the desert without some major issues.

The truth of the matter was being a hunter was lonely work. No one knew what I did, and they never would if I did the job right. Granted, I wasn't as lonely now that I had Fluffy to keep me company. I'd spent the night crawling in and out of places that would make the guy from *Dirty Jobs* blush, but at least I wasn't alone.

Not that the imp would get in the trash. She had higher standards.

Some smells wouldn't wash out of clothes. Climbing in and out of every damn trash can at the mall was a good way to grind some not-so-fresh scents deep into the fabric. The only things not ruined were my hoodie and the shirt beneath it. The jeans and boots I'd never be able to wear again.

It wasn't like I could strip them off now. People tended to frown on pantsless men running around downtown. Instead of stripping completely, I removed my hoodie and used it to protect the driver's seat.

There were some things even Scotchguard wouldn't protect against.

I sat in the Jeep and thought about what had happened. Saul's information had been off, and that was a normal occurrence. I would need to call him and tell him "no dice" on the fanger, and he would tell me to keep looking. He had an entire little speech about it, and it revolved around his favorite movie.

The Matrix.

"Most people couldn't handle the truth" was Saul's famous opener. They'd rather stay plugged into the Matrix. The simulation was safe. The simulation was known. Life made more sense when things that went bump in the night only did it in movies and books. Seeing someone getting their throat torn out wasn't a sexy thriller when the thing that did it hunted you next.

When I did my job right, no one had to be unplugged.

The guilt trip would be real, but I was satisfied the fledgling wasn't here. If it was, Saul would need to get Watchers down here to pinpoint its location because I couldn't do it. All I wanted to do was shower and get in a game of *Madden* before bed, but I still had to drive to Saul's place. If he wanted to see me in person, it meant he had some new information on Krista.

"What are you going to tell Saul?" Fluffy couldn't help twisting the knife.

That he owes me a new set of clothes.

"I'm going to tell him he needs better information." It was true. "Whoever put him onto this missed something."

Fluffy laughed. "You're going to get the speech again."

"Hey, this time it's not my fault." I pointed at my pants as evidence of a hard day's work. Then the low gas light flickered on.

When it rains, it pours.

Was there anything worse when you're having a bad day than the fucking gas light? Sure, a flat tire would have been more irksome, but I had a full-sized spare, and Discount Tire would repair the damaged one for free. Gas always cost money, and despite what I'd read as a kid, cash didn't grow on trees.

Wouldn't that have been nice? I would have been the king of the money tree farmers.

Vampires who lived long enough tended to be wealthy. All they needed to do was get enough money to buy land or stocks, wait a couple of hundred years, and presto, instant wealth. With what Saul paid me, I had a leg up on stability.

I'd invested all of it in the market, and over the last twenty-five years, I'd turned that hundred thousand into a million dollars. I also owned two small homes and an apartment.

I still had to work a few jobs along the way. Vampire hunting wasn't a cheap business. No insurance company covered a werewolf tossing your Jeep off a cliff. It would make one hell of a commercial, though. The actor could point at the werewolf statue and say, "We covered that."

Who decided werewolves should be so damn strong, anyway? No one should be able to toss a Jeep like a Tonka truck.

On the plus side, I didn't have to pay for health insurance. That was a real killer for most folks. How was it that insurance companies were for-profit organizations? It seemed to me people's health shouldn't be tied to something as trivial as money.

Getting sick shouldn't be something that bankrupted you. People should never have to choose between leaving something for their children and staying alive. Easy enough for me to say when I had perfect health and no family to worry about.

I was pretty sure there wouldn't be anyone to leave an inheritance to anyway.

I'd had many sexual encounters over the last twenty-five years, but they were always short flings. I couldn't risk people figuring out what I was so I couldn't get too close to anyone. The fact I didn't age would be a dead giveaway. No one had sent any letters about paternity, so there was a better than even shot having children was off the table.

It was probably a good thing. My life was too big of a mess to bring a woman into it, let alone a child. I could see it now. "Hey kid, I know Fluffy is a demon, but she's family too." The therapy bills alone would bankrupt me in a month.

Not to mention the fact I had plenty of enemies. Killing off fledglings didn't make you a lot of friends in the vampire community. A family would be something the fangers could use against me.

At least I had Fluffy. No one fucked with the Fluffster.

The Gas-N-Sip had the lowest gas prices in town and the least number of customers this late at night. Sure, Quick Trip had all the fancy stuff. Fluffy and I downed a dozen spicy chicken taquitos the last time we made an Herbal Sciences run, but QT always had cops in the parking lot. Gas-N-Sip never did. Rule one was still no cops when hunting, so spicy taquitos were off the menu.

I pulled into pump number two and looked at Fluffy. "Please, don't steal anything."

"As if." Fluffy flew out of the Jeep and headed toward the store.

In any other encounter, a person would assume "as if" meant they were insulted that you would even consider the fact they would steal. With Fluffy, it meant she'd steal even more to show me she could do it without getting caught.

Most humans couldn't see the imp unless it wanted them to, so Fluffy could get away with pretty much anything. Next time you're alone at the computer and the wife slips out of the house, understand that while *she* may never know about your quick Internet trip to Busty Asian Beauties, Fluffy would.

It was amazing how much I'd learned since Krista turned me twenty-five years ago. Before then, my life was all about the Path to Greatness and getting into college. Now I had to worry about whether my demon watched me masturbate. Life didn't always turn out how you expected, but if you watched closely enough, there was a beauty to the madness. It was the beauty of certain moments that eluded me.

Like spending the night searching through the trash.

I laughed as I put my card in the machine and hit the good old eighty-seven button on the pump. Despite the ups and downs, I wouldn't give up being a half-vamp for anything. I loved it, and the fact I could walk in the sun and eat human food without dying only made it better.

The green lights flashed on the console, and I got busy pumping the gas. Then I needed to go inside and buy snacks for after the hunt. I never kept food on hand at the apartment. It was too tempting to eat. The last thing I wanted was to eat human food and get one of Saul's red cards with an oncoming case of IBS on steroids. Werewolves didn't care if you had to take a dump in the middle of the fight. They'd keep trying to bite your head off.

I laughed at the thought of the older man.

Saul was always getting into stuff he shouldn't, but since he'd taken over as Van Helsing, the Watchers provided more accurate information than ever. That was why tonight was such a mystery. He had let Greg form a faction of Templars, men and women willing to risk their lives to kill a vampire. If the vamps had it out for either of the brothers, it was Greg. He might not be the Van Helsing, but he was the one creating problems.

Their father would have been proud of what they'd done, even if they hadn't done it together.

It wasn't as if the masters noticed the loss of a few fledglings here or there. Most older vampires didn't care about their spawn's offspring or foot soldiers. They thought of the people under them as tools to achieve greater success. Kill a few closer to the top of the food chain, and they took notice.

Getting noticed by a master was bad news. The Helsing Society spent most of their time taking out the low-hanging fruit, but Greg was ready to expand their purview.

I'd been killing vampires for a quarter of a century and never tested my mettle against a master. Part of me wanted to try it to see if I could win, and a larger part wanted to know if they had information on Krista. Twenty-five years was a long time to wait for answers.

I still hadn't found much in the Helsing Society's literature. It seemed half-vampires were about as rare as Nephilim. As in, it rarely happened. Only one record shed some light on my condition. Even that was a passing reference.

In 1348 AD, there was a record of a small village with a mysterious visitor. The man walked in the sun, but at night people went missing. When the villagers returned, they were different.

People began to die in larger numbers, but the plague rattled everyone. Van Helsing wrote that he'd never seen anything like it, and when he killed the stranger, the rise in new vampires stopped. That allowed him to kill the rest of the fledglings with ease.

I hoped to find out more, but I could only read so many books at a time.

What was that awful smell?

I found the source of it pretty quickly. A homeless man was walking through the parking lot. Jesus, he looked like someone needed to hose him off. I watched his shuffling progress as I waited for the gas to stop pumping.

Then it hit me like a truck. Could that be the fledgling?

How did the guy make it all the way here from downtown? I didn't have the answers, but they didn't matter right now.

The only good biter was a dead biter.

This revenant didn't look like much more than a walking zombie. All it wanted was to find its next meal and darkness to hide from the sun. This particular biter was having trouble opening the door, and the cashier inside had already noticed. Holy shit, did he have a shotgun? The Gas-N-Sip didn't strike me as the kind of place with a rough clientele but answering the door with a gun in your hand would certainly explain why no one was ever here.

Smelly finally got the door open, and the cashier yelled at him. Something about getting the fuck out so he wouldn't have to mop the entire place. It was the kind of thing that might have worked on someone who was strung out, but the revenant wasn't on drugs.

He was looking for a snack.

Smelly grabbed the man and sent him flying across the store. I was impressed when the cashier didn't drop the gun or fire it accidentally.

It was even more impressive when he snapped the weapon up and fired before Smelly ripped his throat out. Blood splashed across the store like rain in a hurricane. The front windows shattered, and an arm stuck to the comic book rack. The revenant wasn't in sight, but I saw some of his intestines on the floor as the cashier ran behind the counter and picked up the phone.

A call to the police wouldn't give me much time to get in and out, but I couldn't leave the revenant behind. There were cameras on the pumps, but this wasn't the kind of place that had more than a hard drive in the security hub.

Still, it would be better to rip out the entire system than leave anything behind.

Saul spent some serious time teaching me how to avoid detection. My best protection was that my face blurred in every photo, but my Jeep and its license plate didn't have the same protection. I sprayed them with that reflective stuff to stop freeway cameras, but it wouldn't stop a regular camera.

Part of me expected to see flames incinerate the fledgling, but they didn't appear. It was odd. When a newly turned vampire took enough damage, they went up in flames and turned into ash like someone had staked them.

The older they got, the harder they were to kill. The fact that this one didn't burn up after the clerk shredded his insides and he lost an arm meant it wasn't an average fledgling. Was this a vampire punishment?

Starving one of them to the point of stupidity would surely send a message to other vampires to get in line.

The fanger stood and walked around the counter. He had the clerk in his grip, and I realized I'd been watching when I should have been running. This bastard was determined to live, and I had to end him before the cashier had an irreversible life change.

I didn't want two piles of ash left behind.

Glass *crunched* under my boots as I ran through the door. Fluffy hovered above the scene, eating a tube of Pringles. The imp wasn't going to be much use in a fight. She never directly contributed unless I was about to die.

There was no real way to do this without exposing the cashier to the truth, so the direct approach was better than having to ash him. The revenant had the poor guy down on his knees and was leaning in to feed as I vaulted the counter.

The stake felt as natural in my hand as a pen or a baseball bat. I picked my spot on the revenant's back and struck without hesitation or doubt. The silver tip burst through his chest. A few small bits of his heart went with it. Not exactly a fair fight, but it was over.

I looked at the cashier. "Stay there."

Lugging the body outside took me a second, but I couldn't let it burst into flames inside the store. When older vampires exploded, they went big. I tossed the body out the door and looked back at the store. Sadly, there was nothing I could do about the blood and guts, but I plucked the arm free from the comic book stand and tossed it on the body as it burst into flames.

The best kind of vampire evidence was no evidence.

Unfortunately for the kid behind the counter, he was in for a long night of answering questions. Not an enviable position, but one I didn't have to share. I looked for the security system, but Fluffy flew to the Jeep carrying it. She might not be much use in a fight, but she was a boss when it came to stealing shit.

I was starting to love the little fucker.

"Let's roll." I tossed the keys to Fluffy, who started the Jeep as I climbed inside.

The imp grinned from ear to ear as she peered at the security system from her place on the heated seats. "Did you see that guy's expression when your stake burst through the vamp's chest? It was priceless."

"I was too busy making sure the store didn't burn down." I put the Wrangler in gear and pulled out onto the street, hoping I had enough time to escape unnoticed before the cops arrived.

It was either sheer luck the revenant ended up at the

Gas-N-Sip, or someone was sending them to places I frequented to send a message. Either way, it wasn't a great sign. This many attacks so close together could be the start of something bigger.

Saul would have the answers, or at least whatever answers we could find. There were still a few hours left before the sun came up, which meant I had time to make the trip. I got on the I-17 and headed north.

Something wasn't right, and it was time to find out what.

CHAPTER NINETEEN

Saul's office was inside an old warehouse.

There were tons of rundown warehouses off I-17, but Saul liked this building because it was closer to the people. Nothing brought folks together like Castles and Coasters. It was like the Golf 'n Stuff from my childhood, but with roller coasters. A super cool water park wasn't much farther down the road, and almost directly behind the amusement park was Metro Center. It used to be a mall, but now it was a super hip shopping-slash-urban area.

My mentor in all things supernatural said he liked to hear the screams and laughs from the people at the park. It reminded him of what he was fighting for. If he had a few too many drinks in his system, he'd say the sounds of laughter helped him drown out the bad memories. I knew what he meant. You couldn't be part of this world without losing someone close to you, and we all had different ways of coping.

Saul Van Helsing was my lighthouse in the darkness. To say I struggled coming to terms with my new existence would be an understatement. Having friends like Fluffy and Saul helped, but even Saul didn't know the whole truth about me. He knew I wasn't human, and by now he knew that I fed on blood. Of course, not aging a day since my late twenties made me the best-looking forty-five-year-old in Phoenix history.

It was also a dead giveaway.

I should have asked Saul for help. It must have been my pride or the fact I was still worried he'd toss me out once he confirmed the truth. For the last ten years, Greg hadn't done anything but shoot threatening glances in my direction. I couldn't afford to lose Saul, too.

The only one who knew all my secrets was Fluffy, and that was because I couldn't get rid of her, no matter how hard I tried. I kept the imp full of Herbal Sciences from the local dispensary, and she kept her big fat mouth shut. She loved cannabis, and it stopped her from antagonizing my neighbors. Nothing got a family fighting like missing food from the fridge and toys in the wrong sibling's rooms. Fluffy could be a brat, but we were working on it.

Saul was too smart to think I was the first human who magically stopped aging, but the fact that I could eat human food and didn't burst into flames in the sunlight went a long way to ease his concerns. He looked past my quirks because we made a difference. Knowing how sly the grumpy old bastard was, he had probably chronicled me for their archives.

I was the de facto champion of Van Helsing until the next real champion emerged from among their ranks. Saul was worried the power might never come back, but I knew it would return. The universe wouldn't be cruel enough to keep a champion away forever. It would choose someone when it was ready. The light needed someone to fight for it.

When the Helsing Society didn't have a warrior to lead them, their charge was to chronicle the darkness. Saul kept this tradition alive while Greg used the information to plan attacks. Creatures that hunted humans no longer had free rein to walk the night.

The Helsings had notes on vampires, werewolves, witches, and a smattering of demons. The Helsing Society didn't stand a chance in a real battle until their true champion appeared, but every single member, Templar or not, was ready to stand and fight.

Their belief that they could rise and win was inspiring.

The Templars were still a mystery to me. Greg didn't trust me enough to include me in his plans, and Saul didn't like to talk about it. I thought Greg's idea was ballsy, but it seemed to be working. They recruited many former military members to fill their ranks, and those guys didn't fuck around. Saul only said we had our own path to walk if I pushed the issue.

I pulled off the freeway, enjoying the look of the roller coasters as they ran. The sounds of delight coming from the park had the opposite effect on me. So many people in one place put me on edge. It was like walking next to a Five Guys and smelling the scent of French fries in the air. The aroma of fresh golden-brown deliciousness drove a person's hunger, like smelling humans sparked mine if I hadn't fed enough.

It must have been too long since my last meal.

Fluffy appeared on my shoulder with a warm bag of blood in hand. "You better drink this if you don't want to drain the grump."

Damned considerate for a demon.

"Thank you." I accepted the bag of blood and finished it off faster than a college freshman hitting a beer bong during Rush Week.

Fluffy was growing on me. Small things like this let me know that while she enjoyed tormenting everyone else, she cared about me for some reason. I'd tried talking to her a few times about why she was here and what she wanted, but Fluffy wouldn't answer. While Saul had his Watchers and Greg had his Templars, I had my imp.

I put the empty bag in the tailgate before checking my mouth in the rearview. It wouldn't do to walk inside Saul's place with a mouth full of blood. He might understand that I had to feed sometimes, but he wouldn't appreciate me rubbing his face in it. A few quick sips of water cleaned my teeth off enough to be acceptable, and I was ready to roll.

"Sorry, you can't come inside." Saul would never understand my relationship with Fluffy. "I'll make it up to you when we get home."

Fluffy crossed her arms. "There is only one thing I want."

"But it's so expensive," I whined.

Damn imp always wanted the good stuff.

Fluffy pouted as she buzzed around my head in a circle. "Not as expensive as eating him would be."

She had bailed me out with the blood, and I owed her one. "Fine, I'll buy you the ounce of bigs, but I don't want to hear any complaints about the smell from the bathroom after I eat my super nachos."

The imp side-eyed me. "It's not called Netflix and diarrhea for a reason."

"Please. You know that without my account there wouldn't be a Netflix for you to watch." I crossed my arms.

"California burrito. Add potatoes." Fluffy landed on the hood of the Jeep and danced. "And a horcha, cha, cha, ta. I love that shit."

"I'll get you the big one." I grinned at the imp, imagining the taste of the sweet cinnamon milk.

I wanted to trust Fluffy. She was so damn cute. Doing the cha-cha for a horchata was downright whimsical. Still, she was a demon. As much as I wanted to trust her, I couldn't give in until I knew why she was here. Not that I could ever get rid of her. Good or bad, she was my constant companion.

The Fluffster was always good for a chuckle.

Saul's door had a fingerprint scanner. The crazy old bastard tried getting his hands on a retinal scanner, but people began asking questions when you had one of those on your door. Like why does a guy running an antique business need a retinal scanner? What exactly was he hiding? Where did he import-export from?

Those were all questions Saul would rather avoid. The retinal scanner was off the table for now.

The panel *beeped*, and the door *clicked* open as the system recognized my prints. I walked through the entrance, and it sealed shut behind me. I was trapped in a hallway eight feet wide and ten feet long. Saul had installed several deterrents, ranging from bean bag pellets to liquid silver in the sprinkler heads. Anyone he didn't want inside didn't get in.

A speaker crackled overhead, and a mechanical voice filled the air. "Twelve separate twists turned twice."

I could never keep up with Saul and his code phrases.

"Four pumpkins found hollow." I tried my best.

The clue had to do with fall. I knew it.

Saul stood in the doorway as it opened at the far end of

the corridor. "Jesus, you're worse than Greg. Get in here already." He walked into the building. "Did you find the fledgling?"

"I didn't find anything downtown." The second door closed behind us. "But I did run into a little surprise at the Gas-N-Sip."

Laughing, Saul walked between rows of priceless Helsing artifacts. "So that was your little mess all over the news. Cops are calling it one hell of a prank."

"The revenant wasn't laughing when that clerk blew half his guts out the front windows. Then he got back up, Saul. This wasn't our normal zombie mode encounter." I still didn't know how the revenant made it so far from the target zone.

Saul waved as if to say it wasn't as important and I was making it out to be more than it was. "Come on. I've got a couple of things I want to show you."

"It better not be some stake you purchased from a museum." My heart beat a little faster, but it always did when I thought he might have information about Krista.

"I wouldn't call you down here for something trivial."

He had, and he did.

If this meeting wasn't about one of his new acquisitions, it had to be Krista. "Don't leave me hanging, Saul." No one ever accused me of being the most patient of individuals.

Grunting, Saul thrust open the door to his innermost sanctum. "Trust me. I've got an entire presentation planned. You're going to love it."

PowerPoint. Ruining lives since forever.

My first thought was this better not take too long. The Fluffster would soon get bored with making the arcade games malfunction and disabling people's rides in the middle of an epic bumper boat battle. She might like the chaos of the amusement park, but it wouldn't keep her entertained forever. I had to stay long enough for Saul to feel appreciated but not long enough for Fluffy to feel neglected.

This is why people become hermits.

I smiled like there was no place I'd rather be because Saul deserved to feel good about his accomplishments. "I can't wait to see what you've cooked up for me this time."

Saul squawked like he knew I was full of shit and had video games on the brain. He pointed at a chair. "Sit the fuck down and listen to what your elders have to say."

I sat. It never paid to screw with Saul when he felt feisty.

"I've got a new lead," he stated triumphantly.

"Is that the entire presentation? I have to say it's not your best work." Sometimes my mouth was set on smartass.

He clicked a remote, and a picture appeared on the wall in front of me. "I think I've finally tracked down a recent sighting of Krista."

There she was on the wall, the woman who killed my parents. Rage rolled off me in waves. It almost made my fangs drop. I couldn't do anything but stare into her soulless eyes. Everything changed the day she came for us, and I still wanted revenge. I might get a chance at her if Saul knew where she was.

"How'd you find her?" I whispered. "We've been looking for so long."

Saul poured a glass of tea. "See? I told you, you'd like the presentation."

"Like" might not have been the right word for how I felt. It was more like I needed this presentation. Hell, after twenty-five years of chasing shadows, I'd earned this fucking presentation.

I didn't know if killing Krista would make me feel any better, but the only way to know for sure would be to do it. I was game if she was. I dreamed of the day I'd be strong enough to take her on since she murdered my parents.

This might finally be my moment.

I wanted to know everything, but Saul had set up to do his thing, so I let him continue at his pace.

Saul pointed at Krista's projected image. "The incident you told me about occurred in St. Charles in 1999. A local sandwich shop owner and his family were wiped out."

Saul pulled up a picture of my parents and me outside the shop when Dad first opened it. I was fourteen, and there was no missing the resemblance. The screen flashed through a few local news stories and my high school picture. All the secrets were out now. I should have known better than to give him the St. Charles connection, but we'd run out of other leads.

Saul had to know what I was, and by showing me the pictures, he was letting me know he knew. At the same time, he called me here to help me out and wasn't shy about dropping his letter off earlier. Despite the fact he knew and probably had for some time, he didn't cut me off. All of a sudden, I felt all warm and cuddly.

It was almost as good as when Saul helped me find Thomas Michael Sweeny. It had been five years since then, and I hadn't thought about Sweeny a single day. He didn't know anything that made him special. He was a go-fer, a human the vamps didn't deem special enough to turn. Part of me still wished I had taken him out. Why should he get to live when my parents were dead? But Sweeny was only a tool.

"I still think I should have offed him." Any human willing to sell other humans out to the vamps deserved a similar fate.

Saul shook his head, wordlessly asking if we were going to have that conversation again. "If you killed him, we wouldn't have this new lead. More importantly, we don't leave collateral damage. Dead humans are messy, and they make people ask questions."

Saul didn't know I could have bitten him and ashed the greasy little fucker. No body to deal with then. So he hadn't figured out the entire truth about me yet. I should fill him in on what I could do, but I wasn't ready to completely bring down that wall.

"What is rule number one?" Saul was in full instructor mode, and he wouldn't continue his presentation until I answered him.

"Rule number one is no cops and no activity that brings the cops." It came out of my mouth like a wet fart when I'd spouted the same words to Fluffy like poetry hours ago.

Saul nodded and smiled. "Dead humans bring more attention from the cops. Same with extensive property damage. So, no dead humans and no destroyed gas stations." He pointed at the wall. "Keeping Sweeny under observation led us to Pinky Lamoan.

"Pinky is a low-level nothing. The kind of guy a landlord calls when he needs bullies to sweep out the homeless or to scare tenants. He's not a nice guy." Saul looked rather pleased about it.

"He had a transaction with this man." Saul clicked a new

image onto the wall. "Alexander Grant. For all intents and purposes, he's the new Sweeny."

That slimy goat-licking whore.

I stood and scrutinized his face from every angle as I committed it to memory. *We'll meet soon, Alexander. I'm dying to ask a few questions about your employer.*

"Guess who's coming to town to scope out a few properties?" Saul grinned.

It couldn't possibly be this easy after all this time. "Alexander is coming here?" Our eyes met. "For her?"

Saul nodded.

Holy shit. My date with Krista got a whole lot closer.

"Are you sure?"

"As sure as I can be. I take it you want to meet him?" Saul sipped from his cup.

That was for damn sure. "We might have a few things to chat about."

"I thought you might." Saul winked. "Just don't forget rule number one."

"Yes, Dad!" I laughed when his face scrunched up. Saul hated reminders about his age. "You have other information?" It was hard to believe my luck could be this good.

Saul's face turned grim. "I have information on the master who killed my dad."

Just like that, Fluffy wouldn't be the only one enjoying Herbal Sciences tonight. I would need something to relax. Facing down a master was the scariest thing I'd ever done, and I spent most of it simply running away. Dealing with Krista was one thing, but a master was a whole different ball game.

"Did you find him?" I hoped the fear didn't bleed through into my voice.

It had been twenty-five years, but I could still see the master sprinting after our van with his face full of determination and arms pumping like pistons. There was no doubt in my mind if he had caught us, we'd all be dead. The master was even scarier than the coven of witches Saul caught experimenting on werewolves.

The master made that nightmare look like a walk in the park.

Saul nodded. "I think so." It wasn't like him to sound so unsure.

"But?" I knew whatever came next wouldn't be good.

Saul deflated like an overripe melon left in the sun. "I can't risk getting my people closer than they are now."

He didn't say he wanted me to try, but he didn't say not to. "You want me to see if I can get closer? I'm not sure that's a great idea."

The master knew what I looked like.

"I know it's a big ask." Saul's face flushed with anger. "You know what that monster did to our father."

I couldn't forget it.

It was my turn to offer a little comfort. "I know if you could go, you would."

"Damn fucking straight." Saul looked chagrined about swearing so much. "All I've wanted since that night was to make my father proud and knowing there might be something I can do about it… I'd take that chance in a heartbeat to take the damn weight off my shoulders."

He patted my hand gently to let me know he was okay. "First we work on this. Rule one of grabbing Alexander is?"

"Don't kill Alexander." I sighed.

It wasn't like I was a maniac out killing people willy-nilly. People like Alexander had bodyguards with guns. Sometimes they had guns themselves.

When people shot me, I tended to get overdramatic. What happened at the Gas-N-Sip was nothing compared to me after a few ammunition rounds burst through my chest. Shooting a vampire had to be the dumbest shit I ever heard of, but people tried it all the time.

They'd be in for a real surprise with anything other than a fledgling.

Saul stood and slapped a hard copy of the file against my chest. "I know you've mostly checked out on me, so take that with you. Don't do anything until we talk again."

The implication being, don't murder him. It'll bring unwanted attention.

My mentor in all things was right. Despite the TV shows that wanted us to think our dedicated police departments caught all murderers, the average number of murders solved was closer to sixty-five percent. Those killers couldn't bite someone and turn them into ashes moments later. I could commit the crime and avoid police attention, but the vampires would notice.

Krista would know if someone killed one of her servants, and so would any other vamps who paid attention to such things. Taking a Renfield off the board—a human who sold out other humans to vampires—would be the shots that started a war between nests. Not that they cared about the human, but any provocation was the chance to have a little fun. The slightest insult had to meet with immediate retribution.

Shit. Now I was half-tempted to kill him to get the vamps fighting each other, but a vamp war wouldn't be good for the people of Phoenix. Too many human casualties.

Killing the Renfield was off the table, but it didn't mean I couldn't hurt him.

Saul walked toward the exit. "We've waited a long time for this chance. Let's make sure we handle it correctly."

I was all in.

The last time we went in half-cocked, it had cost lives. That was the night the title of Van Helsing passed to Saul. He was right to insist. I hated how often he made the correct call, but it was nice to know the guy making those calls was in your corner. He'd never let me down. This was another example of how much I needed him.

Saul pulled out a phone the size of a notepad and waved it. "Call me, and we'll do this together."

"What about Greg?" He would be pissed we were working so closely together again.

Saul smiled. "I'll loop him in when I'm ready."

I watched as he tucked the phone into his pocket. It still amazed me how far technology had come since I'd been born. Back in the early '80s, personal computers were a dream. Shit, most people only had one TV, and cell phones looked like two giant bricks taped together with walkie-talkie antennas.

Don't even get me started on the cost of those cellular phone calls.

That's why Zach on *Saved by the Bell* was so shocking. He used that phone like it was nothing at a time when even Wall Street bankers were afraid to use them.

The one thing I missed about the '80s and '90s was the lack of connection. It was nice to leave the house, and no one could find you until you wanted them to. The amount of time parents spent calling all their kids' friends when they didn't come home on time bordered on absurdity. People thought you died if you didn't leave a big enough digital footprint these days.

Being connected was great when you wanted to order takeout but real shitty when you wanted to duck someone.

Not that it mattered so much for me.

Part of my lifestyle was keeping myself at a casual distance from almost everyone I met. Getting attached meant questions. It meant explaining why I spoke like I was in my mid-forties but looked like I was under thirty. Where was my family? Who did I work for? All great entry-level questions I couldn't begin to answer.

Hi, my name is Dylan. I hunt vampires. It was a great way to end the first date before the drinks arrived. Not that I tried. After my first time lying through the normal meet-and-greet questions, I gave up dating. I was a love 'em and leave 'em type by necessity. It was for their protection.

Honest, I swear.

Saul stopped me before the outer door. "Take this one slow. Do the job right. They might have eyes on Alexander, and he might have protection. If he does, whoever is protecting him might be more valuable."

If the guard was a bloodsucker, it also made them expendable.

"I'll take my time. I promise." When I worked with Saul, it always felt like I was talking to my dad.

He rested a hand on my shoulder. "Be safe and send me your plan before you go."

Stop it. You're going to get me all choked up.

"I'll see what I can come up with." As much as I wanted to handle everything, his ideas always saved the day.

I was looking forward to decompressing with some Herbal Sciences and Biggieburto's. People could talk all the shit they wanted about my favorite drive-through burrito chain, but they didn't know what they were talking about. Fluffy was right. Eating burritos and smoking a little weed was living the high life. Even though I'd pay handsomely later for eating human food, it was worth it.

It wasn't like I had anything to do during the day. If Krista was coming, I would go nocturnal.

The door opened, startling both of us. Saul reached inside his jacket and pulled out a gun. Taking my cue from him, I pulled out a small tactical baton.

It wasn't the kind of thing a normal person would bring to a gunfight but getting shot didn't matter to me. With a flick of my wrist, the one-foot baton became three feet of solid pain. With my strength behind it, every strike would be a killing blow.

"Get behind me." I growled and pushed Saul to the side with my free arm.

Greg walked in with his daughter and another woman dressed in full Templar garb. It took a second to place her, and I groaned. There was a time Cassandra and I could have been called an item. In the end, I couldn't trust her enough to tell her my secret, and I couldn't lie to her forever. She nodded at me politely and pulled Saul into a brief hug before standing behind Greg and crossing her arms.

Cassandra still looked as spectacular as the day we met fifteen years ago. I heard she had a family of her own now. Not something I would ever have been able to give her. It never occurred to me to find out if I could have kids. *Didja hear the one about the vampire who walked into a fertility clinic?* Being the butt of a joke wasn't something I had time for.

Cassandra did her best to ignore me, but I had Megan's full attention. One corner of her mouth twisted in a curious smile. I could work with that better than the deep frown her father aimed at me. I would have to break the ice, and since she was the only receptive member of their party, I turned my attention to her.

A few flippant remarks went through my head, but this didn't feel like the right time to poke the bear.

It took me a second to realize I wasn't looking at the gangly teenager I'd expected. I hadn't seen Megan in twelve years. She was twenty-five now and fully grown. Seeing her bright blue eyes filled with mirth staring back at me, I almost couldn't speak. It was starting to get awkward.

This was the moment they talked about in the love stories. When you met the right one, you knew. I'd been waiting for it my entire life and the last puzzle piece was in front of me. My heart skipped a few more beats. Before I could recover from staring helplessly into her eyes, she spoke.

"Uncle Saul, your handsome friend seems to have lost the ability to speak." The most beautiful woman I'd ever seen had a voice to match. There was a hint of a Southern accent, which made her feel exotic.

Saul wrapped his arms around her. "You'll have to forgive my friend, Megan. I'm sure he's never seen a vision as beautiful as you."

My mentor doted on the girl like she was his daughter.

"I don't think he's your type," Greg snapped, not liking that we were speaking.

Megan looked me over and lost interest immediately. "Shame."

Whoa! I needed to right the ship if I was ever going to

have a shot at asking her out. If she thought I wasn't her type, that would likely put me too far in the friend zone to recover.

All of this seemed crazy. I didn't know the girl. The last time I saw her was so long ago she was an entirely new person. Megan was a child back then, but now she was grown. Just looking into her eyes, I knew I was in deep trouble.

"I think Greg was trying to say that I don't date very often." I turned and winked at Saul, then wagged a finger at him. "And this one has used the words 'nonexistent' and 'picky' to describe my dating habits."

Oh, holy Mother of Mercy, this was not going how I wanted it to.

"Awfully handsome not to have a full dance card. Must have some serious character flaws."

I thought she might have been flirting with me. *Did she say I was handsome?*

Cassandra snorted, and I crashed back down to Earth.

"That will be enough of that." Greg brushed past me. "Saul, whatever you have to discuss with Dylan will have to wait. We have important family business to handle."

Cassandra swept past, pulling Greg with her into Saul's inner sanctum.

"At least I'll always have you, Saul." I looked at my mentor, but he watched his brother until the door closed behind him.

Megan looked at Saul and me. "If Uncle Saul likes you, and the personality isn't that bad, it must mean one of two things. So, what is it? Micropenis or serial killer?"

Saul coughed.

I walked right into that one. "If those are the only options, I guess I better grab my hockey mask."

Saul cleared his throat, uncomfortable with our flirtation. "I'll hear from you tomorrow night?"

"Yes, of course." I looked into Megan's bright blue eyes and smiled like I'd found the last PlayStation Five during the pandemic. "I hope to see you again sometime."

"I'll be around." Megan wrapped an arm around Saul's shoulders. "We better hurry or Dad will blow a gasket."

Saul pushed me through the door and closed it in my face as I continued to stare at her. There was something there. A twinkle in her eye, a take no prisoners attitude. No surprise when her dad was the head of the Templars. She'd probably already killed her first vamp.

Dangerous and sexy. I watched the door for a few more moments, willing it to open. When it didn't, I turned and headed for the Jeep.

It had been a long night, and the sun would be up soon. It was time to get some rest. Fluffy was curled up on the passenger seat, looking content. If she was that happy, someone else was having a bad night. The imp was kind of like a Niffler from *Fantastic Beasts* world. Too damn cute to hate, but she made life way more interesting than it needed to be.

I owed Fluffy some dank, and only super nachos, a burrito, and a giant cheese quesadilla could fill the rumble in my stomach. Food called my name, and I'd have plenty of time to look over Saul's information while I sat on the commode.

There was a real lead to look into for the first time since Krista's attack, and it filled me with hope.

CHAPTER TWENTY

Megan

Uncle Saul's young friend was super cute.

The fact that my father didn't want me to talk to him might have made him even cuter. There was something about him, a flair for violence. He wasn't good at talking himself up. He already admitted to being a serial killer and not great in relationships. I bit my bottom lip as I thought about his arms.

Maybe a little danger was worth it.

"So, Uncle Saul, tell me about your friend." I pulled him close, making it feel like we were sharing a secret.

Saul patted my hand. "Dylan is a more complicated story than we have time for now."

So, he was also a mystery.

"Don't think I'll let you off the hook that easily." I tugged him forward faster now that the fun was over. "We better hurry. Dad has something exciting to share."

It was funny how my dad was more excited about it than

I was. I had killed my first fledgling and experienced an awakening. No one wanted to be the next champion less than me.

I was almost out. Three more years and I would have put enough time in to take a sabbatical from the Helsing Society and my father's Templars. It was supposed to be time to do what I wanted before deciding whether to commit my future to the cause. Hunting vampires was Dad's thing. I wanted a normal life and maybe children someday.

That was over now.

If I couldn't leave to find my passion, I would tweak Dad's nose a few times along the way. A date with Dylan would piss him off. He didn't like him, and I wanted to know why. Dad would never tell me, but maybe tall, dark, and handsome would. Something about him caught my interest, and when I was interested in something, I didn't stop until I had it or knew enough to stay away.

The inner sanctum sealed, and Dad started in on Uncle Saul. "Did you have to bring him here?"

"Dylan's done as much as either of us to keep this city safe." Saul looked at him. "He's not perfect, but he's always there to help us."

Dad looked triumphant. "We don't need him anymore."

"What are you going on about?" Saul looked like he'd had enough of this and wanted to go to bed.

Smiling like it was the best news I'd ever heard, I looked deep into Saul's eyes. "I'm the champion."

"Well, this changes everything." Saul took my hand and squeezed it in reassurance.

Yes, yes it does.

THE STORY CONTINUES

The Helping Society story continues with book two, *Past Bites*, available at Amazon.

Claim your copy today!

AUTHOR NOTES - BRADFORD BATES

MAY 25, 2022

Hey everyone, Bradford Bates here. I just wanted to say, I hope you enjoyed the story. This one was near and dear to my heart. I've always liked people that are kind of flawed who want to do the right thing despite how it would be easier to do the wrong one. They don't always make the best decision but find a way to come through in the clutch.

I'm an Arizona guy myself so it's fun to write something set in my own backyard. The southwest is a great place to live despite the fact in Arizona we only have two seasons. Extremely hot, and downright perfect. Thankfully the heat is only unbearable for about four solid months, giving us eight months of really great weather.

You haven't really lived until you've seen a hundred degrees in October.

These books wouldn't be possible without my wife Becky. She supports me in every way conceivable to ensure I'm successful. I couldn't do this without her. Our four furry companions Blizz, Jackson, Cisco, and Lucyfur sometimes make things difficult with their shenanigans, but bring way more joy into our lives than dogs have any right to.

I wanted to give a special shout out to Matt from Grow Sciences. In the book you might see references to Herbal sciences. That's my nod to Matt and the team over at Grow Sciences just for being super cool people. He is always willing to help people out with grow advice, and just really seems to care about the community in ways no other retailer does. When you find good people, who run great brands it always feels nice to support them.

A couple more folks I'd like to thank. Daz from Night-Owl. The man is a next level breeder. If you wonder where I get some of my ideas in my books, it's enjoying his genetics. I'd also like to give a shout out to my guys in the meat department at AJ's. They are always taking time out of their day to BS sports with me, and ask about the books. That's super cool.

Oh, and then there is Michael The Dreammaker Anderle. He lets me run off on my own a little bit with these ideas. They aren't always his thing, but he is always incredibly supportive. He also isn't afraid to pump the brakes when I go off the rails. I'd call that the perfect partner in crime. I hope we have many more novels under our belts together.

Let's not forget Tracey. She takes my words and cleans them up in a way that makes them more palatable. It's not an easy job, and she is greatly appreciated.

I can't wait to see all of you again at the end of book two.

AUTHOR NOTES - MICHAEL ANDERLE

MAY 27, 2022

Thank you for not only reading this book but these author notes as well!

I really appreciate Bradford giving a shout-out in his author notes. The interesting thing is sometimes a story idea works, and I'm right on and gung-ho…and then there are times I'm scratching my cheek and saying, "If you thinnnnnkkkk sooooo."

But I'm a huge fan of Van Helsing.

More from the Van Helsing movie with Hugh Jackman and Kate "OMG" Beckinsale than the Dracula stories.

I realize that for many, she annoys the ever-loving crap out of them. I don't follow her on any social media or anything, but she can wear the ever-loving Q$%# out of those outfits in *Underworld* and *Van Helsing* movies.

Mind you, it doesn't hurt she has an English accent (being English and all). She absolutely sells the bad-ass female action star in my mind. I honestly couldn't tell you about her other work. I know she did some sort of Shakespeare thing and did some modeling. That's about it.

AUTHOR NOTES - MICHAEL ANDERLE

Beckinsale presently has a new movie out called *Jolt* that I'm on the fence about watching. The premise seems a bit hokey to me (homicidal killer using an electric straitjacket to stop her desire to kill people. When someone kills the first guy she's truly fallen for, the jacket comes off.)

Seems like a weak reason to go around and kill a bunch of people. It's not that I need deep storylines, but even that seemed weak to me.

However, the script is supposed to be funny, and I'm a sucker for funny action-adventure movies with explosions. Hell, I even liked the hokey-as-hell *Commando* with Arnold Schwarzenegger just because of his stupid quips.

All of this to explain that when Bradford wanted to do something riffing off the Van Helsing character, I was all-in. Good, bad, or indifferent, he had me hooked.

I hope you liked this story and will join us for book two.

Talk to you in the next book!

Ad Aeternitatem,

Michael

If you want, you can read a couple of my short stories in my STORIES with Michael Anderle newsletter here: (No requirement to sign up.)

https://michael.beehiiv.com/

OTHER BOOKS BY BRADFORD BATES

Rise Of The Grandmaster Series
(with Michael Anderle)
Rise of the Grandmaster (Book 1)
The Trials of Tristholm (Book 2)
Deserts Of Naroosh (Book 3)
The Eyes of Prophecy (Book 4)
Battle for the Kingdom (Book 5)

Ascendancy Legacy
The Arena
Jar of Souls
Guardian of the Grove
Demon Stone
The Rising Darkness
Redemption

Ascendancy Origins
Rise of the Fallen
Butcher of the Bay
Night of the Demon

The Bozley Green Chronicles
Possessed

The Galactic Outlaws
Forced Compliance

Genetic Purge

Smuggler's Legacy

Fortune Hunters
Star Talon

Lost Signal

A Galactic Outlaws Story
The Marchenko Incident

Smuggler for Hire

Origin Ice

The Fairy of Salem
Witching Hour

The Wild Hunt

Standalone Titles
Crimson Stars

BOOKS BY MICHAEL ANDERLE

Sign up for the LMBPN email list to be notified of new releases and special deals!

https://lmbpn.com/email/

For a complete list of books by Michael Anderle, please visit:

www.lmbpn.com/ma-books/

CONNECT WITH THE AUTHORS

Connect with Bradford Bates

Facebook:
https://www.facebook.com/bradfordbatesauthor/

Twitter:
https://twitter.com/Freetheblizz

Website:
http://www.bradfordbates.com/

Connect with Michael Anderle and sign up for his email list here:

Website: http://lmbpn.com

Email List: https://michael.beehiiv.com/

https://www.facebook.com/LMBPNPublishing

https://twitter.com/MichaelAnderle

https://www.instagram.com/lmbpn_publishing/

https://www.bookbub.com/authors/michael-anderle

ABOUT BRADFORD BATES

Bradford Bates is a full-time author, husband to an incredible wife, and father to four furry rescue dogs. He lives in sunny Phoenix, Arizona, trying to not melt in the oppressive heat of the summer. When he isn't busy writing the next book, you can find him playing video games and watching scary movies.

www.ingramcontent.com/pod-product-compliance
Lightning Source LLC
LaVergne TN
LVHW041905070526
838199LV00051BA/2504